Strebor ON THE Streetz

SK

OCT - - 2016

W9-BNQ-791

WIDE
OPEN

WIDE OPEN

San Diego Public Library
Skyline Hills

OCT - _ 2016

S.K. COLLINS

3 1336 10138 4569

SBI

STREBOR BOOKS

NEW YORK LONDON TORONTO SYDNEY

Strebor Books
P.O. Box 6505
Largo, MD 20792
http://www.streborbooks.com

This book is a work of fiction. Names, characters, places and incidents are products of the author's imagination or are used fictitiously. Any resemblance to actual events or locales or persons, living or dead, is entirely coincidental.

© 2014 by S.K. Collins

All rights reserved. No part of this book may be reproduced in any form or by any means whatsoever. For information address Strebor Books, P.O. Box 6505, Largo, MD 20792.

ISBN 978-1-59309-552-9
ISBN 978-1-4767-5225-9 (ebook)
LCCN 2013950648

First Strebor Books trade paperback edition February 2014

Cover design: www.mariondesigns.com
Cover photograph: © Keith Saunders/Marion Designs

10 9 8 7 6 5 4 3 2 1

Manufactured in the United States of America

For information regarding special discounts for bulk purchases, please contact Simon & Schuster Special Sales at 1-866-506-1949 or business@simonandschuster.com

The Simon & Schuster Speakers Bureau can bring authors to your live event. For more information or to book an event, contact the Simon & Schuster Speakers Bureau at 1-866-248-3049 or visit our website at www.simonspeakers.com.

This book is dedicated to everyone who decided to read what is beyond this page. I hope to have your eyes for life. Thank you.

Enjoy

When it comes to love, the truth isn't trusted
and that which is trusted isn't true.

—S.K. COLLINS

ACKNOWLEDGMENTS

First, I thank God for blessing me with my most precious asset—my mind. Without that, I'd be a walking mass of nothing. You made me who I am for a reason and I'm extremely grateful for that.

I want to thank my parents, Ruben and Darlene, for all the support you've given me over the years. You didn't question my dreams and just let me run my own course. Maya, you are my number one supporter! You've been rocking with me from the beginning and I couldn't ask for a better person in my corner. Mary Jean, thank you for being my other mother and loving my work. You give me the endurance to keep going. Zakari, you are the best son ever! I'm trying to do everything in my power to make sure you turn out to be a great man. You are my biggest investment and I will always put you first. To my sisters, Amicia and Cherise, y'all already know what it is. Thanks for all of your support.

I want to thank Kristen, you helped me so much with my film casting and now you are right here again to help me with my novels; you are a blessing. Larnell, you told me to make sure you're the first one who reads my books before anyone else. I got you, big homie! Gina, thank you for always eagerly inquiring when I'm going to have something else hot for you to read—it's coming!

Kareem, thank you for reading my manuscript numerous times until my next one was ready. You gave me extra insurance that I was on to something big! Latoya, thanks for offering to invest in what I was trying to build. You were willing to put a lot on the line just to help me get started. Thank you, thank you, thank you!

To my BEST friends, Carl, Ricki, and Ashley. Your friendship and support is unmatched. Whatever is mine is yours. Believe that. Shout-out to the following families: Collins, Goolsby, Jackson, and Franklin. I love you all. Clarence, Kobe and Corey, thank you for keeping me grounded. Special shout-out to the city of Pittsburgh, PA where I was born and groomed. I am what you made me and my stories truly reflect that.

Shout-out to Tawna, Robin, Shawn, Tanaill, Shaunte, Rasheeda, Torrie, and all of the rest of the Nine-Six Clique. What up, DP! What up, Gene Wild'em! What up, Ramina! Tony Rome, I couldn't forget about you. I always know who to see when I come to Baltimore. You got the key to the city. To Shade, (whole time!) thanks for understanding my grind.

I want to give special thanks to Keith Lee Johnson, author of the Little Black Girl Lost series. The conversations you had with me about being a writer were so valuable. You didn't have to call me at all, but you did. You are much appreciated.

I want to give extra special thanks to Teri Woods, author of the True to the Game series. You put me on to what was going on in the game when no one else would. The information was priceless.

Thank you to my agent, Joylynn. I still can't believe it! I love the way you work!

I want to give a BIG thank-you to Zane and Charmaine! I'm so glad to be a part of Strebor and Simon & Schuster! I will not let you down!

Last but definitely not least, I want to thank Maurice "First" Tonia. Without you I don't think this novel would have seen the light of day. You understood my vision and helped me reach the next level. I know your children mean the world to you, so here's your chance to tell them with the final words. I told you I keep it real.

Message from Maurice "First" Tonia: *This goes out to my wonderful children, Jazmyn, Montre, Bryce, and Asia. Please always remember that anything and everything daddy ever set out to accomplish was done because I love all of you.*

CHAPTER ONE

Early Spring 2004

"Damn! I can't be late for work again!" Zeek cried as he slammed the door behind him and sped off down the street. He had only two minutes to catch the 8:35 a.m. bus, so he ran desperately to the bus stop. His heart raced as he broke out into a heavy sweat, praying he would reach his destination in time. His red Staples shirt blew in the wind as he forced himself to run faster knowing his job was on the line. He made a sharp left and took a shortcut through a vacant park. He knew taking the detour would give him the best chance at making the bus. He tucked the back of his shirt in so he wouldn't get it snagged on the fence he had to get over. He jumped the fence, but he somehow managed to bang his knee on one of the raised rusted posts. He ignored the pain and rushed and made it to the corner.

Zeek's pupils enlarged as his eyes zoomed in on the last passenger stepping onto the bus. He knew he only had seconds to make it there before the bus pulled off. "Hold the bus, please! Miss, can you please hold the bus?" he yelled as he ran desperately.

The woman rolled her eyes and let the doors close behind her. "Yo, driver! Hold the bus!" He immediately started to wave his hands in the air, hoping to obtain the driver's attention.

Unfortunately, the driver never checked his rearview mirror, so the bus proceeded to pull off, leaving Zeek utterly down and out.

While holding his knees in an attempt to catch his breath, Zeek hopelessly yelled, "Aww, come on, man! Come on! Damn...I know you seen me... How the hell could he not see me?"

Now with the bus gone, he had to think fast. He knew he could either wait for another bus or run another twenty blocks to Brookline Metro Station and catch a train. Right then a bus that ran a different route pulled up in front of him. He knew it wouldn't take him to his job, but he would be close, at least in running distance. Without a second thought, he ran up the steps and sat as close to the front as possible. He wiped his clammy hands off on his shirt as he thought about being late.

"I hope there ain't no traffic," he said nervously to himself as the bus pulled off.

The twenty-minute ride into town felt more like hours as Zeek sighed heavily. Before the doors of the bus were fully open, he squeezed out of the tight space and took off running. He dodged and weaved through crowds of people who were on their way to work as well.

"Sorry!" he yelled as he ran out in front of a taxi as the driver smashed down on his horn in anger.

He checked the time on his phone and became even more nervous as Staples was now only a short distance away. *What the hell am I going to say this time?* he thought hopelessly. He'd pretty much run out of excuses for being late.

Zeek quickly entered the store and tensely peered around for his manager. "He must be in the back." He sighed in relief as he headed for his register.

His co-worker, Tara, was finishing up with a customer when she looked up and saw Zeek trying to creep in. She shook her head and waited for the customer to be out of earshot before she spoke.

"Boy, why you late again? You know Dan gonna go off on you, right?"

"Dan can kiss my ass," he said in a hushed tone as he tried to clock into the register.

"If he can kiss ya ass, then why you whisperin'?" she said after sucking her teeth.

"I ain't whisperin' shit. Dan's tight shirt-wearin' ass know what it is. Fuck...why can't I clock in?"

"Boy, you always be fakin'. You are such a bama." Tara quickly cut her eyes to the back of the store and happened to see Dan making his way to the front. She smiled and looked back over at Zeek. "Here come Dan. Let's see you talk that shit now."

Zeek's eyes widened as Dan made his way over to his register. Dan's yellow, overly round frame walked tall in his snug-fitting shirt as he had Zeek in his focus. Zeek's lips started to quiver as he thought about what excuse to use. All he could do was tap his shaky fingers on the cash register keys as Dan moved closer.

Zeek swallowed hard and said the first thing that came to his mind. "Hey, what's up, Dan? I've been trying to clock in for the longest time, but it's not working. Is there a problem with the system?"

"Nope. Ain't no problem with the system. The problem is you," Dan said as he stared at Zeek with his hands placed firmly on his hips.

Zeek swallowed hard as the realization of what was happening started to set in.

"I decided to let you go."

"Come on, Dan. I need this job. Just give me another chance." Zeek begged.

"I'm sorry, Zeek, but you brought this on yourself. I can't give you any more chances," Dan said, standing his ground.

Zeek knew Dan was overly tired of his call-offs and late-to-work routine. It was clear to him after being late this morning that it was his fault that he was fired. He looked over at Tara and became even more embarrassed after he saw that she had been laughing at him. With nothing else to be said, Zeek lowered his head and slowly walked toward the door. He looked back at Dan one last time to see if there was any slight chance he could salvage his job, but Dan had already walked off. He shook his head in disappointment that he had to move on.

Zeek forcefully pushed through the doors and started to walk fast down the busy street. He tightened his lips and balled up his fists as he thought about what had happened. "Damn, I shouldn't have been late! I can't do shit right!" He cursed himself after failing to try to be more responsible.

He'd intended to stretch his twenty-first birthday weekend until the crack of dawn and still get up for work on time. He had hoped this morning would have been the start of a more mature Ezeekiel Harris, but yet again, he was dead wrong. "What the fuck am I going to do now?" Zeek said as he wiped his eyes.

His mind was racing a mile a minute and he couldn't help but feel worthless. He headed back to the bus stop and looked enviously at everyone who drove past him. The summer hadn't even begun and with the money he would've made working, his mind was set on buying a car in September. Now losing his job had ruined his plan. Zeek needed to come up with another way to get a car, but for now, he wanted to go home and sulk in his sorrow.

Once the bus arrived, Zeek stepped up on the bus and took the first available window seat. He still couldn't believe he'd been fired. He shook off the thought as his eyes started to water again.

"Damn, I'm such an asshole," he said as he thumped his head against the glass.

He peered dejectedly out of the window as the bus left downtown and headed back to his neighborhood. His surroundings altered drastically as the business buildings turned into rundown row houses, and the professional working class shifted to corner boys and drug addicts. Zeek shook his head as the U.S. Capitol came into view. The immaculate structure represented a country that attracted millions of tourists from around the world. It also symbolized the power and security that every country respected.

Damn, there's such a thin line between wealth and poverty. I gotta find a way to get in between, Zeek thought as the bus moved deeper into the hood.

Zeek arrived back at his house but didn't bother to go in. He sat down on the porch steps and tried to clear his head. He was so distressed from losing his job that he didn't want to make it worse by sitting in an empty house. All Zeek's friends were at work so it made him feel even worse about being unemployed again. Zeek decided to call his girlfriend and tell her the bad news. He knew she would understand. Zeek needed someone to talk to, someone who could console him.

Zeek pulled out his cell phone and was about to dial her number until he saw his best friend, Lonzo, walking toward him. Zeek forgot Lonzo went to work around this time of morning, and was caught off-guard as Lonzo quickly approached. He pushed his phone back into his pocket and decided to wait until Lonzo was gone before he called his girlfriend. *I can't let him know that we're back together yet*, Zeek said to himself as Lonzo crossed the street.

"Zeek, what are you doin' here, man?" Lonzo asked as he approached the walkway.

"Young, I got fired," Zeek said, giving him a defeated look.

"What you get fired for?" Lonzo asked with slight irritation in his voice.

Zeek started to shake his head out of disappointment as he waited for the words to leave his mouth. "I was late for work again. I missed the damn bus. I tried to hurry up and clock in, but fat ass Dan caught me. I was only like five minutes late. I don't think he should have fired me over that, though."

Lonzo shook his head in amazement that Zeek didn't see his job termination coming. "Come on, Slim. You know you was fakin' wit' that job. You were always late or not showin' up. People see that as being irresponsible."

Zeek knew what Lonzo had said was right, and that was his whole reason for wanting to make a change. Zeek wished he could be more like Lonzo; he always had it together. He'd had the same job for over five years and never missed work. Even though Lonzo had been Zeek's best friend, they were totally different when it came to their work ethic. Zeek could have easily admitted he deserved what he got, but he didn't.

"I ain't sweatin' it," he said, shrugging his shoulders. "I can always get another job. That place wasn't for me anyway," he assured Lonzo.

"Man, you know how hard it is to find a job right now? It took you months to get the one you had."

"True, but what 'bout ya spot? Ain't they hirin'?" he asked curiously.

"Yeah they hirin', but I'm not tellin' them about yo' ass. You ain't gonna have me lookin' bad. Shit…you need to see if you can get your job back at the copy center."

"Come on, man. I knew you since kindergarten and you won't stick ya neck out for me?" Zeek asked as he held his arms out wide, completely stunned by Lonzo's disposition.

"Nope. The way you carried every job in the past gives me enough reason not to. So if I was you, I'd try to get back in that rental office you used to work for."

Even though Zeek badly needed a job, he knew for certain that going back to the rental office wasn't an option. "Naw, I'm good off that. There was nothin' but bamas in that place. Those people got on my damn nerves."

"Well, any job beats sittin' on this hot-ass porch for the summer. If I was you, I'd get off my ass and make it happen. Ya dig?" Lonzo rebutted.

Instead of Zeek taking heed to what his boy was saying, he decided to blow him off. "Yeah, whatever," Zeek said as he waved Lonzo off and looked away.

"Maybe you should look into doing some modeling or acting. You already got the body for it and the ladies think you're cute. Shit, if anything, you can at least be able to work with beautiful-ass women. What man wouldn't want that perk?"

Zeek did have that butter-brown skin and muscular physique that the ladies appreciated. His only drawback was that he never had any money.

Zeek looked up at Lonzo and shook his head. "Me be a model? Man, that's the dumbest shit you ever came up with."

"Yeah, whatever," Lonzo said as he checked his watch. "I'll get up wit' you later. I got to get to work before I'm late my damn self."

Lonzo gave him dap and made his way down the street, while Zeek stayed on the porch with plenty to think about. Zeek then bent over, placed his hands on his face, and sighed. "What the hell am I going to do?"

CHAPTER TWO

"Okay. We'll be out in two minutes," Chelsea said and then hung up her phone. "All right, they're outside now," she turned and told her best friend, Dya, as she tossed her BlackBerry back in her purse.

They were on their way to Philly for the night and couldn't wait to get out of the house. Chelsea checked herself in the mirror one more time and was pleased with the final result. Her curly black hair was pulled back into a ponytail that allowed her studded diamond earrings to dazzle. The Revlon mascara she used gave her big volume lashes that added flare to her already delectable face. She applied an even coat of Purple Passion lip gloss that blended well with her rich stygian-colored skin. When they walked outside, a Black Yukon was waiting curbside. Both of their heels dug hard into the ground as they strutted over to the truck.

Dya got in the front with her boy, Murf. One of Murf's dark-skinned hands gripped the steering wheel as the other one fumbled with the CD changer. The amount of jewelry he wore had been easily visible as his wife beater clung to his well-carved frame. Dya loved his style and couldn't keep herself from looking at him. To Dya, he was a good piece of eye candy.

"What's up, boo?" Chelsea said after laying eyes on Shady, her hookup, who was already posted up in the backseat.

"There go my baby," Shady said as he pulled Chelsea into his arms.

"Long time no see," she said, grinning once they broke their embrace.

"Girl, who you tellin'? You a hard one to keep up with ya damn self," Shady said jokingly.

This was the second time they were able to hook up after several months of miscommunication and rescheduling. Chelsea had too many guys on her roster, and Shady was always on the road. She knew their encounter tonight was long overdue. Chelsea liked that Shady was a little taller than Murf, and his frame was on the slender side. His dress code was the same as Murf"s except for the jewelry. He wasn't all flashy with his. He was indeed someone she would keep around for a while.

They had over a two-hour ride from D.C. to Philly ahead of them in order to get to a club called Chrome, which would give them more than enough time to talk. The audio system blasted, the noise pushing them close enough to have an intimate conversation. Shady rolled up four blunts filled with hydro, which was a very strong grade of marijuana, and passed two of them to Dya. Now, they were smoking and riding.

"So you never been to Philly, huh?" Shady asked as Chelsea played with the tails of his freshly braided cornrows.

"Nope. I always wanted to go but never got the chance. I can't wait to get there. Thanks for taking me, boo," Chelsea said as she continued to run her hand through his braids.

Chelsea noticed his high-yellow skin blush as soon as she started flirting with him. She knew Shady loved every minute of it by the way he smiled back at her. She then put her leg over his to give him more of a reason to turn red. Chelsea took another pull from the blunt as she and Shady continued to converse. They were really hitting it off well.

Once in Philly, they stopped at Pat's King of Steaks. Philly was famous for having the best cheesesteaks, and Pat's was one of the favorites of the locals. Some say Geno's was the best in town, but that's a debate that will never end.

The weed gave them the munchies and made them devour the hoagies and fries like they had never had food before. They all thought the cheesesteaks were the best they ever had, except for Shady. He liked the ones at The Great Steak better and didn't see the point in riding all the way to Philly for one. Murf ignored his claim and ordered another one to go.

After leaving Pat's, they drove to the other side of South Philly to check out Chrome. Murf had been there before and knew this club was off the hook. Cassidy had performed there once, which had caused him to have to wait in line for over an hour. He knew the rap group he was trying to see tonight would have them waiting almost as long. Murf hoped the girls wouldn't be turned off because of the long wait. He really wanted to impress them with the club he'd chosen. He really didn't want to have to find something else for them to do.

Once they arrived at Chrome, they noticed the parking lot was almost filled, but there were only a few people standing in line. Murf was relieved. This gave them enough time to smoke another blunt before they got out of the truck.

"Damn, Chelsea. I'm gettin' a little nervous about what we got on. These Philly bitches dress aggressive as hell," Dya said, as she observed the girls in line for the club.

"I was thinking the same thing. Those hoes are damn near wearing two-piece swimsuits and four-inch heels. We about to look like some straight out-of-towners," Chelsea answered back.

"What the hell y'all talkin' 'bout?" Murf said as he shook his head. "Y'all both got designer shit on. Y'all fit right in, if not better."

Murf was right. Dya had on everything Fendi. Her shirt, jeans, and pumps were all black with matching accessories. Chelsea wore a Marc Jacobs denim dress along with denim sandals and a leather navy blue Chanel bag. Like always, the girls were definitely looking fly, but they didn't know if they met Philly's approval until Murf stamped it for them. Chelsea and Dya looked at each other briefly before getting out the truck and then immediately regained their composure. They were both now ready to make their presence known that the D.C. girls were about to be in the building.

The girls made it past security after they quickly flashed their fake ID's that they had been using since the tenth grade. They still had two more years before they turned twenty-one. Murf and Shady were well into their twenties and had no problem entering any establishment.

As soon as Chelsea entered the club, she was disgusted. "Damn, it's tight as shit in here," she said as they tried to move through the small crowded area.

"Wait, I think I see some seats over by the bar," Dya said as she pulled Chelsea behind her with Murf and Shady following closely.

Chelsea and Dya sat on the only two unoccupied stools at the bar, while the guys stood around them. "Y'all want some Moët?" Murf asked the girls when he finally got the bartender's attention.

"Naw, that shit is bitter as hell," Dya said as she turned up her face.

"Yeah, it is," Chelsea countered with the same expression.

"You can get us something dark," Dya suggested.

"Cool. We gonna be drinkin' brown all night then. I got a couple bottles of Remy in the truck for later, too."

"That's fine with us," Dya said, answering for both of them.

After a few drinks, the girls were feeling it and couldn't wait to hit the dance floor. "Drop It Like It's Hot" blasted through the club, giving them more of a reason to get out of their seats. "Oh, this is my joint! Come dance wit me, boo," Chelsea said as she pulled Shady away from the bar.

Chelsea got Shady to the middle of the dance floor and wasted no time on showing him what she was working with. She repeatedly popped her butt up against his waist as she grooved to the music. When she felt his manhood rise, she backed up on him even harder. "If feels like I'm going to be in trouble later, huh?" she said as she tilted her head back and whispered in his ear.

"You already know." He laughed and started kissing her neck.

"We'll see about that. I don't think you can handle this," Chelsea said as she dipped down to the floor and came back up.

"There's only one way to find out. As soon as this group Murf wanted to see performs, it's going to be a wrap for you," Shady said as he whispered with Chelsea's earlobe between his lips. The warm air that passed through Shady's lips sent a chill down her back. She wanted Shady so badly after that and couldn't wait to leave the club. She hoped the performance wasn't too long so she could put on her own show. Chelsea was determined to make the best out of her night.

The crowd got restless waiting to hear their favorite street anthems from the rap group Crime House. Crime House was one of the best groups out of Philly and had the streets on lock for the last two years. Half of the crowd shouted out lyrics from the group's hottest songs, while the other half demanded for the group to get on the stage. After a few more minutes of anticipation, the crowd thought their wait was finally over when the DJ cut off the music.

"Damn. I didn't want to be the one to say this, but we just found out Crime House can't make it tonight due to undisclosed circumstances. The club owner apologizes for your inconvenience and promises that Crime House will be here next Friday night." The DJ's voice boomed over the mic as he stunned the crowd. Most of the disappointed patrons quickly left the club, cussing and pissed off at having to find somewhere else to go.

"Shit. Crime House just fucked my whole night up," Murf said in disappointment. "I ain't got shit else planned for us. Fuck it. We gonna head back tonight and get a room around the way."

"That's cool with me, but I want to go past my crib when we get back. I want to get my car before we go to the telly," Chelsea informed them.

"What you need your car for?" she asked. "You wit' me."

"True, but shit happens and I would rather have my car." Chelsea wanted to get her car in case they got left at the hotel. It had happened to them when they were younger and she always made sure it would never occur again.

"A'ight cool, whatever. Let's be out," Shady said as he grabbed Chelsea's hand. They all headed for the exit so they could get back to D.C. and finish the rest of their night.

Chelsea pulled up in a parking space next to Murf"s truck in the hotel parking lot. Shady rode with Chelsea to make sure she came to the hotel with them. Murf grabbed two bottles of Remy V.S.O.P. from the trunk, along with a six-pack of Coca-Cola. Once they got their room keys, they split the Cokes and got on the elevator. When the doors opened, Chelsea and Dya gave each other a quick smile as they stepped out of the elevator. From that point, they both walked in opposite directions, and automatically knew they wouldn't see each other again until the morning.

In the room, Chelsea found something to watch on HBO while Shady made two drinks for them. Chelsea took a sip of her drink and decided to add more cognac to give it a stronger kick. As she tipped the bottle over her glass, a strong tang of marijuana filled the room. Shady took a few pulls from the blunt and then passed it to Chelsea. As the night went on they ended up smoking two more blunts and had replenished their glasses several times. Before they knew it, two in the morning had come and passed. A throbbing sensation built up below Chelsea's mid-section and she wanted Shady to make the first move. It didn't take long for him to read her body language, as she gave him one lustful gaze after another.

"So are you gonna stare at me all night or are you going to do something?" Chelsea asked, getting straight to the point. Chelsea wasn't shy to play the aggressor. She had been drinking all night and her sexual urges couldn't be contained. She wanted Shady to give her everything he had.

Shady turned off the main light and got on the bed beside her. "So you really ready for me?" he asked as they started to kiss while his large hands glided along her body.

"I'm ready," she said softly.

The more Shady touched her, the wetter she became, as a warm gasps left her mouth. The throbbing below her waist was getting the best of her so she stood up and slid her tight-fitting dress off her body. She remained standing over Shady in a white bra set so she could show off all her assets.

"Damn, girl. I didn't know ya ass was that fat…I mean I knew it was fat but *goddamn*," he said in amazement. "Well, I guess I'm about to find out something else about you?" he asked as he removed his shirt.

"Yeah. I guess so," Chelsea said as she slowly took off her bra while he finished getting undressed.

Chelsea was now completely naked and waited in the bed until Shady got himself ready. He crawled on top of her and licked all the peach-flavored lotion off her chest and stomach that she'd applied to her body earlier that day. He breathed in her sweet smell as his tongue traveled down to her navel. She could tell by the way he was licking her that he was going to go down on her. Nobody could resist tasting her, and Shady would be no different.

Chelsea squealed as Shady pressed his tongue against her vertical lips getting a good taste of her clit. He rapidly flicked his tongue along her juice box like he wanted to catch every drop that poured out of her.

Chelsea moaned as Shady slid his tongue in and out of her tight slit. "Oh shit," she gasped. She bit down hard on her lip and tilted her head back as far as it could go, almost hitting the headboard. Shady was pleasing her the way she liked it and she couldn't wait to get him inside her. Chelsea then felt the heavy throbbing below her waist and knew what was about to happen. She quickly wrapped her legs around his neck and expelled all over his face.

"Damn, boy," Chelsea said while trying to catch her breath. Her legs fell off his shoulders. "You sure do know how to work that tongue...shit," she continued to pant.

Shady sat up and wiped off his mouth. "I know how to work my dick too. Wait one second," he said as he retrieved a condom from his pants pocket. Shady's thick rod pulsated as he rolled the condom over it. He licked his lips as he positioned himself on top of her.

"Umm," Chelsea grunted as she felt Shady's mass fill up the space between her walls. Shady's heavy stroke was doing Chelsea right. He was doing everything the way she expected. Chelsea was getting so into the way Shady was crushing her insides, until he suddenly pulled out.

"Turn over," he commanded.

"Is doggy style your favorite position?" Chelsea asked seductively as she rolled over onto her stomach and arched her back.

Shady's eyes widened after seeing that her butt looked even fatter now that it was all spread out. Doggy style was his favorite position and this way would work better for him. "You'll see," he said as he slid his pole back inside her. Shady quickly started to dominate her with his powerful penetration until she started popping back. Chelsea's butt cheeks rippled as she repeatedly crashed hard against his pelvis.

"Oh shit. Girl, ease up. Damn ya shit is good as hell," Shady said as he held onto her waist to keep her from pounding into him.

I knew he couldn't handle it, Chelsea said to herself when Shady wanted her to stop moving. Chelsea held still as Shady glided in and out of her almost at a snail's pace.

She figured that if they stayed in that position too much longer, Shady would finish prematurely. Chelsea was disappointed that Shady wasn't as good as she had hoped. She felt he had more than enough inches to please her but his technique needed some work. She figured while he still had it up that she would try and get another orgasm. She decided to help him out.

"I wanna get on top," she demanded.

Shady wiped his brow and then rolled over on his back so Chelsea could get in position. Chelsea eased up on his waist and began to ride him slowly. "You like that?" she asked after seeing the tension leave his face.

"Yeah, I really like it like this. Just keep doing it like you doing it," Shady said as he let Chelsea do all the work.

Chelsea continued to gradually grind her hips as she controlled her own movements. She soon felt her walls tighten. "Oh, I'm about to cum again," Chelsea said as she started to grind harder.

She kept moving until her insides locked up and her knees wrenched.

Before she knew it, her juices were bursting from within. "Oh shit, that felt good. All right, it's your turn. I want you to fuck me so you can bust," she commanded.

She was satisfied, and he no longer had to fake like he was able to keep up with her. He pushed Chelsea down on her back again, spreading her legs wide as he slipped back inside her. Shady liked kissing while he climaxed, so he quickly locked lips with hers, as he penetrated deeply, thrusting harder with every stroke. Chelsea couldn't wait to see his body shake after exploding inside her warm space.

"Cum for mommy," she said with passion. "Come on…cum for mommy."

After he heard her seductive commands, he almost instantly released his load. Shady felt so fulfilled sexually after freeing himself that he wanted to repeat the act all over again. He couldn't wait to rejuvenate so they could continue with round two, but exhaustion got the best of him and he fell asleep as soon as he rolled over.

Chelsea shook her head as she looked over at a passed-out Shady. "I really didn't want any more of that weak dick anyway." She laughed to herself. She took two shots of Remy and went to sleep, too.

CHAPTER THREE

C helsea sat up in the bed and let the sheet fall under her soft breasts. She realized Shady was not in the room with her as she stretched out her arms and yawned. Chelsea took in the strong scent of marijuana that filled the room. She looked on the table and saw an ashtray with a small trail of smoke coming from it. Chelsea realized that Shady had left and made her way over to the ashtray. She was disappointed at the leftovers. "Damn. That nigga smoked it down to the fingertips. He ain't leave me shit." She shook her head and then rubbed her throat as she looked around for something to quench her thirst. She went for an unfinished can of Coke that was on a tray by the television. Even though there was a little bit of Remy left, she preferred to drink the flat soda than burn her throat from the harsh alcohol. Unsatisfied with the no longer carbonated, syrupy-tasting soda, she decided to use whatever remaining ice that was left in the bucket to pour some water over it. She filled up her cup before walking into the bathroom.

On the sink, she noticed some money and a note left by Shady. She read the note.

Sorry I had to leave you. I had to get my day started early. I left a hundred and twenty dollars if you slept past checkout time. I can't wait to see you again. Call me later.

Chelsea had already figured he was going to leave anyway. Shady was a hustler and she knew he wouldn't stick around for anything except money. That's why she'd brought her own car. Chelsea didn't want to depend on no man, especially one who took her to a hotel on the second hook-up. "Niggas is gonna be niggas," she said. She sucked her teeth and sat on the toilet to take her morning tinkle.

After using the bathroom, she looked over her naked body in the mirror, mostly examining along her neck and around her chest. She had to check to see if there were any sucker bites on her. That was the last thing her boyfriend needed to see. She was so relieved there weren't any. She threw the note away and scooped up the money, folding the bills in her purse that sat on the nightstand beside her phone.

As money-hungry as she had been, there was no way that paper would be spent on a couple more hours of sleep. She wasn't expecting anything more than a good time from Shady, but if he wanted to fill up her pockets she considered it a bonus. Once she showered and got dressed, she called Dya to see if she was up yet. To her surprise, Dya had already helped herself to the breakfast buffet in the lobby since she was by herself, too. Murf and Shady had left both girls at the hotel. Wanting to hurry up and join her friend, she put the unfinished Remy bottle in her purse and left out the door.

After checking out of the hotel, Chelsea spotted Dya pouring some orange juice at the counter in the buffet area. She walked up to her. "Hey, what's up, girl?"

Dya was happy to see her. "Hey, boo. I'm trying to hurry up and eat. I'm hungry as hell."

Scrambling with her plate, Dya quickly sat down to work on her food. Even with a full mouth of food, she talked to Chelsea. "You better get something to eat, girl. This is good."

Looking at how much she was enjoying her food, Chelsea couldn't help but to get hungry herself. Once she made her plate, she was still thirsty from the unsatisfying soda and water, so she got two cups of apple juice with her meal. They ate and talked about the night they'd had.

"So how was it?" Dya asked.

Chelsea knew what she was getting at, but decided to play dumb with her. "How was what?"

Dya rolled her eyes. "The dick. You hit it, right? How was it?"

Chelsea was disgusted. "That nigga couldn't even handle it, girl. After I rode his ass, he went straight to sleep…Bama-ass nigga."

"Damn, girl. You didn't even get yours off, did you?"

"Yeah. He ate the box first. Then after that I forced myself to cum; had to squeeze my muscles all around him and shit. You know how it be." The girls shared a laugh.

There was no reason for Chelsea to even ask Dya about her and Murf. They'd been messing around for a few months now. Dya already had told her his sex game was out of control. Chelsea was hoping Shady shared the same quality, but unfortunately he didn't. It was too common that Chelsea had sex with someone who couldn't handle her, so she didn't hold anything against Shady for having bad sex.

After breakfast, the two friends walked out of the Courtyard hotel in Landover, Maryland, which was right outside of D.C. The car was in the front of the parking lot so they didn't have far to walk. Once in the car, Dya rolled a blunt from the bag of weed Murf had given her before he'd left.

Shady didn't leave Chelsea any weed, but he did leave her money. She could buy her own weed if she wanted to, but she didn't need to. She already had enough weed at home waiting for her to last her an entire week. Chelsea could remember only three times in her life that she actually had to buy weed. Guys were always so willing to give it to her.

They pulled up to Dya's house and before she got out, Dya offered Chelsea some more of the weed she had. "Do you have a lot? 'Cause I got some in the crib," Chelsea informed her.

"Girl, I'm not trippin' off that. Here…I'll wrap you up some in a napkin," Dya said as she reached for the glove compartment.

"Well, at least let me give you some of the money ol' dude gave me," Chelsea suggested, knowing Murf didn't leave her any money. She'd found that out over breakfast.

"No, you keep it. You know how we roll anyway. It's always going to come back around."

Chelsea and Dya were like sisters. They always looked out for each other, even if they didn't have it to give themselves. There was definitely no up-and-down friendship with them or any jealousy.

When Chelsea finally got in her house, she noticed her mother had already gone to work. She smiled and then kicked off her shoes as she headed to the living room. Even if her mother were still there, she'd stopped asking Chelsea not to stay out all night a long time ago. Chelsea practically did whatever she wanted. That's why her mother considered her a lost cause.

Chelsea sat on the couch and searched endlessly through the channels, not finding anything interesting to watch. She yawned and thought it would be better if she took a nap instead. Not even a good five minutes into her sleep, her phone rang. She assumed it was Dya and decided to answer as she reached for it. Chelsea was surprised to see her boyfriend's number appear and didn't know why he would call this time of morning.

"Hello," she said in her pale voice, trying to sound like he had interrupted her sleep. Chelsea didn't feel like talking to him at that moment, but what he said next got her full attention.

She sat straight up and knew something was wrong by the sound in his voice. "You got some bad news? What happened?" Chelsea asked, bracing herself for the worst.

"I got fired," Zeek said, sounding depressed.

"You got fired? What happened, Zeek?" Chelsea inquired as she sighed out of distress. She fell back into the arm of the couch and listened to Zeek tell her how he'd lost his job.

"Zeek, baby, you really have to get it together."

"I know I do," Zeek said as he continued to explain. "It was totally my fault why I was late."

Chelsea really didn't want to hear the rest of his explanation because she had heard it all before. She wondered when it would ever stop with him. Chelsea really had mad love for Zeek; he treated her well and always made her his first priority. Emotionally, he was a girl's dream guy, but when it came to staying on top of his business, he lacked the skills and then some. The fact that he couldn't keep it together was the exact reason why she had to make sure she always had a side piece. When it came down to it, what Zeek couldn't do, another one would.

CHAPTER FOUR

Chelsea had a feeling this was going to happen again. Her boyfriend couldn't keep a job long enough to get a full paycheck. Sometimes, love or not, she didn't know why she still bothered to waste time on him. He was nothing like the other guys she talked to. They were hustlers. Getting money was easy for them.

Chelsea and Zeek had been together off and on ever since she was thirteen. He was her first everything. There would always be a soft spot in her heart for him. Although, in spite of everything going on around her, it was getting harder and harder for her to keep accepting him for whom he was.

Zeek sounded very depressed over the phone. He wanted her to come over to keep him company. She couldn't refuse. When she was in a time of need, she would want the same thing from him. As frustrated as she was with him, she was about to leave in the same clothes from last night, and show him the type of chick he really had, but her conscience came into play. Not concerned with being on time for Zeek's pity party, she took her time finding something else to wear.

Eventually, Chelsea decided on a plain white T-shirt and some black Express jeans. She threw on her latest pair of Air Max and went out the door. She got into her gray Nissan Altima and pumped her Lil' Kim bootleg all the way to Zeek's neighborhood. The "Get Money" lyrics that poured out of the speakers really had Chelsea feeling like a Queen Bee, and she only wished she was off to see her King.

Zeek was still sitting on the porch holding his head when Chelsea pulled up. Chelsea slowly walked up the steps, then came over and kissed him on the forehead. "Poor baby. It will be okay. You'll get another job in no time," Chelsea reassured him as she rested her chin on the top of his head.

Zeek knew she meant well, but he wasn't ready for her fortification. It took him a while to get his last gig and that's what worried him. If a job did come along, he'd be lucky if he got to start working by July. The likelihood of him getting a car in September, which was his goal, seemed way out of reach now. Instead of dwelling on the car situation, he turned to Chelsea to talk about his job loss.

"I had every intention of being to work on time. Today was the day I would make a change for the better. Before I could even start, I get fired...damn...I really messed up."

Chelsea sighed. "So I guess you're not going to be able to get me those shoes, huh?"

Zeek couldn't believe those words had come out of her mouth. *The nerve of her*, he thought. He was instantly upset. "Did you hear anything I said? I just told you I got fired! And you worried about some material shit!"

Chelsea got defensive. "I heard what you said, but you promised me those shoes two weeks ago."

"And?" Zeek asked sarcastically.

"You ain't get 'em. Don't say you can do somethin' if you really can't." She then let out a deep sigh. "I knew I should've asked my mom for 'em instead of you."

Zeek hated when she flipped it on him. It made him feel bad that he couldn't support his girl like he was supposed to. Her mom didn't have it like that, either. She made enough money to cover bills and take care of a few miscellaneous things. He knew her mother would sacrifice for her only child, as long as Chelsea pressed the issue enough. He would say anything to help lighten the burden on her mother.

"Look, I'm sorry, but shit happens. Once I get on my feet, I'll get ya ass two pairs of shoes, but right now, it's all fucked up."

"I understand you goin' through hard times, but you got to start makin' some real money, boo," she rebutted. She couldn't understand how making money was easy for others, but hard for him.

What she was saying was right, he thought. He did have to find a job that could satisfy his needs along with hers.

"Yeah, you're right. I'm going to get it crackin' soon. I got to find the right hookup. I was thinking about getting in construction or somethin'… And—"

Chelsea cut him off and focused her attention on the SUV passing by. "Damn! Is that Rodney? He got that Escalade chromed out. That nigga must be sittin' on some gees. You got to have money to get a truck like that." Chelsea took her eyes off the truck. "Oh…I'm sorry, baby, what were you sayin'?"

Zeek couldn't believe she'd cut him off to comment on Rodney's truck. She knew how bad he hated Rodney. Rodney used to always beat him up in the fourth grade over a girl named Shawnna Holt. Shawnna was Zeek's girlfriend, and Rodney couldn't stand it. Now Chelsea was feeling his style? Zeek's upper lip tightened as he quietly growled and stared at her.

"Damn! You on the nigga's dick like that? I'm tryna tell you how I can build, and you zone out on that nigga's shit?" Zeek spat.

Chelsea decided to down play it. "Come on now. I said the truck was hot. Damn, do you know how many niggas out here got those? I ain't sweatin' his shit…for real."

Zeek wasn't trying to hear it. "Yeah, whateva, let's go in the house," he commanded, not wanting to chance seeing Rodney ride past again.

She kissed up to him with a smile. "Good. I don't feel like sittin' out here anyway," Chelsea said as she stood up and dusted off her jeans.

After Chelsea walked into the house, Zeek looked around to see if Rodney was near. Not seeing his truck in sight, he went in the house and shut the door, as jealousy still loomed in his mind.

Lonzo left work and stopped by to see how Zeek was doing. He was about to knock on the door, when Chelsea came out. *What is she doing here?* he thought. *They were supposed to be broken up for three weeks now. Maybe she stopped past because he needed someone to talk to.*

Before Lonzo could try to put the whole thing together, she spoke to him. "Hey, Lonzo."

"What's up?" he said nonchalantly.

"Where have you been? I haven't seen you in a while."

Not knowing why she cared, he answered anyway. "I've been on the low. Handlin' business, you know what I'm sayin'?"

Chelsea assumed he wasn't doing anything but the same old thing. "So I guess you still work at that warehouse, huh?"

He turned defensive. "Yeah. Why?" Before he could hear her answer, Zeek came out on the porch. Lonzo couldn't help but to give him an irritated look, focusing back in on Chelsea's words.

"I'm sayin'. That's cool and all. I mean if that's what you want. But, I guess you doin' you. Right?" Chelsea said callously.

Lonzo was pissed off by her comment. *She doesn't even have a damn job! Who the hell is she to say something to me?* He had given her an evil look, but Chelsea didn't even notice him grilling her. She was all over Zeek kissing him goodbye.

"Okay, boo. I'll see you later. Aight, Lonzo. Hey, tell Jewel to call me so we can go out sometime," she said, going down the steps.

Lonzo was disgusted by the thought. He would never approve of his girlfriend hanging out with a girl like her.

Chelsea got in her car and drove off. Lonzo couldn't wait to hear what Zeek had to say about what was going on with them.

"Why was she over here, yo? I know you ain't messin' wit' her again?"

Zeek paused. "You know what, man? I ain't even gonna lie to you, Slim. I've been keepin' us on the low for a couple of weeks now. There's somethin' about that girl that keeps me coming back."

Lonzo was upset to hear. "I don't understand how you keep fuckin' wit' that girl, even after all the dirt she do."

Zeek was in denial. "Man, I don't believe none of that, young."

"All that shit you be hearin' in the hood, and you don't believe any of it?"

"Hell no. Niggas is jealous 'cause they ain't fuckin' wit' her."

"Now, it ain't only niggas talkin'. Broads be talkin' too," Lonzo reminded him.

"These bitches out here be hatin' on her. They mad 'cause they ain't on her level."

With that said, Lonzo was no longer able to bite his tongue. "They ain't on her level? Nigga, you ain't on her level, either."

Lonzo could see the tension in Zeek's face that he was terribly offended. "So what the fuck are you sayin', Slim?"

Lonzo thought he was speaking perfectly clear, but since Zeek couldn't see what everybody else saw, he had to break it down to his friend a little bit more. "I'm sayin' Chelsea don't want no nigga wit'out no paper. She's in to hustlas if you haven't noticed. Niggas wit' money. And on some real shit, homey, you ain't her type."

"What you mean I ain't her type? That girl gonna love me no matter what…for richer or poorer. She can be wit' any nigga out here, but she chose me, so obviously I'm doin' something right."

"For now you are. But soon she'll be havin' some baller get her what you can't…unless you plan on hustlin'?"

"Hell no. I ain't wit' that shit. I'm not riskin' goin' to jail to please her. Shit, no girl is worth me gettin' locked up."

Lonzo smiled. "Well, I'm glad to see you haven't lost all ya damn sense." Lonzo checked his phone for the time. "Yo, Slim. I'm about to get out of here, but do me a favor?"

Zeek could only wonder what was on his mind. "What's that?"

"Pay close attention to your girl. Examine her ways. After that, hopefully, you'll see what I'm talkin' 'bout. But I'm gonna hit you up later. I got to go meet Jewel."

They dapped each other up before Lonzo walked off the porch. Zeek smiled and made a last remark as Lonzo got to the bottom of the steps. "I don't know why you wasting ya time. You ain't her type."

"Yo, you real funny." Lonzo laughed as he kept on walking. Zeek thought a while about Lonzo's strong dislike of Chelsea.

In due time you gonna see. She ain't all about money…she's all about me, Zeek said to himself as he watched Lonzo stroll off.

CHAPTER FIVE

I t was Saturday morning, and Chelsea liked to spend the early part of her day watching movies and eating cereal. Today would be no different, except she had to wake up earlier than usual. She had two Blockbuster movies due back and didn't want to get any late fees. There was no time to watch them later, since she and Zeek were going out to the movies. A week had passed and Zeek still hadn't found a job yet, but that didn't matter to her. When it came to going to the movies, she didn't mind paying for him. Zeek was the only one she knew who liked going to the movies as much as she did. They would spend the whole day at the cinema sneaking into movies. She couldn't wait to get to the Cineplex. Once her movies, *Ride or Die* and *Biker Boyz*, were over, she would get dressed and pick up Zeek.

As soon as she put the last movie back in its case, her mother called her down into the living room. She was surprised there was a letter for her. It was sent from a James Wheeler, but better known as Wheelz. He was RoRo's best friend. RoRo was her ex-boyfriend who had bought her the Altima. She also had been seeing him for the last four years.

The only time Wheelz wrote if he was sending her money, and the last time she'd received a letter from Wheelz was in February. She couldn't wait to open it. She found a note and $800 inside the envelope. He usually sent her $300. She didn't mind receiving the extra money, but hoped the note would explain why. She began to read it.

Whatz up Chelz,

I hope everything a'ight wit' you. I'm chillin'. But ya boy Ro may be lookin' at life. We got to wait and see. He goes before the man at the end of August. I wish my nigga could be out for the summer but that shit ain't happenin'. Anyways... He told me to send you extra money. I won't be around for a while. I'm goin to Decatur to handle some business but I'll write you when I can. Ro will probably write you too. I can't promise you 'cause he got a lot of shit on his mind. But stay up, boo. And don't be fuckin' wit' no weak-ass niggas. I'm out.

Wheelz

RoRo had been locked up for over a year now. There was no bond set, and he had to sit in jail until his trial. He was facing charges for double homicide and attempted murder. There was a good chance he would be found guilty. Chelsea wondered what business Wheelz had going on in Decatur. All his drug connects were up North. *Maybe he was tryin' to get a different connect,* she thought. *Or maybe he was goin' to see a relative or somethin'.* Whatever it was, it wasn't important enough to keep her holding on to the thought.

She quickly counted out $400 and put it in her wallet, placing the other four in her Dutch Master blunt box that she retrieved from under her bed, which contained the rest of her stash. Her plans were different now that she got the money. She wanted to stop at the mall to get a new outfit before going to the movies. Since she was in a good mood, she would buy something for her mother and Zeek as well.

After getting out of the shower, she quickly got dressed and called Zeek to tell him to be ready in ten minutes. Before leaving out the door, she stopped short and gave her mother a hug. "I'm about to leave. I'm going to bring you something nice back from the mall, okay?"

"Girl, when you come back, we gonna have to talk about where this money be coming from," her mother said, giving Chelsea a troubled look.

Chelsea playfully rolled her eyes and sighed. "Okay, Mom, but I already told you not to worry. It's all good."

"All good nothing. Ain't nothing out here good if you ain't working for it. So that makes me wonder what you're doing to get it," she asked suspiciously as her eyebrows raised.

"Okay, Ma, you got me. I'm a prostitute. Instead of paying my pimp today, I'll bring you back all the money, okay?" Chelsea said, laughing at her joke.

"Girl, you are too damn smart." her mother said as she took a playful swing at Chelsea.

"I love you, Mom. We'll talk when I get back, okay? I'm still going to buy you something. Bye." Chelsea shut the door and ran to her car.

Her mother shook her head in frustration. It wasn't that her mother didn't appreciate anything her daughter did for her; she simply didn't approve of Chelsea getting money from men. *Why couldn't she get a job like everybody else?* she thought. *Only Chelsea knows the answer to that,* she said to herself, completing her thought. She peeked through the window and watched fretfully as Chelsea drove away.

CHAPTER SIX

helsea got to Zeek's house in exactly ten minutes, but he still wasn't ready yet. Chelsea waited in the car for another fifteen minutes, but Zeek still hadn't come out. *What the hell is he doin'?* she said to herself.

She was about to call his phone again when Zeek hopped in the car. "What's up, boo?" he shouted while shutting the door.

"Damn, nigga, what took you so long? Was you in there takin' a shit or somethin'?" she said jokingly.

"Yeah…my fault…my stomach's been messed up for the last two days," he said, cringing up his face.

"Well, I hope you wiped ya ass good 'cause if not, it's gonna start itchin'," she said, laughing.

"Oh, hold up…I know you ain't jonin' on nobody? Ya ass is so big you can't even wash the whole thing by yourself. I know ya drawls be stankin'."

"Come on now…you know my ass smells betta than ya mama's, nigga. Quit playin'."

"Why you got to go at my moms, yo? I should tell her what you said, too."

"Go 'head, tell her. You know she looks like the type that don't wash her ass."

"Damn, that's fucked up." Zeek got so pissed that Chelsea busted out laughing.

"I'm just playin' wit'chu. You know ya mom's my girl. She don't look like her ass stink."

They always enjoyed cutting up on each other. This was probably the best part of their relationship. They liked making each other laugh. For the past few weeks, they hadn't joked with each other as much as they used to, although Zeek happened to be the only one who noticed.

As Chelsea drove down the street with a blunt curled between her fingers, she felt Zeek staring at her hard, as if he was attempting to see straight through to her soul.

Chelsea caught Zeek looking at her when she passed back the blunt. "What's wrong wit' you?"

"Nothin'," he said unconvincingly.

"Then, why are you looking at me like that?"

"I'm just wonderin' what you are thinkin' 'bout."

"I'm thinkin' 'bout if I'm goin' to get these movies back to Blockbuster and what I'm gettin' from the mall."

"Wait a minute. The mall? I thought you wanted to go to the movies today?" Zeek asked, giving her a confused look.

"I did, but my godfather sent me some money this morning," she said with a straight face.

Chelsea had always told Zeek about RoRo but never the truth. She had him believing Ro was an old friend of her dad's who lived in Seattle. Chelsea always showed Zeek pictures of an older man whom she claimed was her godfather. Yet, RoRo was only a few years older than Zeek. He also never knew Ro was her ex-boyfriend. By the look on Zeek's face, she could tell he was mad about something. He didn't think anything suspicious had gone on between her and Ro. The problem was that she was getting money, and he wasn't.

"So I guess you gonna finally get those shoes you been wantin'?" he said sarcastically.

"No, I was gonna wait 'til you got 'em for me."

"Well, you gonna be waitin' a long-ass time, 'cause I ain't got no money," he angrily reminded her.

"I know you ain't got no money. Get 'em whenever you can. I ain't trippin' off that."

"See, that's the shit that pisses me off about you. You always want to spend my money before you spend yours. I'm tired of that shit!"

Chelsea could easily think of a hundred things about Zeek that she was tired of. Out of all the guys she'd messed with, Zeek was the only one who didn't give her any money. *At least, he could buy me a pair of shoes every so often*, she thought. Other than their interest in movies, Chelsea couldn't find any other reason why she'd kept him around so long. Now, her tolerance for him had run short.

"What? I'm always spending my money! You never have any money to give me! And I ask you to buy me one pair of shoes and you bitchin' about it! Fine! Don't worry 'bout 'em. I'll get 'em myself! And to think...I was 'bout to buy you something nice! I would have felt like a damn fool! Shit! Arguin' wit' ya dumb ass, I passed Blockbuster."

After turning around and pulling into Blockbuster's parking lot, they both remained silent. Chelsea grabbed the DVDs from the back seat and slammed the door when she got out.

"Damn, that nigga pisses me off so much! Why do I even bother wit' his broke ass! Uggghhh!" she said to herself. She dropped the movies in the box and stomped back to her car. She didn't want to be around him right now so she sat on the hood for a second. She realized she would rather be sitting in the mall instead of under the hot-ass sun so she got back in the car.

Before Chelsea started to drive again, Zeek felt bad and wanted to apologize. "Look, babe. I'm sorry for what I said. I didn't mean any of it. I'm depressed about how my life has been goin' lately. I guess I'm just a little jealous of you. You got money and I don't. That really affects my manhood."

Chelsea sighed. "Why didn't you say that? I would've understood."

Zeek shrugged his shoulders. "I don't know. I probably would have been embarrassed to admit I was jealous of you. But I really am sorry. I hope you forgive me."

Chelsea couldn't help but feel bad for him. Yet, she couldn't relate to his problem. She didn't remember the last time she'd gone without any money; someone always gave her some.

"I'm sorry, too," she apologized softly. "Let's try to have a good time today."

"Okay, I'm wit' that." He leaned in to kiss her as she met him halfway. After a few short pecks, they got back on the road and headed to the mall.

Chelsea sparked the blunt back up that had burned out during the argument. She hit it a few times and passed it to Zeek. "So what movie you tryin' to see first?"

"I was hoping we could see somethin' funny first."

Chelsea nodded. "I was thinkin' the same thing. I want to save the scary ones for last."

They were happy they'd come to an agreement for the first time today. Hopefully, their attitudes wouldn't change for the worst again.

They had finished smoking when they arrived at the mall. Chelsea reached into the glove compartment to get her Endless Love body spray. She hated smelling like weed, yet Zeek on the other hand, couldn't care less. She sprayed herself a few times to make sure she was straight. Once she popped some gum in her mouth, she was ready to hit the stores up.

Their first stop was Hecht's. She wanted to make sure she bought her mother something first, before she spent all her money on her and Zeek. Chelsea and her mother shared the same love for perfume, so they headed straight for the fragrance counter.

Chelsea thought it would be nice to get her mother something that was soft and sexy. There was a new fragrance that the sales associate told her about that smelled like candy. Chelsea sprayed the Tony & Tina perfume on her wrist and told the sales associate she was right. It did smell like cotton candy. She ended up buying her mother a bottle and got one for herself. The sales associate also gave her a few sample bottles to take with her.

After Chelsea completed the purchase for her mother, it was time to find something for Zeek. When he had money, Up Against the Wall was his favorite place to shop. Zeek immediately decided on a Rocawear outfit that was on display. Chelsea couldn't wait to see her man in some new clothes, so she was happy to get it for him. There was also a Baby Phat outfit on display that caught her attention as well. The only way she would get them both was if she got a deal, so she talked the salesman into giving her both outfits for a hundred and fifty. She ended up getting an eighty-dollar discount.

The movie theater was connected to the mall, so they decided to take their bags to the car before going to the theater. Chelsea popped the truck and threw the bags inside. Before closing the trunk, she added some Remy to a bottle of Coke and put it in her purse. Getting drunk at the movies had become a ritual for them. Chelsea also enjoyed going through the main entrance to see the Egyptian-styled designs outside of the Muvico theater. Whoever thought to make the theater look like an Egyptian temple was a damn genius in her eyes.

Chelsea and Zeek were disappointed that the three movies they'd watched so far weren't that good. They heard the next movie was scary as hell from someone leaving from it. They were hoping they had saved the best one for last. Halfway through the movie, Chelsea's cell phone was blowing up. She wondered who would be calling her that many times. *I hope nothin' happened to my mom. Maybe I'm trippin'. It's probably just Dya bein' nosy.*

Chelsea wanted to answer her phone badly, but she decided to wait in case it was one of her hookups. "I'll be right back. I got to go to the bathroom," she said, whispering in Zeek's ear. Zeek didn't think anything of it, since she had drunk so much soda.

Before she even made it to the bathroom, her phone vibrated again. She pulled it out of her purse and saw that it was Dya. "Hello."

"Girl, what you doin'? How come you ain't answerin' ya phone?"

"I'm at the movies wit' Zeek."

Dya sucked her teeth. "Girl, if you don't take that bum-ass nigga home so we can go out wit' some real niggas."

"All right, hold up. The movie's almost over. Hey, how many times did you call me?"

"About three times. Why?"

"I got like eight missed calls. Who we supposed to be hookin' up wit anyway?"

"Poundcake and Lunchmeat," Dya said proudly.

Chelsea was cool with that. Poundcake was Dya's hookup. Poundcake was tall with a maple syrup complexion and had a baby face like Usher. Lunchmeat was as tall as Poundcake, but he was light-skinned and chubby...really chubby.

Chelsea didn't mind hooking up with the fat boy. He spent well and loved eating her out. Out of all the times they'd hooked up, she only had to have sex with him once, which was the only time he'd ever asked. She hoped tonight it would stay that way. Besides, she wasn't in the mood to be trapped under all his weight anyway. Chelsea decided not to dwell on it since the likelihood of him asking was very slim. She still wasn't even sure if he was her best option for the night.

"Aight, hold up. I got to check the rest of my calls. I'm tryna see what else is crackin'," Chelsea informed her.

If someone was better on her callback list, Dya's hookups would have to wait.

Dya thought she was crazy. "Come on, girl, stop fakin'. You know nobody payin' like them niggas, and they from out of town, too. You can see them other niggas later."

"Yeah, true. But let me call you right back real quick anyway."

"Okay, but hurry up."

Chelsea looked at her missed call log. Dya was right; everybody was local. They had money and good dick, but none of them had paper like the Chicago boys. She hurried up and called Dya back and had everything hooked up for later on that night. The only thing now was for her to get rid of Zeek. She got back to her seat and Zeek had a "what took you so long" look on his face.

"Are you okay?" he whispered.

"Yeah. I'm fine," she whispered back.

"So, what took you so long?"

"I was talking to Dya. She wants to go to the club later."

Zeek's demeanor changed for the worst, almost seething while remaining silent for the rest of the movie. Chelsea didn't notice until they got back in the car, and on the road, that Zeek had an attitude. "What's your problem?" she asked, unsure what was going on.

"Are you goin'?" he asked, not looking at her, or showing any emotion.

"Goin' where?"

"With Dya," he said, rolling his eyes like she'd asked a dumb question.

"Yeah...she's tryin' to go kick it...why?"

"I thought we was chillin'? We've been together all day."

That was the problem. *We have been together all day*, she thought.

He had already cost her time and money, and now he wanted more. Zeek was about to get his feelings hurt. "We are chillin', but I'm tryin' to have some girl time. I'm sayin'…I'll stay wit' you for 'bout another hour, but then I gotta go."

She tried to explain to him nicely, but Zeek wasn't pleased. "You fuckin' always out wit' Dya goin' to some fuckin' club all the time! That's all the fuck y'all ever do! Y'all act like y'all lost somethin' up in them fuckin' places the way y'all always be up in there! Y'all young asses really ain't even old enough to get in them joints!" he shouted, in a tone Chelsea had never heard.

Zeek never got into clubbing like Chelsea had. He'd never understood the whole vibe. He didn't realize how the club was such a social haven where anybody could come to drink, dance, socialize and be seen by everyone who was anyone. He preferred to spend his time with Chelsea and only Chelsea. Zeek was frustrated that he was unable to get his way with Chelsea. At the same time, Chelsea was erupting on the inside.

After all the irritating things Zeek had said to her all day, her words flowed out of her mouth like lava. "Who the fuck are you raisin' ya voice at, nigga?!?!" she shouted. "Who are you talking to like that??? I'll go out to the club as many times as I want, and you won't do shit! Dya is my mothafuckin' girl, and I'll be wit' her as long as I want! Fuck that! I spent my money and bought you shit, and you start bitchin' 'bout me goin' out! You weak as hell for that, yo! Fo' real!"

"Oh, so I'm weak as hell for that? You supposed to be my girl and you talkin' shit on me!"

"Yeah…you weak! And broke! I'm tired of your shit!"

"So it's like that? 'Cause I ain't got no money? You feel you can disrespect me—"

"You damn right," she interrupted.

"Well, fuck you then. Take me home right now!"

Chelsea rolled her eyes. "Where the fuck you think I'm goin'?" she said sarcastically. "I can't wait for you to get the hell out my car!"

As they pulled up in front of Zeek's house, he couldn't wait to get out and tell her he was done with her. Chelsea was thinking the same thing, only on a whole different level. She had a baller waiting to fill her pockets back up and didn't need to deal with his unnecessary drama. Zeek's tantrum wasn't about to spoil her night. Her mind had been elsewhere when she heard Zeek's voice piercing through her thoughts.

"And you can keep that outfit you bought me. I don't want shit from you," he said as he slammed the door shut. She was about to curse him for slamming her door, which she hated, but to get him out of her face, she let it ride.

Before one of his feet could hit the porch, Chelsea sped off.

Zeek walked in the house and went straight to his room. He lay on his bed thinking about what could be wrong with his girlfriend. Despite all that happened, he still hoped they could salvage their relationship. In a few days, he looked forward to everything being forgotten so they could start fresh again. All he wanted was the old Chelsea to come back. He wanted the Chelsea that he could talk to without money becoming the main subject, the Chelsea who always had time for him and wouldn't let a day go past that they didn't see each other. The Chelsea who always told Zeek she loved him. He knew if he could get that old Chelsea back, he would be happy.

CHAPTER SEVEN

Before Zeek could put his key in the door, Chelsea was out of sight and already on the phone with Dya. "What's up, Dy? What's crackin'?"

"Is you away from that nigga yet?" she whispered, not wanting Zeek to hear her talk reckless.

"Yeah...I dropped his ass off a few minutes ago. So what's the plan?" she asked impatiently.

"They want us to meet them at the Friday's in Greenbelt. Come over my house, and I'll drive."

"Aight, I'm on my way. Give me like five minutes."

"Cool. I'll tell 'em everythang is all to the good." They both hung up the phone.

Dya waited in her car while Chelsea got the rest of her things out of her car. She popped the trunk and lifted up the spare tire cover. On top of the tire was a Donna Karan overnight bag containing a bra set, deodorant, socks, body lotion, toothbrush, and a Sean John velour outfit. She grabbed the bag and got in the car with Dya. They both came equipped with overnight bags for situations like this.

"Girl, we seen so many movies, but most of them were dumb," Chelsea told Dya on the way to Friday's. Chelsea sighed. "But let me tell you what was really dumb. Zeek's dumb ass blew the shit out of me."

"Damn, what he do now?" Dya asked.

"Girl, he got all in his feelings 'cause I told him we was going out. Then he started talkin' to me out the side of his head and I had to carry his broke ass. I swear he makes me sick."

"I don't understand, Chelsea. You got all these other niggas that got paper, so why do you even bother with him?"

Chelsea shrugged. "I don't know. I guess it's complicated."

"Do you think he even know how you really get down?"

"Nope. That nigga think I'm an angel without wings." Chelsea smiled.

Dya shook her head. "Ya boy's either blinded by love or he's too slow to catch on. Either way he's fucked."

"I couldn't agree more," Chelsea said as they pulled into Friday's parking lot.

Lunchmeat and Poundcake were already posted up in a booth, long before the girls even showed up. They chose Friday's because it was close to their hotel and they could blend well in the overcrowded restaurant. They both sipped on Crown Royal while discussing business. Business was actually the only thing they really ever conversed about. They were both big-time drug dealers from the South Side of Chicago. They were also members of the notorious street gang, the Organized Crime Gangstas.

Larry Gatton got the name Lunchmeat while growing up under extremely harsh conditions as a child. Both his parents were on drugs and he had to take care of himself by any means necessary. He wore the same clothes to school every day and the others kids said he always smelled like old bologna. It wasn't until he started selling drugs and making a name for himself that he started to embrace the cruel name he was given. Now with his overweight stature, his name suited him like never before.

Jamie Nelson had it hard, if not harder, than Lunchmeat did as a child. He lost his mother to drugs and his father to prison before he turned ten years old and was forced to live with relatives along with his younger siblings. He sold anything from stolen car stereos to marijuana to get money to put food in all of their stomachs. It wasn't until he got his hands on crack cocaine that his poverty-stricken days would come to an end. One day after hustling for twenty-four hours straight, Jamie decided to weigh all the money that he'd come home with.

He stacked all of his assorted bills on a triple beam scale, and to his surprise, his money weighed in at 456 grams, which was equivalent to weighing a little over one pound. That's when young Jamie realized he was starting to make some serious money, or cake, which everyone in the drug game called it.

"Getting cake by the pound" would be the motto he lived by and that's how he got the name Poundcake, given to him by none other than Lunchmeat himself.

Business had been good for Lunchmeat and Poundcake for some time now. They owned a few luxury apartment buildings on the better part of Michigan Avenue along with various properties throughout the city. There had been no beef between them and their rival gang, the Black Viking P. Fosters, which was good for both organizations. Despite everything that was going right for these two powerful hustlers, Lunchmeat and Poundcake still wanted more. They were at the table trying to cook up a hot new plan.

"Are you sho' you wanna make a move on Forty-Ninth and Ashland?" Lunchmeat asked, while swallowing the remainder of his strong drink.

"Hell yeah, I want that block. That's the first thang I think about soon as I wake up," Poundcake said with a straight face.

"Oh, yeah, I could understand that. There's mad paper on that strip." Lunchmeat saw how bad Poundcake really wanted it. "But you know them Vikes ain't givin' that up easy."

"Man, fuck them niggas. I got somethin' for they ass."

"Hey, if you want to go bum-rush them niggas, you know I'm wit' it." Like Poundcake, Lunchmeat had killed a few niggas in the past to take over another area. Murder was no problem for them when it came to getting more money.

"Nah...that's only goin' to cause a war. Not that I really care. But I want to hit them niggas from the blind side."

"How we gonna do that?"

"We'll pay some fiends to do a drive-by on 'em niggas. As long as they shout out 'Gammas' and throw up signs, the Vikes will think the Gammas are being disloyal and strike back."

The Black Viking P. Fosters and Rolling Gammas were under the same family. Poundcake thought he'd come up with the perfect plan to catch the Vikes off-guard. Starting a feud between them would cause chaos and allow O.C.G. to move in on the Vikes' territory. He knew his plan was bound to work.

As they put a close on their conversation, Dya and Chelsea walked over to the booth.

"What up, boss playas?" Dya said as she threw her hands up.

"What's goin' on, fellas?" Chelsea said with a smile as she took a seat.

"It's about time y'all got here," Poundcake said jokingly.

"Yeah, we were 'bout to eat without y'all," Lunchmeat added.

While the girls got themselves comfortable in the booth, the fellas got them whatever they wanted. They all ate and drank while they laughed and flirted with each other. Lunchmeat was starting to enjoy all the extra attention Chelsea was giving him. She had rubbed her hand around his crotch a few times, making him harder than a pistol.

Chelsea's sudden interest in Lunchmeat didn't come by accident.

In the car, Dya had told her about how much money Lunchmeat was really working with. Poundcake had mentioned to Dya that they were making over $70,000 a month off the apartment buildings alone. Chelsea grew curious on how much Lunchmeat was making in the streets. What she really wanted to know was how much could she get out of him in the long run.

The elevator took them up to the top floor of the Marriott on Ivy Lane, which was down the street from Friday's. Poundcake and Lunchmeat already had rooms there since they were in town on other business. They were in the process of opening a night-club in the D.C. waterfront area, which would be another way to legitimatize their drug money.

When the girls got in the room, they couldn't believe how big the suite was. It was the biggest hotel room they'd ever been in. Dya thought it was bigger than a three-bedroom apartment. They had really stepped their game up. As soon as Poundcake entered the room, he started rolling up some weed they'd gotten from a local dealer. Who had also been their biggest client in the area. Lunch-meat positioned himself in front of an assortment of liquor bottles that were on the counter and started making drinks to help the girls feel more at ease.

"Ladies, we're goin' to all have to take a trip together real soon," Lunchmeat suggested.

"Lunchmeat, baby, you know I'm wit' it," Chelsea said, holding up her drink.

"Where y'all wanna go?" Dya asked.

"We were thinkin' about goin' back to Cancun," Lunchmeat mentioned. Cancun was where they had met Dya and Chelsea during Memorial Day Weekend last year.

"But we might try somewhere different, like Belize," Pound-cake added.

Chelsea knew that she and Dya loved Cancun so much and they would be ecstatic to go back again. She'd never heard of Belize, but if these big-time ballers knew about it, then it was a place she had to experience.

"Yes, Belize. That sounds nice," said Dya.

"Yes. We would love to go there," added Chelsea.

It was settled. They would all go to Belize. Poundcake and Lunchmeat would use this trip to celebrate after they successfully took over the Black Viking P. Fosters' corner.

Lunchmeat watched how his boy was all over Dya. Watching them made him want to have a little fun of his own. "Come on, baby. We goin' to let these two be alone." Chelsea grabbed her purse and night bag and followed Lunchmeat into the connecting room, which was an identical suite. Lunchmeat spread his large frame across the king-size bed and turned on the TV.

"Yeah, baby, get comfortable. I'm gonna go take a shower," Chelsea said while flashing a devilish grin.

The look she gave him would have made a rabbit get an erection. His manhood swelled as she entered the bathroom.

Chelsea came out of the bathroom wearing nothing but a towel. As she walked, she left a scented trail of her strawberries and champagne body splash that quickly filled the room. Lunchmeat lay in his boxers, admiring Chelsea's body as she dropped her towel and crawled on the bed like a cat. "Damn, you sexy than a mothafucka. Lay down, girl, so I can show you what my tongue's been missing all these months."

Chelsea rolled on her back and spread her legs for Lunchmeat to come get it. He ate out her middle so vigorously that she had no choice but to climax right away. It was too soon for him to be done, so she didn't let on that she'd busted already, hoping she could get off another one. She grinned when she did, but what came next took her by surprise. After he was finished, he lifted his head to wipe his mouth, then reached in the nightstand for a condom. This caught Chelsea so off-guard, she didn't know what to do.

The odds of him actually wanting to have sex were slim to none in her eyes. If she really wanted to play ball now would be the perfect time to take a swing. Chelsea swallowed her pride and began to handle her business.

Crack! Urp! Crack! "Come on! Give it to me, baby! Give it to me!" Dya yelled as she and Poundcake were getting it on.

Dya's naked body was positioned on the dresser as Poundcake repeatedly rocked her up against the mirror. "You like that shit, don't you? You like that shit, huh?"

"Yeah! Give it to me! Pound me out, baby! Pound my shit outttt!" *Crack! Urp! Crack! Urp!* Dya played her part well.

Back in the other room, Chelsea was holding her thing down, too. Chelsea was riding Lunchmeat like he was her prize horse at the Kentucky Derby. His eyes rolled into the back of his head, as he let out strange noises and thought to himself. *Damn! This sexy bitch got me open like a mothafucka. She got me up in here whinin' n' shit. I don't want to cum yet. No, no, no! Don't cum yet! I want this shit to last…oh shit!*

Chelsea pounced on him rapidly, thinking the complete opposite.

Come on, you fat mothafucka! Hurry up and bust! Hurry up! Yeah!
Yeah! Let that shit out!

Lunchmeat grabbed firmly on her waist for a few seconds,
trembling from busting his nut. He huffed as he spurt the last of
his seed, his hands sliding off her waist and onto the mattress.

Chelsea rolled off of his weak body and onto the bed. Lunchmeat lay almost motionless while gasping for air. He had been
with many women in his lifetime, but Chelsea's sex game made
him look at her differently. She would probably be the death of
him, but he couldn't help falling in love with her. With the trip to
Belize coming up, he was already making plans for their future.

"Damn, girl. You got me fallin' for you hard," he said, staring
into her eyes.

"You don't have to game me up, you know? You already got
what you wanted." She smiled. She might have thought it was all
fun, but for Lunchmeat, this wasn't game at all. Chelsea was the
type of girl he needed. Once he got her to trust him, he could
wife her up.

"Nah, baby…I'm serious…this ain't game. I'm goin' to prove it
to you. I got plans for us," he said as he kissed her on the forehead.

Chelsea couldn't help but smile. "What type of plans you talkin'
'bout?"

"Be patient, sweetie. You'll be the first to know before every little
thing happens. I promise. I ain't gonna let you miss out on nothin'."

"Okay. I'll be patient, Meaty baby." He loved when she called
him Meaty. It made him go crazy inside.

"I want you to come to the Windy to see me."

"The Windy? Chicago? I wouldn't have anything to wear. I hear
them girls up there be show-stoppin'. I wouldn't want to make
you look bad."

"Look, girl. Don't worry about all that. I'll handle that in the morning. I want you to tell me you'll come."

Chelsea didn't have to think hard about it. "Okay, Meaty. I'll come see you. I would like to know when."

"I'll send for you in a few weeks. We 'bout to open up another spot around the way. I want to wait a while to make sure everything's runnin' smooth. Then I'm goin' to show you how we do it in the Chi."

He put his arm around her so she could rest her head on his massive-size chest. Shortly after, he fell asleep, leaving her awake with all of her thoughts. The truth of the matter was Chelsea had enough new clothes she hadn't worn to start her own boutique. She wanted to see how bad he wanted her to come to Chicago. She looked at it as an opportunity to take a business trip of her own. The perks were great.

She would get to visit a new city, receive a few expensive outfits, and stuff a couple of dollars in her pocket. If she was able to break out on her own, maybe she could run into some other ballers while she was there, too. Right now, her life was looking sweet and about to become sweeter. She rested her hands under her face, then closed her eyes and went to sleep with a smile on her face. She hoped to have dreams of spending Lunchmeat's money.

Zeek's face continued to fill up with frowns as he stared at the ceiling. He'd been up all night thinking about how he'd left things with Chelsea earlier. He also hoped that she would have called him by now as he checked his phone again. *I overreacted. Was it possible that I'm too insecure? Maybe I have to trust her and allow her*

to have her own space. Damn. I don't even know if I should be the one to resolve our conflict, he thought. Zeek wanted to make things right with Chelsea any way he could. He ultimately knew that getting a good-paying job would be the starting point. Zeek decided he would call her the next day, then begin looking for a job. He prayed that everything would be back to normal for them, soon.

CHAPTER EIGHT

"One, two, three, four, five, six, seven, eight, nine, ten. A thousand. One, two, three, four, five, six, seven, eight, nine, ten. Two thousand," Lunchmeat whispered to himself as he continued to count his money.

Chelsea woke up to the pleasant sound of money being shuffled and the sexy smell of Issey Miyake cologne. She rubbed her eyes to see a well-dressed Lunchmeat sitting at the table counting out hundred-dollar bills. His white and blue Nautica button-up shirt and stone denim Diesel jeans fitted the overweight thug nicely. He smelled so good that if he had been someone of her physical standards, she would have ripped his clothes off and sexed him right in the chair he was sitting in. Instead, she simply enjoyed the smell.

"Good mornin'." Chelsea smiled as she stretched out her arms.

"Hey, good mornin'. I was about to wake you to see if you wanted breakfast. Are you hungry?"

"Yeah…I am," Chelsea said, thinking of her growling stomach.

"Me too. Soon as you get dressed, we can go downstairs. Poundcake's already dressed. He's waitin' on ya girl," Lunchmeat added.

"Okay…I'll get in the shower now. I won't be long."

She walked past him naked and smiled when she went into the bathroom. He liked the fact that she didn't even eyeball how much money he had on the table. *She didn't even take a glance*, he thought.

He knew she wasn't a gold digger and he could start trusting her a little bit more.

Chelsea had flipped out in the shower after seeing all the money that was on the table. *There must have been thousands*, she mused quietly to herself. *How much was he goin' to give her? What was he plannin' on using it for?* So many questions came to her mind, but no answers.

Hopefully, he will hook me up with a g or two, she imagined. She stepped out of the shower and dried herself off. "Damn, that shower felt good, but an extra thousand in my pocket would feel even better," she said, looking at herself in the mirror. Chelsea came out of the bathroom and made sure she didn't look at the table. She sat on the bed and started to put her bra set on. To her surprise, Lunchmeat walked over to her and put a handful of money in her face. "Here. Put this in your purse," he commanded.

Chelsea tried to play dumb. "Do you want me to hold it for you?"

"No, it's yours." He smiled.

Chelsea was in shock. "What? Are you serious?" she asked with a smile from ear to ear.

"I wanted to ensure that you'll come to Chicago. You don't have to spend it all on clothes. Save some for a rainy day."

"You really don't have to do this. I was gonna come anyway. Besides, I wouldn't feel comfortable takin' this much money from you."

Now even Chelsea knew that not taking money from hustlers was an insult to them. Every hustler never wanted to feel like they didn't have it like that, or that they were giving away their last. Lunchmeat just fell deeper into her game.

"Baby girl, this ain't shit. You gonna start seein' a whole lot more than this here. Get used to it, baby…take it."

She slowly grabbed the money, then put it in her purse. She got off the bed and gave him a tight hug and kiss. "Thank you."

Lunchmeat rubbed her back as they embraced. "You welcome, baby."

Chelsea finished getting dressed while Lunchmeat put the rest of his money in a small luggage bag. "Make sure you don't lose that purse. You just put five stacks in there." He smiled. *Did he say five thousand? There's no way he gave me that much.* If he did, there was no way she was letting that purse out of her sight. She threw the purse on her shoulder and was ready to leave out the door.

At breakfast, Chelsea was too excited to finish her waffles and bacon. She wanted to know how much money Lunchmeat had really given her. When the time was right, she excused herself from the table and went to the ladies room. She ran into the first open stall she saw and sat on the toilet to count her money. She felt weird sitting on the toilet without actually having to use it, but once she started counting the hundred dollar bills, she quickly got over it.

She finished counting and couldn't believe she was holding $5,000 that was now her own money. She felt like she had become rich overnight. Five thousand dollars would be more than enough to buy all her summer clothes. She thought about all the sandals and outfits she could get as she rubbed the bills between her fingers. Her thoughts turned to all the fake broads that she didn't like as a wily grin formed on her face. *If I gave 'em a reason to hate me before, they're gonna get more of a reason now*, she predicted.

Dya came in the bathroom to see what was taking Chelsea so long. She started looking under the stalls. "Hey, girl, where you at?"

"I'm in the next to the last stall."

Dya walked to the end of the bathroom and stood in front of the stall. "What you doin' in there?"

"I'll show you when I come out."

"Nah, that's okay, girl. I don't need to see that shit. Did you eat somethin' bad?"

"No, girl. It ain't like that." Chelsea opened the door and showed her the money.

Dya was shocked. "Girl, if he finds out you robbed him, he's gonna kill you."

"I didn't rob him. He gave it to me."

Dya took a step back. "He gave you all that?"

"Yeah… This mornin'."

"How much is it?"

"Five gees."

Dya couldn't believe it. "Five gees? Damn, bitch! What type of pussy you think you got?"

"One that's worth a couple million," she said while doing a little strut. Chelsea was really feeling herself now. According to Lunch-meat, she was going to start getting pussy payments like this on the regular.

Dya was extremely happy for her friend's quick come-up. Although Poundcake didn't give her any money, he did promise they would go shopping. She was sure to try and get $5,000 worth of clothes out of him now. The girls took a quick look over themselves before leaving the bathroom and couldn't wait to get to the mall.

Back at the table, Lunchmeat had told Poundcake how much money he'd given Chelsea. Poundcake agreed to give Dya the same amount. It wasn't hard to tell that they were heavily influenced by each other. "If he could do it, I could do it too" were the words that they lived by. In the future, those words wouldn't mean anything to either one of them.

They both watched the girls prance back over to the table. "Damn, ladies, we was about to send someone in after y'all. We thought y'all might of fell in," Poundcake said with a grin.

"Nah…we were havin' girl talk. Besides, our asses are too big to fit through those little toilet seats." Dya laughed. Chelsea giggled along with her.

Poundcake couldn't argue with that. They soon finished eating breakfast and were now ready to tear the mall up.

The fellas convinced the girls to shop in Baltimore instead of around D.C. They told them they knew D.C. like the back of their hands and wanted to explore new ground. The truth was that they didn't want to take a chance being seen by the other girls they messed with.

Chelsea and Dya looked at this as a chance to stunt in front of some B-More girls. An hour later, they found themselves at the Towson Town Center ready to spend some dough. Almost all the stores Chelsea and Dya liked to shop in were at this mall.

Nordstrom had a wide variety of designer bags. They wanted to pick out purses before they bought any clothes. They decided on Amy Hobo by Marc Jacobs. The Amy Hobo bags only came in green and black. Chelsea got the green one and Dya the black. Before the purses were paid for, Poundcake handed Dya a large stack of money.

She was so glad she didn't have to kiss his ass every time they went into a store. She blew him a kiss, then made her purchase. The purses cost $995 each, which meant they had a little over $4,000 left to spend.

Chelsea bought two pair of BCBG pumps for $175 each, while Dya paid $550 for one pair of Dolce & Gabbana sandals. Chelsea and Dya usually had different shopping habits, and today it showed. Chelsea bought a couple of Polo shirts for her and a Tommy Bahama shirt and cologne set for Lunchmeat, and then she was done. Dya, on the other hand, bought a $500 pair of Dolce & Gabbana jeans along with all the matching accessories. She then topped it off by getting a $1,200 diamond tennis bracelet from Gordon's Jewelers.

Dya was definitely living for the moment, but she could afford to. Dya always had someone giving her money more often than Chelsea did. She could spend her whole $5,000 today and get $500 more tomorrow. Chelsea more or less would have to ration hers out.

Lunchmeat and Poundcake didn't buy anything. They watched and observed the girls' actions. Poundcake thought that both girls had style, but Dya was a lot classier than Chelsea because of her expensive taste. Lunchmeat had a different outlook about both girls altogether. He saw Chelsea buy one expensive item, and the rest of her purchases were average. Chelsea even bought him a few items. Then, she saved the rest of her money like he advised her to do.

Dya didn't buy Poundcake a damn thing. Lunchmeat didn't have to worry about giving Chelsea money and having her come back broke two days later. Dya would have been nothing but a pain in his ass; he was trying to rid himself of girls like her. However, Poundcake felt empowered by a girl like that.

At the end of their escapade, Dya only had $735 left from heavy spending, while Chelsea still had over $3,000. They decided to have lunch at the Rainforest Café, but before they did, the girls wanted to take another lap around the mall, so the haters could see them again.

Some girls gave them dirty looks as they carried their shopping bags. Lunchmeat and Poundcake wanted to floss their chicks as hard as the girls did with their shopping bags. They didn't mind other cats looking at their women. 'Cause game recognized game, and no man had enough of it to strip them of their women.

Lunchmeat and Poundcake's flight was scheduled to leave at 4:38 p.m. from Ronald Reagan National Airport. After lunch, they still had two hours to get back to the airport. They were only an hour away from the airport, so this gave them plenty of time to get back and check their bags. Poundcake rode with Dya in her car, while Chelsea and Lunchmeat trailed them in the rented Cadillac. Both couples wanted to have their last little bit of quality time together before said their final goodbyes.

Dya and Poundcake talked about last night and how much fun she had shopping with him today. Lunchmeat and Chelsea weren't only talking about last night and what happened today. They talked about their future together.

Lunchmeat kept telling Chelsea how much he enjoyed her company, and all her responses to him were vice-versa. He told her that when she came to visit him, she was going to be one of the baddest chicks Chicago had ever seen. She took what Lunchmeat said as a compliment, as well as a big challenge. Chelsea knew she had what it took to be highly favored in D.C., but to go into Chicago and become the talk of the town seemed hard for her to imagine. She thought Dya would have a better chance than she would.

Chelsea always thought Dya was more beautiful than she pictured herself. Chelsea had the pretty looks, long curly hair, and hour-glass-shaped body, but Dya had the beauty. Dya had high cheek-bones and vanilla glowing skin that always looked like she applied the right amount of makeup. She had mysterious smoky-gray eyes that forced men to be sexually captivated by her. Dya's looks were extremely ornamental, simply beautiful. Beauty was what Chelsea was after, but she knew that was something you had to be born with. It wasn't something you could buy in a store. It had to be natural.

If Lunchmeat thought she was that chick, she needed to find out what he thought about Dya. "That would be nice, but I think Dya would turn more heads than me. Don't you think?"

Lunchmeat twisted his lips. "Yeah, right...I know that's your girl, but Dya ain't got shit on you." He laughed.

This was strange for her to hear. Dya always got more attention than she did. *What was he tryin' to say about my friend?* "What? You don't think Dya's pretty?" she asked, watching his eyes to see if he would lie or not.

"Nah...she's pretty, but she got too much attitude and not enough presence. You got all that shit and a betta body." Lunchmeat paused. "On some real shit...niggas from the Chi would kill for a chick like you."

The thought of someone killing over her made Chelsea feel eerie. *Who would kill over me? Were Chicago niggas that crazy and I didn't know it? Or was I a diva and didn't know it, either?* Chelsea had always been self-conscious of her looks. She always felt inferior to Dya. She lacked all the self-esteem a pretty girl should have. Maybe her going to Chicago was more valuable than painting the town red or picking up a couple more ballers. She would find identity in herself. Maybe, Chelsea would kill for that.

During the remainder of the drive to the airport, Chelsea started to take Lunchmeat's words to heart. She always came second to Dya, except for one time. They both had attended Amidon Elementary School all the way up until the sixth grade. When it came to lining up to go to lunch, Chelsea came before Dya. This was actually how they met. It was the first day of kindergarten, and all the children had to line up in alphabetical order for everything they did. At the head of the line was Michael Adams, followed by

Tiffany Atkins, then came Chelsea Brose standing in front of Dya Burke.

They instantly became friends when Chelsea's shoe came off on the way to the cafeteria, and Dya helped her put it back on. Ever since then, they were inseparable. Dya was always one step ahead of her. She had sex first, smoked weed first, drank alcohol first, and even had a car first. It didn't matter how hard she tried, Chelsea could never get one up on Dya. Now with her overweight lover filling her up with confidence, she might have a chance to be on top.

The airport wasn't crowded like it was when the fellas first arrived. The rental wasn't due back for another ten minutes, so Lunchmeat talked to Chelsea in the car before turning in the keys. Before he could get out a word, Chelsea's phone rang. She knew from the ring tone who it was. *Shit! It's Zeek. He's always callin' at the wrong time.*

She dug in her purse and stopped her phone from ringing. "I guess that was ya boy, huh?" Lunchmeat asked.

"Yeah…that was him. I'll call him back later, though." *Damn, I forgot I told him about Zeek. I need to stop running my mouth so much*, Chelsea said to herself.

Lunchmeat knew everything about Zeek that he probably wouldn't want him to know. Chelsea always aired him out when she was upset with him. But Lunchmeat didn't care about Zeek; he cared about her. He was always the type that wanted someone else's woman. There was no desire for him to go after a woman without a man. He got no challenge from it. Chelsea had been with Zeek off and on for five years now. Lunchmeat knew she was going to be the challenge of a lifetime.

They continued to talk for a few more minutes. Before they got out the car, Lunchmeat gave her another $1,500.

She was surprised all over again. "What's this for?"

"I want you to get some nice dresses. There are some fancy restaurants in the Chi I wanna take you to."

"But I still have a lot of money left from earlier. I think that will be enough," she said with a smile.

"No, I want you to save that. Take this to spend," he demanded.

She put the money in her purse, and then they got out the car. She ran over to his side and gave him a big hug and kiss. "Thank you, Meaty. I really appreciate everything you done for me," she said while her face pressed up against his large chest.

"I know. That's why I don't mind doin' things for you. Stay the way you are and soon you're gonna think you're dreamin'."

Not knowing what to say to that, she giggled and squeezed him tighter.

Lunchmeat and Poundcake got all of their belongings from the Cadillac Seville and returned the keys to the booth. The girls walked them to the arriving flights entrance and said their last goodbyes. The next time Dya would see Poundcake would be in Belize, unless she came with Chelsea to Chicago. Chelsea would soon talk Dya into coming. There would be no way Chelsea would be able to leave town without her road dog.

Chelsea was in no hurry to call Zeek back. She waited until they got back on Interstate 295 North before she placed the call.

"Hello," he answered quickly.

"What's up, Zeek? Sorry I missed ya call," Chelsea said as Dya nudged her for even calling him.

"That's okay. What are you doin' right now?"

Chelsea shrugged her shoulders. "Nothin'…comin' back from takin' Dya's aunt to the airport."

"Hi, Zeek!" Dya yelled loud enough for him to hear, knowing he didn't like her that much.

"Tell her I said, what's up."

"He said, hi."

"Tell her I said, what's up, not hi," he commanded. "You make me sound like I'm gay or somethin'."

Chelsea rolled her eyes. "Whateva. He said what's up, Dya. Now, are you happy?" she asked in a playful tone.

"Yeah, that will do." He laughed.

Zeek decided to press his luck. "What are you doin' later on?"

"I don't know yet. Why, what's up?" she asked, already knowing what he wanted.

"We need to talk. I want to apologize in person. I would like to see you if you didn't mind."

Her mouth wanted to say no, but her heart forced her to speak otherwise. She gave in to him once again in order to protect his feelings. She promised Zeek she would be over to see him once she left Dya. Maybe tonight, she would get everything off her chest to rid her of all the guilt she kept inside. That's only if Zeek would be able to handle it; the truth, that is.

Chelsea put her clothes back on after she and Zeek's intimate encounter. The kind words from Zeek as soon as she'd arrived at his house allowed one thing to lead to another. Soon, she found herself embodied with his light passionate stroke. Yet, her pleasure never matched his, as he lost all his stamina while she contained all of hers. *Maybe that's why I fuck other niggas. I can never bust with this mothafucka. If he can't fuck me right, he could at least pay me for my time. But this broke-ass nigga can't even do that. Let me get my ass out of here.*

When Zeek came out of the bathroom, he noticed that Chelsea was fully dressed and putting on her shoes. "Where are you goin'?"

She thought it would be better to lie. "I gotta go. It's gettin' late."

"Oh. I thought we could watch a movie?"

"Nah…maybe tomorrow would be better," she suggested.

Chelsea was acting strange and Zeek knew it. "I don't please you? Is that it? Tell me what it is. I promise I won't get mad." He hoped to get an answer to his question.

"No, Zeek. Everything is fine. We already talked about this earlier. I'm tired, that's all."

"So if there was a problem, would you tell me?"

"Yes, Zeek, I would tell you. But everything's okay. There's no problem." Chelsea lied to him again. As much as she wanted to tell him everything she felt and bring their relationship to a tragic end, she was unable to tell him the truth that would set her free, and ultimately, destroy him.

Zeek settled for her answer and let her leave at her own will. He still thought there might have been more to her story, but he wasn't sure. Chelsea called him as soon as she got home like she'd promised.

Once she hung up with him, she found herself frustrated; her body was on fire. Thanks to Zeek, she faced the prospect of masturbation to release all her sexual tension. Even if she played with herself, she would still be restless. She needed someone with a swift stroke to make her sleep like a baby, so she called up her old friend Mister to come scratch her itch.

Mister was a tall, dark-skinned thug with a nice body and a long pipe. He was really into Chelsea. Whenever she called him, he would drop everything he was doing and come running. This time was no different. He left his girlfriend at the club to have a midnight quickie with Chelsea. He told his girl he had some business to handle and would return to the club. Instead, he ended up meeting Chelsea at the Super 8 hotel in College Park.

As soon as they got in the room, they went straight to it. They stripped each other down and wrestled their way onto the bed. Mister hurried to put on a condom, then pushed himself inside of her and quickly began to pound her out nonstop as quivers traveled up her spine.

"This is what I been waitin' on," she moaned. *Zeek never gives it to me like this*. Zeek always attempted to make love to her, but she clearly wanted the exact opposite. Although, Chelsea never told Zeek how she wanted it, she knew that Mister never had to ask. He gave it to her the only way he knew how, fast and rough. He finally emptied himself of his powerful load. She'd lost count of how many orgasms she'd had.

When it was all said and done, Mister went back to the club while Chelsea stayed in bed. Mister left her no money, but this particular time Chelsea didn't care. She had taken part in this act for mere pleasure all on her own. She'd gotten what she'd come for and much more. Her body continued releasing juices as she drew into a deep sleep. She hadn't had sex like that in a long time, and she loved it.

CHAPTER NINE

It had been two weeks since Lunchmeat and Poundcake had been back in town. Now it was time to put their plan into action. The target area was Forty-ninth and Ashland. The cats that ran that block were the Black Viking P. Fosters. They were led by a crazy thug named Bumble.

Bumble was medium height and dark-skinned with a long scar running down the left side of his face. He'd grown up in the dangerous Robert Taylor Homes where he'd gotten his name after he'd committed his first murder at the age of eleven. Killa Green, one of the former leaders, now deceased, had given him his name. He said the way he attacked his enemies was like a killer bee.

The block seemed normal to Bumble as he watched his crew handle transactions from across the street. Bumble posted up on Forty-ninth Street and observed everything that went down on Ashland. He made sure he stayed away from the money and drugs that his workers carried. He kept his burner inside the top of a fire hydrant in case something popped off.

Since everything was cool, he went to holler at some girl who was getting in her car. After saying a few smooth lines, he was able to get her number. He had promised to make plans with her later that night, when suddenly his attention focused on a fast-moving black Ford Taurus heading toward his strip. He noticed inside the car were four men wearing ski masks with guns in hand. He imme-diately sent the girl on her way and went for his gun.

Before he made it to the fire hydrant, it was too late. The drive-by was already happening. Gunfire rang out, while his crew ducked down behind cars and proceeded to fire shots back. One of Bumble's soldiers was able to shoot out one of the car's front tires, causing the driver to crash into a telephone pole.

Everyone in the banged-up car appeared to be injured. Yet, one of the passengers attempted to make a run for it and got shot in the back of his head, dying instantly as his body slammed to the ground. Bumble and his crew ran up to the car ready to light shit up. Drake, one of Bumble's lieutenants, put his gun to the driver's head.

"So you Gamma mothafuckas tryin' to kill us? I thought we was fam, bitch?" Drake asked.

That's when Bumble looked at everyone in the car a little closer. "They ain't no fuckin' Gammas," Bumble implied.

"That's what the fuck they was yellin' when they ran through this bitch," Drake stated as he still pointed his gun at the driver.

"Nah…look at 'em, hog. These mothafuckas ain't wearin' no beads. Y'all know Gammas wear black and gray beads around their neck. Yo, somebody sent these mothafuckas."

Drake started to take notice. "So somebody wanted us to start beefin' wit' the Gams for a reason. These are some bitches-for-hire-ass niggas. Who sent y'all?" Drake said, pushing his gun into the driver's eyelid.

The driver was so scared that he pissed on himself. The other passengers looked like they were going to do the same.

Everyone in the car was so scared to respond to Drake. This made Bumble madder than he already was. "Didn't none of y'all bitches hear my hog ask y'all a question? Somebody betta say something, before I have one of my niggas put a rocket in y'all head and end up like this faggot-ass nigga y'all brought with you," Bumble said, referring to the dead man that tried to run. Drake pressed his gun into the driver's eye even harder, giving him an instant migraine.

He had to talk now. "It was O.C.G.," the driver muttered.

"Do you know how many O sets there are, nigga? Y'all mothafuckas betta start droppin' some names," Bumble commanded.

"Who the fuck sent y'all?" Drake yelled.

"It was Lunchmeat and Poundcake," the driver cried. "They paid us to do a drive-by to start some shit between y'all and the Gammas."

Drake looked at him like he should be telling them more and the driver knew it. "That's all we know...I swear...they didn't tell us anything else." The driver continued to cry.

After that was said, Bumble signaled Drake to kill the driver. Drake fired his gun slumping the driver's body over onto the passenger's lap.

Bumble was now ready to get rid of all of them. "I want y'all to lose these niggas and throw this ride away, too. Burn this bitch first, if y'all got to," he demanded.

Drake popped the trunk and threw the two bodies in there along with the two living passengers who would later be gagged and duct-taped together. Drake took Gripp with him to get rid of all the bodies. Gripp was about the same height as Drake, maybe an inch or two taller. He was dark-skinned with a lot of muscle definition and had the strength of three men. He was Drake's right-hand man and his killer in crime. While Bumble was driven off in a red Jeep Grand Cherokee, the rest of his members scattered from the scene.

Bumble rode in the back of the SUV and analyzed everything

that had happened. He hadn't expected some bitch shit like this from Lunchmeat and Poundcake, especially since they were top-notch gangsters. They had been trying to buy out his block for the longest. *To do a snake move like this was asking for a war.* What made Bumble even madder was that his block would be hot, and they wouldn't be able to deal there for a while. This may have left the block open for anyone to try and take over now. Lunchmeat and Poundcake had to die.

Ever since Lunchmeat got back to Chicago, he and Chelsea had been texting each other and talking on the phone like crazy. Lunchmeat was watching their little love affair take flight. Chelsea was pumping his head up with everything under the sun. She also sent him pictures of her, some modeling in two-piece swimsuits and some of them in nothing but a thong. Those pictures brought him back to their times of intimacy.

Yet, everything Chelsea told him wasn't all game. She was starting to catch some feelings for him. Lunchmeat talked so smooth and knew exactly what her insecure mind needed to hear. He knew how to make her feel at ease. Chelsea was so comfortable with him that she gave him her social security number to do her passport application. Her expectations of going to Belize grew by the second. She really trusted him and felt like he would cause her no harm.

Drake and Gripp stashed the car with the bodies in it at their chop shop until it was dark outside. By the time they got back to the car, it was almost midnight. They checked to make sure the two men in the trunk were still gagged and duct-taped to each other. After seeing them still bound together, they closed the trunk and headed for the highway. They drove into a wooded remote area about fifty minutes outside of Chicago. Once they made it to their designated spot, the two men in the trunk were each shot twice and killed by Gripp.

After they dug a hole, they dumped all four bodies in it and covered them up. Drake and Gripp laughed at all the graves they had made in the area. They'd dumped so many bodies there it looked like a small cemetery. They were pleased with all the work they'd put in over the years. They later took the car to a nearby junkyard and burned it before they rode off into the night in the car Gripp had followed Drake in. They later broke up the Glocks that they'd used in the murders and threw them into Lake Michigan.

Ten days had passed before Chelsea received her passport in the mail. She didn't like the picture she'd taken, but was still happy she was leaving soon. Dya had received her passport and was waiting for Chelsea's to come. Chelsea had already told Zeek she was going to Myrtle Beach with Dya's family. Zeek had gone with them last year and hated every minute of it. There was no way he would put himself through that torment again. Since he fell for her story, she had a valid reason to leave town without getting questioned.

In two days, Chelsea and Dya would be heading off to Chicago and then Belize. They both went to the Bowie Town Center mall to get some last-minute items for their trip. They went to Victoria's

Secret to get some sexy swimsuits and lingerie. Dya got some Pink perfume, and Chelsea got Very Sexy One. They also picked out some pretty panties to go with the outfits they would buy. Most of the clothes they bought came from Wet Seal and The Gap. They got a few tank tops and several pairs of coochie-cutter shorts. Once they picked up some Gucci flip-flops from Macy's, they were finished with their shopping.

Hunger pangs started to kick in, so they went to the food court and ate at Panda Express. The moment Dya put her fork in the plate of food, her phone rang. She was irritated as she dropped her fork to reach into her purse. "Damn. Niggas always callin' at the wrong time n'shit," she spat. She looked at her phone. "Oh. It's Pound. He's lucky it's his ass, girl. Shit, as hungry as I am… hello? Yeah, what's good?"

Unfortunately, Poundcake had nothing good to say on the other end of the phone, except for sorry. The more he talked, the more disappointment appeared on Dya's face. Chelsea could tell there was something wrong. When Dya got off the phone, she told Chelsea the bad news.

"He said we ain't goin' nowhere."

Chelsea was confused. "We're not goin' where?"

"On the trip… He said they goin' at it with two different gangs out there and shit ain't safe for us."

"What the fuck that got to do wit' us goin' to Belize?" Chelsea asked.

"I don't even know, girl. But, he said we still goin', but not right now. That's still a blower, yo."

The girls couldn't believe their Central American voyage was put on hold for the moment. Dya was so pissed off she wanted to take all her clothes back, but Chelsea wouldn't let her. Chelsea wanted to wait to call Lunchmeat and dreaded to hear the same bad news from him. She decided to wait it out until he called her first. They continued to eat their food hoping that their trip would be back on soon.

The girls left the mall to go to the nail shop. Even though they weren't going out of town anymore, they still wanted to get a manicure and pedicure. Right before they arrived at the nail shop, Lunchmeat gave Chelsea a call. This was the call she'd been waiting for. She hoped that their situation wasn't the same as Poundcake and Dya's.

By the time Chelsea got off the phone with Lunchmeat, she was relieved. Lunchmeat still expected her to come to Chicago to see him, and after that, they would fly to Belize. This was music to her ears. Not only would she get her toes and nails done now, but she would get a Brazilian wax touchup as well. The ball was now in Chelsea's court, but Dya wanted to play defense.

Dya constantly pleaded with Chelsea not to go to Chicago. She felt it wasn't safe and something could possibly happen to her. Chelsea didn't let any of Dya's motherly words sink in. Dya was being protective and jealous at the same time and Chelsea could sense it. Chelsea was going whether Dya liked it or not. She had something to prove and was going to go prove it. This was her big chance to finally be ahead of the pack. No longer would she live walking in Dya's shadow. For Chelsea, this trip wasn't for fun. It was for placement and status. She was ready to put herself on another level.

Lunchmeat never told Chelsea the whole story. In Chicago, a war was going on, and bodies were turning up all over the South side. Bumble put a hundred stacks on each of Lunchmeat's and Poundcake's heads and everybody was trying to cash in, at least those who weren't scared. Poundcake decided to skip town until everything died down. His team was strong and could definitely handle the gunfire, but everybody was only shooting at him and Lunchmeat. There wasn't enough reason for him to stick around, but Lunchmeat did the opposite.

Even after one of his Mercedes was car-bombed and he was caught up in a ten-minute shootout, Lunchmeat still didn't run. He held his soldiers down as much as he could without getting killed. Eventually, his people wanted him to stay out of the field because he was too valuable for them to risk.

Lunchmeat had fallen out with Poundcake because he'd left a war that he'd helped start. "So now you just gonna run like a bitch, huh? After shit backfires, now you scared, bitch?" Lunchmeat had yelled into the phone.

"Ain't no bitch in me, nigga. I'm just lettin' shit cool down before we make the next move."

"Mothafucka, this is the next move! You knew it could come down to this shit before we even agreed to do it! All our soldiers are in the field ready to go, but where the fuck are you? You straight pussy, nigga!"

"Where am I?" Poundcake smirked. "I'm on a beach surrounded by bitches. You need to get like me and stop playin' in them streets, Fatboy. You might get ya self killed." *Click.*

When Poundcake hung up the phone, the feud between two longtime friends had been ignited. Poundcake had turned his back on all his soldiers and Lunchmeat couldn't let that ride. Lunchmeat and the O.C.G.'s promised if Poundcake ever came back to Chicago, they would kill him on sight.

Lunchmeat could've easily fled the city, too, and been looked at being disloyal the same way as Poundcake, but there was too much money to be made, and most importantly, Chelsea was coming to hold him down. Lunchmeat didn't need to make any more money. He was a millionaire a couple times over and owned enough property that he would never have to hustle another day in his life if he was to stop today. Even with all the love from his family of hustlers and killers surrounding him, he still didn't have the love from a woman. Over the last two weeks, no other girl he messed with wanted to get near him. He was too high risk for them. He thought about all the fake bitches that were after his money. They always talked about being down for him but weren't. And the girl that didn't care about his money was.

Chelsea knew about all the drama in his life and it didn't seem to faze her. She didn't care about that. She cared about him. He was convinced she was the ride-or-die chick he was looking for. He'd promised himself if Chelsea kept her word after the war was over, he would get out the game for good and make her his wifey. Lunchmeat was ready to shower her with all the riches he had and love he wanted to give. He only hoped Chelsea was on a plane headed to Chicago Friday morning.

CHAPTER TEN

Zeek rushed through his front door carrying a stack of job applications and darted up to his room so he could fill them out. After two weeks of solid job searching, he was pleased with his results. "I can't believe I got an interview already." He smiled as he put his pen to the first form and wrote his contact information.

He had gone from store to store determined to get his name out there and not come home empty-handed. After talking to every hiring manager that was available, or willing to talk to him, he ended up getting an interview with Settlers Construction Company. His palms started to sweat thinking about how much the job was paying. *I need this job bad. I ain't never made that much money before. I really hope I get it,* Zeek thought as his grip tightened around the now moistened pen to keep it from slipping out.

Zeek finished filling out all the applications he had, but he was still far from finished. Most of the places where he had gone wanted him fill out an application online and then wait for a response. After filling out a few, he decided to take a break. His mind was so fixated on the construction job interview that he felt applying for any more jobs at this point was overkill. There was no doubt in his mind that the job wasn't his. Zeek felt the manager was impressed with his eagerness and would have a hard time not making him a part of the team.

His mind started to drift as he thought about everything he would buy with all the money he would be making. Not only would he have a new car, but his clothes and shoes would be on another level as well. Zeek knew that getting that job would bring Chelsea and him closer together. Them becoming one again was something that he badly desired. Zeek quickly reached for his phone and dialed her number.

Chelsea double-checked her bag to see if she had packed everything. Assured that she had, she headed downstairs to say goodbye to her mother, who was about to leave for work and was looking for her car keys.

"Are you lookin' for your keys?" Chelsea asked.

"Yeah. Why you've seen 'em?" her mother asked while still looking for them.

"Yeah. You left 'em in the door last night. I put 'em in your purse."

Her mom looked in her purse that was dangling off her arm and then laughed. "Thank you, sweetie. Girl, I was so tired last night. That damn job of mine. I came in and went straight to bed."

Chelsea became saddened. "Dag, mom. I wish you didn't have to work. You deserve better. Soon I'm goin' to be able to take care of you. And you'll be able to leave that job for good."

"What you mean soon? You plan on hittin' the lottery or somethin'? Girl, don't worry about me. Take care of yourself. I'll be fine."

"But, Mom, I can't stand watchin' that job take your life away. I want to help."

"You know how you can help? I want you to do better than me...understand? Go back to school and become a pharmacist or even a teacher. Damn, Chelsea. You can be whatever you want. Please don't let these men out here selling drugs make you think that's the best way. 'Cause it ain't. Get your money the right way."

Even after her mother's long speech, Chelsea still looked at her in dismay. *She doesn't get it. Things ain't like it was when she was growin' up. A nigga ain't shit out in the street without no money. What does she want me to do? Wait until I get out of college before I make any money? That would be at least four years wit'out gettin' paid. Fuck that. I need money now. If these niggas are stupid enough to give it to me, then that's on them.*

Chelsea blocked her mother out as she continued to talk. The only thing she heard her say was, "I think Dya is here."

Chelsea looked through the blinds and was glad to see Dya walking up to the house. Normally, Chelsea would sit and listen to her mom go on and on about what she should be doing with her life, but today, she didn't have the time to listen. She had a plane to catch. Her mom opened the door and happily greeted Dya.

"Hey, Dya."

"Hey, Ms. Tina. How are you?"

"Tired, girl, but I'm cool." Chelsea's mom remembered about work after checking her watch. "Look I got to run, but y'all have a safe trip and enjoy y'all self." She gave them both hugs and walked to her car, but not before stopping short. "And Chelsea, remember what I said."

Chelsea sighed as her mother got in her car and drove away. For now, Chelsea wouldn't give her mother's words a second thought. She shut the front door and was off to the airport.

The whole car ride Dya kept trying to talk Chelsea out of going. She was really starting to piss her off.

"Damn, yo. Nothin' you say is goin' to change my mind. I'm just goin' to fuck wit' this nigga for a few days and come back. Ain't shit gonna happen."

"Well, answer this: if y'all still goin' to Belize, how come y'all can't go to Chicago when y'all come back? Or why can't y'all skip Chicago altogether and go to Belize?"

"Bitch, I ain't got time for this. The same reason you not. I ain't get that option. I'm goin' to take what I can get," she spat.

Dya was unable to respond. She was mad that Chelsea had put her in her place. She was also jealous that she wasn't going. Dya didn't say anything else to her until they arrived at the airport.

Dya pulled in front of the airport and wasn't ready to give her girl a happy farewell. Dya stood up on the curb with her arms folded waiting for Chelsea to get her bag from the trunk. Chelsea could see Dya had an attitude, so she tried to psych her up.

"Come on now, bitch. Don't be actin' like that. You supposed to be happy for ya girl. What? You don't want me to bring you back no fly shit? 'Cause I'll go shoppin' for me."

Dya began to smile. "You know what size shoe I wear, right?" They hugged and made up. "Damn, boo, I'm goin' to miss you so much. Please be careful out there," Dya advised.

"I will, girl. But don't even trip off that nigga Pound. We goin' to go to Cancun when I get back, me and you."

"Well, if Belize is like that, I'm tryin' to go there instead."

"Whateva you tryin' to do, I'm wit' it. Stay up and I'll holla at you when I get there."

Chelsea turned to walk away, but Dya cursed loud enough to stop her.

"Wait. What about Zeek? He thinks you'll be wit' me. What if he sees me?" Dya asked.

"That nigga ain't got no whip. You'll be straight. I'm not even worried about it."

"A'ight, cool. Have a safe flight." Dya smiled as Chelsea made her way into the airport.

Dya drove back home thinking that she didn't want to lie for Chelsea, if she did happen to run into Zeek. Not that she was jealous of her girl, but she felt sorry for him. She decided she would stay clear of any place he might be.

Chelsea heard her cell phone ring right before she got to her gate. "Ahhh, not now, Zeek. Damn, why did Dya have to talk his ass up," Chelsea said as she shook her head before answering the call.

"Hey, Zeek," she said, rolling her eyes.

"What's up? What you doing?"

"Me and Dya gettin' ready to go. Let me call you back when we get there," Chelsea said as she approached the security gate.

"Okay, cool. But let me tell you something real quick."

"What?" she quickly asked.

"I got a job interview."

"Oh wow, Zeek. That's great. Where at?"

"Settlers Construction Company. My interview's next week."

"Oh, I know somebody that used to work there. They used to make good money too. I hope you get it."

"Yeah. 'cause you know I need it." Zeek laughed. "Okay, I wanted to tell you that. Go 'head and call me when you get there."

"Okay, I will. Later, boo."

Chelsea hung up the phone and hoped Zeek got the job so he could get himself together. Chelsea quickly put him to the back of her mind as she thought about the wonderful trip that she had ahead of her.

Chelsea boarded the plane and got comfortable in her window seat. She sipped on her strawberries and crème Frappuccino from Starbucks, while waiting for takeoff. As the plane soared at 37,000 feet, Chelsea wondered what Chicago would really be like. She imagined Chicago having as many clubs as D.C. had, but more ballers that went to them. Her competition would be heavy, but she was ready to show Chicago hoes what D.C. bitches were all about. Chelsea couldn't wait to meet them head-on. *It was so easy to get Lunchmeat to fall in love wit' me*. Although, any emotions she might have had for him were only developed for the love of money. Her mother was right. She was about to win the lotto and Lunchmeat was the winning ticket. Soon, she would be able to cash in and run away with her jackpot. She adjusted her seat and enjoyed the rest of the flight.

CHAPTER ELEVEN

he plane landed smoothly at O'Hare International Airport a little after 10 a.m. Chelsea strolled through the huge airport until she reached baggage claim. While she waited for her bag, she called Lunchmeat to notify him of her arrival.

"Yo, what's up, baby. I'm here. I'm waitin' for my bag."

He advised her to go to the arriving flights side of the airport. He also said he would not be meeting her himself. She was to look out for his boy in a green Ford Excursion. He would be the one to bring her to him.

Chelsea stood up against the wall waiting for her driver. A few minutes later, a cat in a green Excursion pulled up to her. He leaned over the passenger seat so he could holler at her.

"Aye, thang-thang! Is ya name Chelsea?"

"Yeah," she responded as she walked over to the truck.

Lunchmeat had sent his young boy Jaws to pick her up. When he got out the truck, Chelsea checked him out, as he popped the trunk to take her bag. Jaws was about six feet even and brown-skinned. He wore a black throwback Jordan jersey, black jeans, and a black baseball cap with a red "B" on it. He also had on a pair of crispy black and red Air Force Ones. Lunchmeat gave him his name because at a young age, he was ready to chew up the streets.

Chelsea thought he was cute and didn't mind riding with him.

"What's up, C-bone? I'm Jaws. Meat sent me to scoop you."

"That's cool. But why didn't he come himself?"

"I don't know, thang-thang. I'm doin' my job."

With no more questions to ask, Chelsea attempted to open the passenger side door, but Jaws opened up the back door for her instead while giving her a smile.

"Nah, thang-thang. Stars ride in the back out here."

Chelsea blushed and hopped in the backseat. She'd never gotten this type of treatment before, yet she thought it looked funny to be sitting in the back, when there was no one else in the front seat. She went along with it and enjoyed the ride. Chelsea felt so lost in the back of the big truck.

Chelsea couldn't believe how big Chicago was. It was so much bigger that D.C., it almost reminded her of New York City. The Sears Tower was the tallest building she had ever seen. She wanted to go to the top of it before she left. Jaws watched her actions through the rearview mirror. It was time for him to see what she was all about.

"Damn, girl. You really picked the best time to roll to this mothafucka."

"Why you say that?" she questioned.

"Didn't ya boy tell you? Niggas is getting stretched out all over this bitch. Ya pretty ass should've stayed home. This ain't a place to be takin' no vacation right now."

Chelsea scoffed. "Nah, boo. I ain't tryin' to have fun out this shit. I'm here to spend time wit' my nigga," she answered wisely, hoping she wasn't falling into one of Lunchmeat's "see if I can trust you traps." Chelsea played it safe not knowing what Jaws already knew about her.

Jaws could sense Chelsea was getting a little uneasy with his questioning. He then offered her something to calm her down.

"Aye, C-bone. You smoke?" he said, holding up a blunt.

"What kind of weed you got up in there, playa?"

"Some Northern Lights. I know where you from y'all ain't got shit like this," he said, passing her the blunt.

"Nah. I ain't never heard of this shit before," she said as she lit the blunt, then took a couple pulls.

Just a few puffs of the thick powerful smoke left Chelsea's chest throbbing. "Damn, that's some strong shit," Chelsea said while wiping the tears from her eyes. "Why don't you sell me some of that shit?" Chelsea hadn't bought weed in years, but was willing to pay for some of what he had. "Nah, thang-thang. Ya boy Meat got this, too. I'm sure he'll give you some."

Knowing that, she was happy she could get the same weed from Lunchmeat for free. This was the best weed she'd ever had.

Jaws continued to look at Chelsea through the rearview mirror. He considered her to be one of the sexiest girls he'd ever seen. She messed with Lunchmeat, but he still wanted to try his hand anyway.

"So, C-bone. Where you from, yo?"

"D.C."

"Oh, yeah? D.C.'s a rough city. How a fine-ass broad like ya self handle livin' out that shit? I guess you must fuck wit' a major nigga down there or somethin'?"

"Not hardly." She laughed. "My man ain't even in the game."

Jaws raised an eyebrow. "Oh no? He don't hustle? Why not?"

"'Cause, man. That nigga ain't built for that shit."

"Damn, thang-thang. You talkin' like you built for it. You ain't ready for that shit, either."

Chelsea sucked her teeth. "What, nigga? You don't even know me at all. Your girl's the one that ain't ready," she said with a playful grin.

Jaws twisted his lips. "You ain't even tryin' to see my girl like that. She'll beat 'cha little ass."

"What? Call that broad right now. Ya girl will get her ass beat. I'll be fuckin' her up so bad, ya ass will jump in it. I'll have to beat both of y'all niggas' asses."

"Yeah, right, you too pretty to be that gangsta."

Chelsea playfully rolled her eyes at him. "Damn. You must have an ugly bitch if she's too much for me to handle. Nigga, my name rings bells where I'm from."

Jaws laughed at her silliness. "Yo, you crazy girl, but you real."

"I know," Chelsea said with confidence.

Jaws would soon see how real she was.

The weed Chelsea smoked was taking a huge effect on her. She felt like she was floating while driving through the depressed South Side of Chicago. The streets were crowded with so many people that it reminded her of Baltimore. Jaws thought by driving through this part of town would make her nervous, but he saw no change of expression in her face, until she smiled. Jaws had taken her through the deadly Stateway Gardens projects and she wasn't even scared. He knew then that Chelsea was gangster.

Chelsea noticed that Jaws turned onto a small, quiet, rundown street. He drove to the end of the dead end way and turned into a lot of an old office building.

"Meat is up in here," Jaws said as he pulled up to the empty vacant building.

"He's in there?" she questioned, hoping this wouldn't be the place where she would be getting dropped off.

"Yeah. That's his truck right there," he said, pointing at a BMW that was parked a few spaces down from them. Before Chelsea could decide what she was going to do, Lunchmeat called her phone.

"Hello," she answered.

"Hey, baby. I see you outside. Come through the door right in front of you and walk straight to the top."

Still hesitant, she hung up the phone and said her goodbyes to Jaws. "A'ight, young. Good lookin' on the ride. I'll probably see you again."

"Yeah. Maybe sooner than you think," he said with a grin. She smiled back not thinking anything of it and got her bag.

When Jaws drove away, Chelsea checked out Lunchmeat's new Maroon BMW X5 SUV sitting on 20s. She could tell it was new; all the stickers were still on the windows. Chelsea liked the truck, but thought it was too small for someone his size to be driving. Chelsea entered the building and proceeded up the dark staircase until she saw a light coming from under a cracked door in the middle of the hallway. She guessed that had to be were Lunchmeat wanted her to go. She decided to keep on walking.

She opened the door thinking she was going to walk into a shit hole, but yet discovered on the other side of the door was a luxury Italian-styled furnished condo. As she walked around, she saw a huge kitchen with a marble floor and an island. The living room had a fifty-inch flat screen surrounded by a long navy blue leather sofa. Chelsea couldn't believe how phat his crib was. Out of nowhere, Lunchmeat grabbed her from behind. "Hey boo," he said while wrapping his arms around her waist, causing Chelsea to smile.

"I was wonderin' where you were. Damn, you got a nice place here!"

"I was hopin' you'd like it. I bought every available house and building on this street and I'm going to redo all of them with this same design. They're goin' to be my new line of luxury condos."

Chelsea was definitely impressed. Lunchmeat stared into her eyes. He really missed Chelsea and couldn't shake her from his mind ever since their last meeting. He was so sexually backed up from not having sex in three weeks he had to have her right then. He picked her up and carried her into the bedroom. He placed her

on the bed and started removing his clothes. She already knew
how bad he wanted to fuck her. Anything she could do to keep
Lunchmeat happy would also help her out even more. That's why
Chelsea took off her clothes and braced herself for what was about
to happen next.

The sex was okay for Chelsea, but unbelievable for Lunchmeat.
They lay in bed facing each other, while wrapped together underneath red silk sheets. Lunchmeat couldn't take his eyes off of her.
He realized he had fallen in love with Chelsea all over again. He
felt she was the perfect woman for him. He could also tell Chelsea
was having a hard time holding back her feelings for him as well.
Yet, Chelsea was not feeling what Lunchmeat had felt. She wasn't
in it for love. She was only in it for money. She couldn't care less
if Lunchmeat loved her. Chelsea was only with him because of his
money, not for what she had for him in her heart.

Chelsea couldn't wait to get out into the city and live it up. She
wanted to see what Chicago was all about and get her hands dirty.
Chelsea was so excited thinking about it that she wanted to leave
at that very moment.

"So when are we goin' into the city? I'm tryin' to have some fun."
She edged closer to him.

Lunchmeat had other plans. "We're not goin' to be able to do that,
ma. I got mad niggas aimin' at my head right now. I can't let you
get in the middle of my shit."

Chelsea was crushed. *Why the hell I got to be missin' out on shit
'cause people shootin' at ya fat ass?! Shit! Just tell me where to go, and
I'll get around my damn self. This is some bullshit!* Chelsea was so pissed,
her whole day was ruined, but she didn't want to expose her attitude.
She put on her worried face. "Damn, boo. It's like that? Niggas
really tryin' to kill you?"

"Yeah, but fuck 'em. They ain't gettin' me. They might get Pound's bitch ass, but they ain't gettin' me."

Chelsea was surprised to hear about how Lunchmeat and Pound-cake had fallen out. After he had told her about all the shootouts and car bombings, she didn't want to go anywhere in Chicago with his ass.

Lunchmeat advised Chelsea to go shower up because they were going straight to the airport and off to Belize. Chelsea was happy again. She thought she would be cooped up until they left the next morning, and forgot all about wanting to go to the Sears Tower. She wanted to go to Belize right now. Chelsea kissed him on the cheek and hurried into the master bathroom. Inside were a big round tub and a separate shower. She wanted to get in the enormous tub to relax, but didn't want to waste time by filling it up. She quickly put her hair up in a bun and jumped in the shower.

Chelsea rubbed the thick washcloth all over her body. She fell in love with the multiple showerheads that sprayed her body from all different directions. She thought it was the best shower she had ever taken and didn't want it to end. When she turned off the water and reached for a towel, she heard several voices in the other room arguing. She couldn't imagine who Lunchmeat would have let in the house.

She quickly wrapped in a towel, then cracked the door to get a peek of the action going on outside. To her surprise, Lunchmeat was getting assaulted by two gunmen. Chelsea could only make out one of their faces. He was a dark-skinned man with a scar running down his face. The other man was wearing a black bandana over his face and had one tied around his head. She could see evil in both of their eyes.

Chelsea was so scared. She couldn't believe this was happening.

She looked for an escape route but was trapped in the bathroom.

"Where's the money, mothafucka?" one of the gunmen yelled as he pointed his .50-caliber Desert Eagle at Lunchmeat's head.

"I told y'all bitches three times I ain't got shit here," Lunchmeat grumbled. "What the fuck you think you gonna do, Bumble?"

Bumble and the other gunman didn't believe him, so he directed the other gunman to dig into a large flowerpot that stood beside the dresser, ripping out the miniature palm tree that was buried in it. He dug his hands in the pot and pulled out a large trash bag. He put the bag on the dresser and tore it open, showing Bumble what was inside the bag. Bumble and the masked man feasted their eyes on what appeared to be over $400,000 in the bag. They could eyeball the amount in comparison to a rival gang's stash house they'd previously robbed. They had taken $100,000 from there, and this pile was three to four times bigger than that one.

Lunchmeat was astonished that someone had found his stash spot. Not only the fact that they'd found it, but they knew exactly where it was. There was only one person who knew about his stash spot, and he hoped that person wasn't hiding under that mask.

Lunchmeat was furious. "You's a stupid mothafucka! You gonna rob me? And this mothafucka's the enemy. What the fuck is wrong wit' you, nigga?" Lunchmeat yelled at the masked man trying to intimidate him. Instead, he only enraged him.

"You's what the fuck's wrong wit' me!" the masked man yelled, before raising his gun at Lunchmeat and shooting him in the abdomen.

The gunshot wounded Lunchmeat, putting fear in Chelsea as her heart continued to beat out of her chest. She knew the masked gunman had some sort of tie to Lunchmeat. The way Lunchmeat talked to the man sounded like they were friends. Chelsea didn't want to accept who she thought was behind the mask, despite only meeting him hours ago.

Bumble cocked back his gun and looked at Lunchmeat. "You gonna die today, nigga. But as much as I want to kill ya fat ass for tryin' to take over my shit, I'm not. My little homie here is goin' to take ya ass out, but before you go, take these with you." Bumble shot Lunchmeat twice in the waist and once in his right shoulder. Lunchmeat's body filled with pain.

"Those was for you lyin' to me about this paper, bitch," Bumble said as he grabbed the bag of money and stood in the doorway. Bumble then gave the masked man the command. "Go 'head and merk this nigga."

The masked man aimed his gun at Lunchmeat and gave him a cold stare. Lunchmeat thought that it was only right that he knew who his killer was going to be.

"So is that how it's goin' to be, you lil' bitch? You goin' to kill me and I can't even see ya face?"

The masked man stood in silence, which only angered Lunchmeat.

"Take that flag off ya face, you fuckin' coward! Take it off!"

The masked man slowly pulled the bandana off of his face. When the man revealed himself, Lunchmeat's body quivered with rage while Chelsea was in total astonishment. *It's Jaws.* She couldn't believe that Jaws was a part of this hit, but she wasn't aware that Jaws had reasons deeper than she knew.

Jaws had harbored bad feelings toward Lunchmeat ever since he'd removed him from a major corner he was running last year. He felt some type of way about Lunchmeat trying to stop his shine. Jaws wanted to be a boss, but with Poundcake and Lunchmeat in his way, that wouldn't be possible. If they both were out of the picture, he could rise to power.

Jaws definitely had it twisted. Lunchmeat didn't want to hold him down. He had taken Jaws off the corner to protect him. Jaws always had the block hot and never learned discipline. Lunchmeat loved him like a little brother and didn't want his reign to end before it ever started. Yet, Jaws never saw it that way and wanted revenge. This was what he'd waited so long for.

Jaws walked up close to Lunchmeat with fire in his eyes. "Sorry, Meat. But you brought this shit on ya self. You should've never took me off that corner. On top of that, you put some bitch-ass nigga in my spot! Nigga, I'm the king on these streets! I was runnin' all you and Pound's shit by myself while y'all sat back and got rich! Fuck that! I'm takin' over now!"

"I hope killin' me gets you everything you ask for, nigga. I always tried to shape you for the top spot, but you was too much of a fuckin' hothead! Wit'out me, ya bitch ass ain't goin' to be shit! Remember this, you lil' mothafucka! You could never be me!"

That was all Jaws needed to hear. He shot Lunchmeat right between his eyes, causing his body to slump against the headboard. Jaws shed a tear for his old mentor, but it was his time to be king.

Bumble was happy to see that Lunchmeat was no more. He had gotten what he wanted and was ready to leave. "Aight, nigga, let's be out."

Bumble's plan had worked perfectly. He had completely brainwashed Jaws into crossing his own family. Bumble had put up $200,000 to whoever killed Lunchmeat and Poundcake, and Jaws wanted to be the one who made it happen. Jaws knew exactly where Lunchmeat would be hiding and he knew where he kept his bail money if he ever went to jail. At first, Bumble thought he was being set up, so he had to put Jaws to the test. Bumble had Drake and Gripp snatch up an O.C.G. member and throw him in the trunk.

Bumble later popped the trunk to show Jaws who he had to kill.

Inside the trunk was Poundcake's little cousin, Pester. Pester was like Poundcake, only younger. He had leadership qualities with a strong ambition to get money. Pester was actually the one that was given Jaw's corner.

Jaws saw his opportunity to get revenge more ways than one. He shot Pester once in the head and that was all he wrote. From then on, Bumble knew Jaws was all about his business and not about family. As soon as Jaws finished playing out his part, Bumble would kill him. Bumble knew Jaws had no loyalty and couldn't be trusted.

Bumble planned on killing him when they got back in the car, but his body suddenly hit the floor before he made it into the living room. Bumble caught two bullets to the back of the head. Jaws was supposed to get $100,000 for killing Lunchmeat, but when Bumble wanted him to kill another one of his own, he knew he wouldn't live long enough to ever collect it. Jaws picked up the bag of money and headed back toward the bedroom.

Chelsea was even more frightened when she heard more shots go off in the house. Her best guess was that Jaws and the man with the scar had killed each other. She had never seen a dead body in her life. It was hard for her to even look at Lunchmeat's body, but for her to walk past two more bodies would be too much for her to handle. Just then, she saw Jaws enter into the bedroom.

"Oh no," she cried out loud. *Jaws is going to kill me!* She quickly backed away from the door and pushed herself back up against the toilet. Her heart pounded as she watched Jaws rapidly approach her through the cracked door.

There was no way she could see herself getting out of this situation. She was going to die and there was nothing she could do about it. All the money in the world wasn't worth risking her life over. She desperately wished she was home right now.

Jaws walked in on Chelsea's trembling body. Tears rolled down her face while he stood over her with his gun in hand. Chelsea's hardcore image crumbled right before his eyes. Instead of him seeing a gangsta bitch, he only saw a young girl playing in the wrong game. Jaws laughed at how pathetic Chelsea looked to him.

"Damn. I thought you were a tuff bitch," he said as Chelsea remained silent.

Jaws raised the gun and cocked it ready to deliver a fatal shot to her head. He suddenly relaxed his trigger finger and lowered his gun. The scared look on her face reminded him of one that his little sister would make. He didn't have it in his heart to kill her. "This is ya fuckin' lucky day, thang-thang. When I leave here, you betta get the fuck out of town and never come back. You ain't see shit. You hear what I'm sayin'?" he threatened through clenched teeth.

Chelsea quickly nodded her head in agreement as tears continued to pour out of her eyes. Jaws ran out the bathroom and continued running until his footsteps could no longer be heard. Chelsea breathed heavily, relieved her life was spared.

When Chelsea finally came out the bathroom, she tried to gather up her things without looking at Lunchmeat's body. Chelsea double-checked everything, not wanting to leave anything behind. She even grabbed all her blood-stained clothes off the floor that were right by Lunchmeat's body. She was so scared and almost threw up when she saw Lunchmeat's belly button on her bra. The scene was the sickest thing she had ever seen. Chelsea began to panic when thinking about how she would get to the airport without Lunchmeat. That's when it hit her. She could drive the BMW SUV.

She scurried around the room looking for his car keys. Still crying, she went through his jeans that were on the floor. The first pocket she checked had a couple thousand dollars in it. This wasn't what she was looking for, but it would certainly help at a time like this. She felt in the other pocket and pulled out a set of BMW keys.

Chelsea moved quickly to get dressed. She checked once more, making sure she didn't leave anything behind. She didn't want anyone to know she was there. She grabbed her bag and walked into the hallway and almost threw up when she saw the back of Bumble's head blown out. She had to gather her strength if she wanted to make it out of this. She tiptoed around the body that seemed to clog the hallway and ran down the dark stairwell.

She quickly started up the truck and was on her way to the airport. The only problem was that she didn't know the direction of the airport. Chelsea had to stop and ask several people for directions. Finally someone suggested she use the car's navigation system since she couldn't remember where to go. Her mind was so rattled she didn't even think about the available GPS. Once she got on her way the flashbacks started to fill her mind, She damn near cried all the way to the airport, thinking back on her tragic moment.

The terminal was finally in her sight and she couldn't wait to get on the first thing smoking back to D.C. Although, when she had to make a decision on whether to go to short-term or long-term parking, she ran into another problem. What the hell was going to happen with the truck once she got on the plane? She suddenly pulled over and weighed her options while she threw her bloody garments in a trash can. Everything had happened so fast that she didn't think about what she would do when she got to the airport. Her first thought was to ditch the truck and never have to worry about it again. Her second thought was to keep it and drive back to D.C.

The new car smell and leather seats would be hard for her to give up. She pictured herself driving through the hood with all eyes on her. A new BMW SUV on some twenties was a sure way to get heads turning. Most importantly, this truck would give her a competitive edge over Dya. Dya's Ford Mustang wouldn't have shit on her new ride. Her mind now made up, she would drive back to D.C.

Chelsea needed the navigation system once again. When she put in the coordinates, she was surprised by the results. *Eleven hours? It's goin' to take eleven hours to drive back to D.C.?* The plane ride would have only been two hours, but Chelsea didn't care about rushing home anymore. All she wanted was that truck and didn't care how long it took her to get there. Even if it took her two days to get back, all she knew was that Beamer was coming home with her.

CHAPTER TWELVE

Chelsea's heart sped up every time she thought about the tragic ordeal, as she bolted down Interstate 80. She periodically checked her rearview mirror. Even though Jaws decided to let her leave, she still felt her life was in danger. She couldn't believe Lunchmeat was murdered right before her eyes. Her friend was gone and so were her chances of being well taken care of. She felt horrible for thinking about all the things she couldn't obtain due to Lunchmeat's demise. Her feelings for him had grown because of his death, but not enough to say that she loved him.

She suddenly noticed the gas light had come on. She had been on the road for five hours straight and needed to take a break anyway. She stopped at a rest stop outside of Cleveland to get some gas, food, and call Dya. Dya was the only person she could call who knew where she had gone. After she told Dya about all the drama that had happened to her, Dya told her about more drama she would likely encounter.

"What do you mean you saw Zeek?"

"I went to Safeway with my mom and his ass was in there. When he asked where you were, I told him you were with my aunt. I don't think he believed me."

After what happened to Chelsea, she couldn't care less about what Zeek thought. "It's cool, girl. I ain't even trippin' off Zeek like that. I'll worry about that 'bama later."

Chelsea was getting hungrier and was ready to get off the phone. "A'ight, Dy. I'll holla when I get back. Oh, Dya. I almost forgot. Wait 'til you see what I'm pushin', girl. I'll show you tonight."

Chelsea was still excited about the truck when she got off the phone. She couldn't wait to see the look on Dya's face when she came around in that joint. It was finally her turn to shine.

Chelsea ordered a double quarter-pounder meal with a vanilla milkshake from McDonald's. She ate all her food inside the restaurant, so she didn't get anything on her leather seats. After she finished eating, she went to the bathroom, then got back on Interstate 80. Chelsea finally got back to D.C. a little after midnight. She was so exhausted after going to Chicago and back in one day. Her hands had been wrapped around a steering wheel since 1p.m. and couldn't wait to get to Dya's house. Eleven hours of driving solo had really taken a toll on her mind and body.

She called Dya to let her know she was only a few minutes from her house. Dya was already outside waiting on her arrival. When Chelsea pulled up in front of Dya's house, she could see the full-blown expression on her face, even in the dark.

Dya's mouth dropped all the way to the ground. Yet, she was still happy for her girl. Dya was so excited. "Damn, bitch! I thought you were comin' back in a stolen-ass hooptie! I ain't know you got away in this! This shit is like that!" Dya then jumped into the truck. "Damn. This is nice. You know I'm goin' to be whippin' this, right?"

"No doubt. Matter of fact, I might have to leave it over your house anyway. You know how my moms be on some bullshit."

"That's cool. But right now we need to drive this mothafucka around the city."

"I'm feelin' that. Let's roll."

"Do you want me to drive? I know you're tired from all that drivin' you've been doing." Dya was desperate to get behind the wheel and Chelsea knew it.

Dya wanted to feel what Chelsea had been feeling all day. Like a bad-ass young bitch pushing a brand-new luxury vehicle. Chelsea ended up letting her drive anyway. She was tired of driving but also wanted Dya to know who really had it going on now.

Dya drove all around the town. She wanted to floss hard in the new BMW truck. Dya wanted Chelsea to keep the stickers on the window, so everyone could see how much it cost. After riding around for several hours, they went down to Adams-Morgan to get some jumbo pizza slices. Besides getting some pizza, there would be plenty of people down there to floss in front of.

When they got down to Adams-Morgan and turned on Eighteenth Street, it was how they thought, even at three in the morning. There were mad niggas everywhere. Dya parked right in front of one of the pizza shops where there was a crowd of people standing around.

They sat in the truck for a few minutes, so they could build up anticipation of who was inside. As soon as they got out, everyone's eyes were glued to them as they went into the pizza shop. Boli's didn't have that many people in line, but after Dya and Chelsea came in, Boli's became jam-packed. It was obvious to Dya that the niggas came in there because of them, and the broads came in there because of the niggas.

"Weak hoes always want more attention than they supposed to be gettin'," Dya said while Chelsea agreed.

After they got their jumbo slices and sodas, Dya didn't want to eat around all the fake girls and preferred to eat in the truck, but Chelsea wasn't with that. But when Chelsea noticed more girls trying to use them to get more shine, she didn't think eating in the truck was a bad idea after all, at least only this once.

The crowd outside built up again once Chelsea and Dya got back in the truck. Chelsea was back in the driver's seat changing CDs, while Dya looked at everyone who stood around the vehicle.

"Damn…these bitches are ji on our dick, young," Dya said with a mouth full of pizza.

"I know, right?" Chelsea put in a Ludacris CD and turned the volume all the way up.

They watched all the corny attention-seekers dance and sing along to the words as they continued to eat their pizza. Chelsea and Dya loved every minute of it.

A few minutes later, two boys out of the crowd gathered up enough balls to come up and talk to them.

"What's up, young? I guess ya man let you rock his whip for the night, huh?" one of them said as he approached Chelsea's driver-side window, while his friend went over to Dya's side.

Chelsea and Dya looked disgusted by both of the boys' appearances. They weren't blinged-up or had on any decent clothes. They looked like regular niggas to them. There was no way Chelsea was going to let them say anything slick.

"Nah, young. This is my shit."

"Yeah, right, that's what they all say."

"Nigga, I ain't none of them broke hoes you know. Nigga, I'm stackin'."

"So is you supposed to be hustlin' or something, girl?" he said sarcastically.

"Yeah. Somethin' like that. But I can tell you ain't."

The boy got into his feelings. "Nah, young, I'm ballin'. You don't know nothin' 'bout me."

Chelsea looked him up and down. "Yeah, right, nigga. You ain't ballin'. You fakin' like shit, boy. You look like you ain't bought new shoes in years, you bum-ass nigga."

"Damn, slim. You goin' to let her carry you like that?" the other boy asked, but the one trying to talk to Chelsea looked like he didn't have anything else to say. Chelsea laughed as the boy walked away.

The other boy stayed and tried to talk to Dya. "So what's up, shorty? What's your name?"

"It's Tasha," Dya said while rolling her eyes.

"Come on, baby. You can't tell me you don't like what you see? I'm that nigga."

"If you that nigga, then how come I can't see you? Get the fuck outta here."

"You fakin'," the boy said after finally getting the hint and walked away.

They looked at each other and shook their heads. They hoped no more cornballs would try to holler at them.

Chelsea's sounds continued to blast, until a pearl-colored drop-top Lexus SC 430 drowned out her speakers. The car pulled in right next to them on Dya's side, taking away all their attention. Chelsea peeped game that the two men in the car were doing the exact same thing as them. She liked their style and hoped they would try to holler.

I need a system like that. A system like that in this truck would take me up a notch. First thing tomorrow, she would go get a better system installed.

"Aye, yo! Yo, light skin!" the driver of the Lexus yelled, trying to get Dya's attention, while turning down his music.

Dya turned down the volume so she could hear him. "Were you talking to me?"

"Yeah, my man tryin' to holla at you, baby girl."

"Well, tell ya man to handle his BI." Dya thought both of the men were cute and didn't mind talking to either one of them.

The passenger got out the car and stepped to Dya. "What's up, young? I'm sorry my man had to plug me in. I would've did it myself, but ya music was up too high."

Dya couldn't keep her eyes off all the gold that was in the brown-skinned thug's mouth.

"Nah, you cool." Dya grinned.

The thug licked his lips. "So what cha name is?"

"Dymond. What's yours?"

"Xtra."

"Xtra? How did you get that name?"

"'Cause I always give more than you can handle," he said, giving her a wink.

Dya was impressed by his smooth swagger and wanted to challenge him on his statement.

While Chelsea was so busy ear hustling on Dya and Xtra's conversation, she didn't even notice the driver was at her window.

"What up, ma? How you doin'?" the driver asked, throwing her off-guard.

"Oh shit. You scared me," she said, holding her chest.

He smiled. "My fault, baby. I didn't know I was that ugly."

Chelsea smiled back. "No. You're not ugly at all. I didn't see you comin'."

"Well, maybe if I got your name. Next time won't be much of a surprise."

She smiled. "It's Chelsea. What's yours?"

"Hummy," he said, showing his pearly whites.

Hummy rhymes with yummy, she thought, staring at the sexy, dark-skinned man in front of her.

He was the best thing she'd seen all night. Chelsea was really feeling his style and liked the way he knew how to talk to women.

They all continued their conversation with each other until Xtra suggested they go to a hotel and chill. The girls were down for it and followed them to a downtown Hilton. After they all parked, Hummy showed Xtra the case of Grey Goose he had in the trunk. Chelsea wasn't concerned with the liquor right now. She wanted to know what type of system he had back there. Hummy told her he had two twelve-inch Rockford Fosgate subs with two 800-watt Rockford Fosgate amps. Everything was all mounted in glass cases on each side of the trunk. Chelsea was really impressed. She had to get a system like that.

The hotel room wasn't as nice as the one's Lunchmeat and Poundcake had, but it was still way above your average overnight stay. They all enjoyed each other's company, while sipping on vodka and cranberry juice, still discovering one another's interests. Chelsea was really feeling Hummy and made sure they would hook up again. After they played a few drinking games, Chelsea couldn't remember anything else. When she woke up, she was surprised that Hummy and Xtra were still there with them. Everybody was still at the table playing Spades, like they were the previous night.

"I know y'all ain't still playin'?" Chelsea asked, just opening her eyes.

"Yeah, young. We pulled an all-nighter," Dya said, laughing.

"Y'all crazy," Chelsea said while sitting up and taking a stretch.

Hummy was happy Chelsea finally woke up. He missed talking to her. "Good mornin' to you," he said, showing off his teeth again.

"I wish I could say the same, but y'all ain't get no sleep."

"It's all good. We were waitin' for you to get up, so we can go eat. You hungry? They got a buffet downstairs."

"Yeah, that's straight. I'm ready wheneva y'all are."

After they finished out their hand, they went downstairs to enjoy a good breakfast.

Once they were done with breakfast, Xtra turned in the room key. They all went to their cars and made plans to see each other soon. Dya passed out on the ride home and didn't wake up until they got up the street from her house.

"Damn, we here already?" Dya said while wiping her eyes.

"Girl, you've been sleep for a minute."

"For real? Damn, I'm bushed."

Chelsea then pulled up in front of Dya's house.

"I'm a go on in here and get some sleep. What you gonna do?"

"I'm gonna go see if I can get a system put in here."

"A system? Girl, this shit sound good already."

"True. But I want somethin' like Hummy got."

"That's what's up. I would go wit' you, but I need to get some sleep."

"That's cool. I'll be back to pick my car up later. Oh yeah. I'll call Qwanda and Fawn to see if they tryin' to go out tonight."

Dya liked the idea and would see her when she came back.

Chelsea drove away thinking about the system she wanted so badly, and Hummy told her where to go for the best deal. She went to Soundstream Audio, which was about fifteen minutes away from her house in Bladensburg, Maryland. When she got to the store, Chelsea saw that there were so many subwoofers to choose from, she didn't know where to start.

"Can I help you?" the young man behind the counter asked.

"Yeah. I'm tryin' to get a system."

"Do you know what you want?"

"I want somethin' that bangs. My friend got some Rockford Fosgates. I think that's what they're called."

"Yeah, I carry Fosgate."

"Yeah. I think I want them."

"What type of car you got."

"I got a BMW. It's a truck, though."

"Okay. I can hook you up wit' some nice shit. How much you tryna spend?"

"Honestly. I don't know a good deal from a bad one. So, you'll have to teach me." She gave a little smile and he smiled back.

"Come here. Let me show you what I got."

The salesman showed her all the low-end subs and the high-end ones. He also gave her a good lesson on picking out amplifiers. After Chelsea thought she had seen enough to make a decision, that's when he took her to another showroom. She saw a Chevy Impala on display with the tightest system she had ever seen. That's the one she wanted.

"That's what I'm talkin' about. I want this right here," she said with her eyes wide.

"This is one of our competition cars. The sounds that we put in here came in yesterday. Don't nobody even got this new line from Audiobahn. Nothin' Fosgate makes could compete with these."

The trunk was lit up by green LED neon rods that aligned all the corners, providing an alien-like glow. Underneath the rods on both the left and right sides were two twelve-inch subwoofers enclosed in a fiberglass case. On front of each case was a chrome plate that had *Audiobahn* stamped in cursive. In the far back were three 1,000-watt amps that hung like picture frames. Chelsea was sold. *If I had this system in my truck, I could make the whole block shake.*

Three hours later, her system was installed and she was ready to cruise the streets. Chelsea decided to get the white lights in the trunk since it was the best match for the color of her truck. She only paid $3,000 for an $8,000 system because the salesman thought she was pretty. Chelsea couldn't believe how loud her system was. She only had the volume turned up six notches, and people three blocks away would turn around to see where all the noise was coming from. Chelsea felt like she was on top of the world.

Chelsea thought her truck needed to be spotless for tonight's outing. She went to the self-service car wash to get a quick soak, wax, and rinse. While she put on her final rinse, she saw a purple Escalade on 24s, pull into the bay right next to her. It was rare to see a purple Escalade in D.C., but she had seen this one several times. She knew exactly whose it was. It belonged to Rodney.

Chelsea had been waiting for her chance to holler at Rodney and now he was right there. Even though she had never spoken to him before, she had to come up with a good reason to say something to him. She reached into her pocket and pulled out the most wrinkled dollar she could find, and walked over to him.

"Excuse me. I was wonderin' if you had change for a dolla? My dolla won't go through the machine."

"Yeah. I think I do. Hold up." He reached in his pocket and pulled out a big wad of money and exchanged dollar bills with her.

"Thank you. Your name's Rodney, right?"

Rodney was surprised. "Damn, Chelsea. I didn't even think you knew me."

Chelsea was shocked herself. "Wait a minute. How do you know my name?"

"You're Zeek's girl. Everybody know that."

"That is not my man," Chelsea fronted.

"Yeah, right. Stop fakin'."

"If I was fakin', do you think I would be over here tryin' to talk to you?"

"I don't know. I thought you came over here for a dolla. I guess that was some game, huh?"

Chelsea was running game, and she knew exactly what she was doing. Chelsea had been secretly lusting for Rodney for the longest and now she had her chance to get at him.

Even though Chelsea always considered Rodney to be ugly in the face, there was still something about his style and reputation which always made him sexy to her. Rodney was indeed a baller. He first started getting money when the purple haze craze came through D.C. a few years back. He was one of the few able to get this type of marijuana, which in turned made him rich practically overnight, hinting him to get a purple Escalade.

Rodney took her number and said he would call her later tonight. Chelsea knew she was playing with fire by messing with someone Zeek had hated ever since childhood. Yet, she still wanted to press her luck and hopefully come out on top. Chelsea thought she was a true P.I.M.P.

Chelsea and Dya were looking so fly cruising in the Beamer truck and so were their friends, Qwanda and Fawn. Qwanda and Fawn were best friends like Chelsea and Dya. They always met each other at different places, but tonight they would roll together. Qwanda and Fawn were both the same height, 5' 5," with caramel complexions. They were so similar in beauty that they were always mistaken for sisters. They also shared the same passion for hustlers as Chelsea and Dya did.

It was Saturday night and they went to one of D.C.'s hottest clubs, H2O. They pulled up to valet to get instantly noticed by the crowd. They were so caught up with the idea that they were the center of attention, Dya thought she saw someone take a picture of them while they were in line. When they finally got inside, the club was packed and full of energy. The club was so crowded the girls had to hold each other's hands to avoid getting separated on their way to the bar. The bar area had very little standing room, so the girls got their drinks and went to one of the available corners.

It didn't take long for guys to come over and try to holler at them. Different guys kept buying them drinks all night, hoping they would go home with them. Chelsea was feeling a couple cats whose numbers she got, but she couldn't keep her mind off of Rodney. It was getting late, and she wondered if he would even call her tonight. As Qwanda and Fawn were being approached by two men, Chelsea's phone vibrated in her hand. She didn't recognize the number, but still needed to answer, thinking it could be Rodney finally calling her.

"Hello! Who's this? Hold on, I can't hear you!" She walked over to the bathroom where it might be possible for her to hear better. "Hello."

"Yeah. Is this Chelsea?"

"Yeah. Who's this?" she said, placing her hand over her other ear.

"It's Rodney."

Chelsea was psyched that he finally called, but couldn't help but notice that his voice sounded so lifelike.

"Where are you?" she asked.

"I'm at H2O."

Chelsea turned around and saw Rodney over by the men's bathroom. He was as shocked to see her as she was to see him. She was happy that he was now walking over to her.

"What's up, young? I didn't know you were comin' down here?" she said.

"Neither did I. It was kind of a last-minute thing. But what brings you down here?"

"Me and my girls are just out kickin' it."

"That's cool. Are you tryna get something to eat wit' me after this?"

"I would love to. But I got all my girls wit' me."

"Can't they come wit' you?"

It was obvious that Rodney really wanted her time. "Well, let me see what they tryin' to do."

Rodney walked with Chelsea over to the bar to find Dya standing alone. "Hey. Where Qwanda and Fawn go?"

"Remember them two niggas that came over here before you got on the phone? Well, those niggas play for the Redskins, and they rolled out wit'em."

Those broads done lucked out again. "Well, my boy Rodney wanna take us to get somethin' to eat. You tryna go?"

"Is it us three goin'?"

"Nah. My little cuz is rollin' wit' us," Rodney added.

"That's what's up. I'm ready when y'all are," Dya announced.

They found Rodney's cousin and headed out of the club.

The girls followed Rodney to Ben's Chili Bowl. Ben's Chili Bowl was famous for its food, especially the half-smokes and chili cheese fries. Chelsea and Dya would come here occasionally after the club let out. Dya was not feeling Rodney's cousin at all, nor did she want him to pay for her food. She didn't want to give him a reason to ask for her number. Rodney ended up paying for everyone's food anyway, including his cousin since he'd spent all his money at the club, as usual.

Chelsea wondered what the rest of her night with Rodney would be like. She pictured herself in a hotel room somewhere getting it rough from the backside. Her little visual got interrupted when

Rodney's phone rang. She could tell the call was about business by the heated expression he had on his face. Rodney hurried off the phone and turned toward her.

"Yo, Chelsea. I got to go handle somethin'. We gonna have to get up later."

Chelsea was disappointed, but didn't want to show it. Dya, on the other hand, was happy they were leaving since Rodney's cousin kept annoying her. Before they left, Rodney assured her that they would be alone the next time around. And Chelsea wouldn't let him get away so easily.

CHAPTER THIRTEEN

Chelsea wasn't in any rush to get up on Sunday morning. It wasn't that she didn't want to go to church or was feeling sick from drinking too much from the night before. She wasn't ready to face the music with Zeek yet. *He would have been called and cussed my ass out already after he saw Dya. Maybe he don't care.* She finally decided to call him to pick at his brain.

"Hello," he answered.

"Hey, I'm back. Did you miss me?"

During the whole conversation with Zeek, not once did she detect him having an attitude. Since everything was cool between them, Chelsea wanted to spend some time with him.

She arrived at Zeek's house with some leftover souvenirs from last year's Myrtle Beach trip.

"Hey, Ms. Harris," she said, walking into the house.

"Hello, Chelsea. How was your trip, girl?"

"It was good. I had a lot of fun. Here. I brought you somethin'."

Chelsea handed her a clock with seashells attached all over it.

"Wow! This is nice, Chelsea. Thank you."

"You're welcome. I'm glad you like it," she said, smiling. Chelsea always had Zeek's mom wrapped around her finger. Ms. Harris strongly felt Chelsea was the right girl for her son.

Chelsea had bought Zeek a shotglass, and a key chain, for whenever he got a car. She believed something would change for him soon.

Chelsea and Zeek spent the rest of the day together. Chelsea ordered pizza and Buffalo wings from Pizza Hut and rented some movies. They were both getting along well. Once Zeek's mom went up to her room, they went down in the basement to have some drinks. Zeek had a few bottles left over from his birthday and needed a reason to use his new shotglass.

They took shots of tequila and chased them with sloe gin. They were both drunk on their asses about an hour and a half later, and Zeek wanted to release some tension. Zeek began rubbing on her body and kissing her neck.

"You feel like doin' somethin'?" he softly whispered in her ear.

Chelsea's legs were shaking and wanted to release some tension of her own. "Only if you are."

Chelsea didn't enjoy having sex with Zeek much, but she was drunk and horny. She didn't want to pass up any pleasure coming her way.

"Take those pants off," Zeek commanded her while he took off his. He slipped on the condom then hovered over her body until he pushed himself between her lips.

Chelsea felt his hardness going in and out of her several times, until she couldn't feel it anymore. "Zeek, what's goin' on?"

He couldn't even look her in the eyes. "You know what happened," he said while pulling himself out of her.

Chelsea was pissed. "Damn, Zeek! Ya dick can't stay hard for five minutes!"

"My fault, baby. It's been a while since we last did it. Just give me a couple minutes to get back up. A'ight?" he said as he pulled off the condom.

"A couple minutes, my ass! It's gonna take you forever to get hard again! I ain't got time for that shit! It took me more time to take my pants off than it did to fuck!"

"Damn, Chelsea. Why are you bein' so harsh?"

"Because I want to be, that's why."

"For someone to look so normal, you damn sure got a split personality."

"I ain't got no split shit! I'm being real! You the one wit' the problem!" she said, putting her pants back on. Chelsea was completely fed up with Zeek. Even though she was drunk, she was still able to suppress some of her true feelings about him. She thought it was better if she left than to stay and say something she would regret.

Zeek wanted to stop her from leaving, but really didn't know how. Chelsea was right. Zeek seldom had success when it came down to lasting long with Chelsea. After what had happened, how could he convince her the next time would be any different?

Chelsea was still mad about her and Zeek's fight when she got home. She was drunk, horny, and frustrated as she sat in her bed. *Why do I keep fuckin' wit' this nigga? Why does he have such a hold on me?* Chelsea thought her life would be easier if he broke up with her, instead of her having to leave him.

She didn't think he could handle a break-up based on how things were going for him. Chelsea was so confused. She wanted to call someone up to scratch the sexual itch she had. Yet, at the same time, she needed to solve her long-going problem with Zeek. Chelsea was so unable to deal with all the pressure that she put her pillow over her head and went to sleep.

The next morning, Chelsea got a call from Rodney. He wanted to apologize for the other night and take her out for breakfast. She gave him her address and said she would be ready in twenty minutes. Twenty-five minutes later, Chelsea came out the house wearing a green Von Dutch halter top with a J-Lo black denim skirt and some matching green Coach sandals. She put her keys in her black Fendi bag after locking the front door and got into the Escalade. Rodney couldn't keep his eyes off Chelsea, taking in her beauty.

Rodney chose IHOP because he loved their stuffed French toast. Over breakfast they learned a lot about each other. Rodney expressed how much he always liked her, but didn't think she would ever notice him. He also told her he once had fought Zeek over a girl that wasn't his and didn't want to make that same mistake again. Chelsea assured him he didn't have to worry about Zeek. Chelsea was coming too close to home by messing with Rodney, but she wasn't sure yet if she cared that much to turn back.

Zeek was at the grocery store picking out a *Thinking of You* card for Chelsea. He wanted to find the right one that explained exactly how he felt about her. He read each one carefully, until he found it. *Four dollars and ninety-five cents is a lot to pay for a card, but she's worth it.*

He also got a half-dozen red roses to complement the beautiful card. Zeek cut his neighbor's grass earlier to get the money to pay for the card and flowers. *It's money well spent*, he thought after checking out of line. He filled the card out right in the store not wanting to lose his train of thought. He wrote out a nice poem and on the available room he had left, he squeezed in an "I Love You." His card was signed, sealed and ready to be delivered.

Chelsea let Rodney come in her house so he could use the bathroom. Since her mother wasn't home, this gave her a chance to make up for what didn't happen the other night.

"I'm in here," she said when she heard him come out of the bathroom.

He walked into her bedroom, where he found her sitting on the bed.

"You got time to chill?" she asked.

"Yeah. I ain't got nowhere to be for a while."

"Good. Have a seat so we can watch a movie."

Chelsea put in a DVD while Rodney lay down to get more comfortable. She stretched herself out in front of him with her ass against his mid-section. A short time after the movie came on, one thing led to another, and they were on their way to making their own movie.

Zeek had been calling Chelsea's phone all morning, but still he hadn't been able to reach her. *Maybe she had a hangover and is still asleep.*

Zeek hoped she would have answered her phone before he started walking over to her house. It was going to take him about thirty minutes to get there on foot. He didn't want to walk all the way there if she wasn't home. Zeek went with his better judgment that Chelsea would be at her house and continued walking to hand her his token of love.

Rodney and Chelsea were grinding halfway naked, as they continued to roll around in bed. After he licked her stomach, he couldn't help himself but to go down on her, even though he thought it was too soon for that. When he lifted his head out of her wet spot, it was still hard for him to believe he was in the groove with Chelsea. He had been secretly plotting on her for years, and now it was really about to go down. Chelsea was actually thinking the same thing. They both were about to get what they'd been so long waiting for.

Zeek was tired as hell from walking by the time he made it to Chelsea's house. His legs began to cramp and his feet were sore. Instead of happiness, Zeek filled himself with rage, once he saw the purple truck sitting in front of her house. He didn't have to second-guess whose truck it was, but wondered why he had come to see Chelsea. He ran up to the truck to see if anyone was in it. Seeing no one, he proceeded up the steps and onto the porch.

He put his ear up to the door to see if he could hear their voices. Not hearing a sound, something told him to check and see if the door was open. Zeek knew Chelsea always had a bad habit of forgetting to lock doors like her mother. Sure enough, he discovered that it was unlocked. His heart raced while his throat felt as dry as a desert. He wasn't sure if he was ready to see what he was about to walk in on.

Zeek opened the door, only to find an empty living room. He got a funny feeling in his stomach when he heard strange noises coming from upstairs. He tiptoed up the steps, trying not to make a sound. Zeek stood in the middle of the hallway, not knowing if he was ready to bust open Chelsea's bedroom door. With all the confusion that had already built up, there was no way he could not. He had to find out what was going on in there. Zeek quickly opened the door to find Chelsea riding on top of Rodney. "What the fuck!" Zeek yelled as he dropped the card and roses on the floor. Chelsea climbed off of Rodney trying to cover up her body.

Zeek stood in the doorway and looked at Chelsea in total disgust. Chelsea looked so scared, not knowing what Zeek was going to do. "Zeek…oh, my God, please let me explain," Chelsea cried as she stumbled over her words. All the bad things he ever heard about Chelsea finally came to surface, bringing tears to his eyes. "Ain't shit to explain! I'm going to fuck you and this nigga up!" Zeek said as he entered the room.

Rodney quickly went for his pants and pulled out his nine-millimeter, stopping Zeek in his tracks. "So you gonna shoot me and you're the one fuckin' my girl?" Zeek asked through clenched teeth.

"I'm tryna protect myself, that's all, Slim. Now, walk away," Rodney said as he gripped his gun tight.

Everything inside of Zeek still wanted to run over to Rodney and beat him down, but he didn't want to get shot. He decided to give Chelsea and Rodney a final stare-down and slowly backed out of the room.

Chelsea was unable to move after she was hit with embarrassment and humiliation. *I forgot to lock the fuckin' door behind Rodney. How could I be so fuckin' stupid?* She never thought in a million years that Zeek would be the one to walk in on her. She thought she had the whole game mastered and could easily outsmart Zeek on his best day, but she was wrong. Chelsea had finally gotten the outcome she was looking for.

Zeek slammed the door shut behind him and stomped his way down the steps. He was so mad he could kill a rock. He wanted to knock over the telephone pole and have it land on Rodney's truck if he could. Instead, he spat on the passenger side window and walked down the street. He planned on never seeing Chelsea again. *This time, I'm really done with her.*

CHAPTER FOURTEEN

Chelsea adjusted her Chanel frames over her eyes as she sat down at the outdoor seating section of Starbucks. Her last forty-eight hours had not been anything nearly as glamorous as she appeared to the patrons that sat around her. The unforgettable thought of her getting caught in the act perplexed her mind as she gradually sipped her white chocolate mocha coffee. Chelsea was stuck on what had troubled her most: the fact that she had finally been exposed as a cheat or that her relationship with Zeek was possibly nevermore. Chelsea wanted another good friend of hers besides Dya to help sort out her disheveled issue. Chelsea knew who to call when she needed someone to weigh in on her problem: Qwanda.

Qwanda paraded happily through Pentagon Row as she swung her Nordstrom bag around the outside shopping plaza. Her tailed bob cut with auburn highlights accentuated her soft heartwood-colored skin. Qwanda smiled heavily as she saw her good friend Chelsea a few feet away. "Hey, what's up, girl?" Qwanda said as she made her way over to the table.

"Hey, Q-Boo," Chelsea said mirthfully as she stood to give Qwanda a hug.

"Uh-oh," Qwanda remarked. "You only call me Q-Boo when you really got something crazy to tell me."

"Yeah, I do, and it's real deep, too."

"Okay, let me run in and grab a drink real quick before we talk. I can't wait to hear this," Qwanda said as she sat her bag down in the chair across from Chelsea.

Qwanda came out of Starbucks a few minutes later with a Grande-sized Caramel Macchiato and hurried to take a seat. "Okay, so what's going on?" she eagerly asked.

Chelsea sighed. "Girlll. I got myself into some shit. Zeek caught me fuckin' Rodney."

"Wait a minute. He caught you-caught you, or did he see y'all leavin' a telly?" Qwanda asked, looking for clarification.

"Nah, Zeek busted my damn bedroom door down and caught me on top of the nigga."

"Are you serious?" Qwanda said as she covered her mouth. "What did Zeek do?"

"Zeek was about to fuck one of us up, but Rodney pulled out a gun."

Qwanda continued to cover her mouth not believing the story that Chelsea was telling. "Girl, I'm so glad Zeek left. That shit could've gotten real ugly."

"Oh my God, Chelsea. That is crazy. Have you talked to Zeek since then?"

"No. I know he won't talk to me. Not after seeing that shit. What would you do? Do you think there's any way I can fix it?"

"I don't know about that one, girl. That's askin' for a whole lot." Qwanda paused as she held her cup up to her lips. She sat her cup back down before she spoke again. "Chelsea, I'm kind of confused on why you would want to fix it anyway. All you ever did was cheat on Zeek because of everything you said he lacked. Why not let him go?"

"Girl, I don't know," Chelsea whined as she held her head. "I do love him, but maybe I always thought he would change. I wish I could've ended it on my own terms. Gettin' caught fuckin' someone else is the only thing he's gonna remember me by."

"So let's say Zeek does decide to take you back, eventually. Would you cheat on him again?" Qwanda carefully asked.

Chelsea let her eyes wander, then she looked up at Qwanda before she spoke. "Probably. I don't think he's capable of giving me what I want."

Qwanda slowly nodded her head as she tapped on her cup before she responded. "Well, I think you should move on. Both of y'all should move on. It wasn't meant for y'all to be together. As tragic as it might have been, maybe this thing with Rodney was supposed to happen. Only something this magnified would have let y'all move on from each other. You feel me?"

"Yeah, I do, but damn. This shit has stressed me out so bad."

"Well, I'm gonna have to help you get unstressed. I'll treat you to Red Door. There ain't nothing better at putting your mind at ease than a good-ass massage and facial. How about that?"

"Girl, I ain't been to Elizabeth Arden in a minute. I could definitely use a massage right about now. Thank you, Q-Boo. You really are my friend, huh?" Chelsea said with blushed cheeks.

"Girl, you won't ever have to question that. I'm down 'til the end. Now let's go so we can hurry up and get beautified," Qwanda said as she stood up from her seat.

Chelsea got out her seat and smiled as they headed to the spa. Chelsea knew her talk with Qwanda had proven to be more than beneficial. Chelsea thought Qwanda knew what to say to put things in perspective. She always valued Qwanda's option, but most importantly, it was her friendship that held all the worth. Qwanda was truly her sister and from that moment forward, their bond would grow even stronger.

Shit. I could at least hear back from that damn job. For the last eight days, Zeek sat around the house looking very depressed. So much so, his mother could even tell there was something wrong with him. She slowly walked into his bedroom and looked down on her troubled son.

"Zeek, honey. What's been troubling you?" she asked like only a concerned mother would.

"Nothin'. I'm tired of this city," he said without giving her any eye contact.

For some reason, Zeek didn't want to tarnish the reputation that his mother had for Chelsea, so he didn't tell her what he caught her doing.

His mother sighed. "Well, if you're that miserable here, why don't you move somewhere else?"

"Like where? I don't know where I would go."

"Boy, don't act like you ain't got family nowhere else. You know the Harrises are everywhere. You even got cousins you ain't seen in years."

"True. I ain't seen Carla or Eddie since I was in high school, and Uncle Huddy or Aunt Denise probably longer than that."

"I've seen 'em. You should have gone to all the family reunions we be having. You being so up under Chelsea got you missing out on family, boy." His mother laughed while putting her hands on her hips.

"You right, Ma. I have been missin' out on family. But you know who I'd really like to see? Aunt Maddy and 'em. I wonder how they're doin'?"

"Well, why don't you call her? I got her number."

As a little boy, Maddy was Zeek's favorite aunt. She treated him better than all his other cousins. Every time she saw him, she either gave him a new toy or some money. Zeek took his mom's advice and called up his Aunt Maddy.

Aunt Maddy was so happy to hear from him, she almost cried when she heard his voice. They talked for hours trying to make up for lost time. She told him she would wire him some money so he could visit her in Pittsburgh, PA. She wanted him to get on a bus by Friday, which only left him two days. She also told him while she ran out to wire his money that she would have Maurice call him.

Maurice was her son and Zeek's favorite cousin as a child. He couldn't wait to talk to him, either. No more than fifteen minutes after getting off the phone with Aunt Maddy, Maurice called. Zeek was psyched up to finally hear from his cousin. "Yo what's up, big cuz?"

"What up, Zeek! My nigga. It's been a long time."

"I know, man. What's good?"

"Everythang. Yo moms said you comin' up?"

"Yeah, I'm 'bout to go book my ticket now."

"Cool. So moms told me you goin' through it a little bit."

"Yeah, man. Some bullshit, but I'll be straight soon."

"Well, I'ma tell you this. When you come up, we gonna do the damn thang. I got the streets on lock up here, cuz. Ya heard me?"

"That's what's up, cuz. I can't wait to see what you got going on." Zeek liked what he was hearing.

"Aight then, I'm gonna get off this phone, but hit me with the time ya bus gets here and I'll pick you up."

"Cool. Aight, cuz." *Click.*

Later that day, Zeek finally got a chance to holler at Lonzo. Lonzo had been out of town with his job and hadn't heard the latest Chelsea drama yet. They both sat on Zeek's porch while Lonzo got an earful.

"You mean to tell me you caught her ass in bed wit' that nigga, and you ain't do shit?"

Zeek had no response so Lonzo went on.

"Young. If that woulda been me, I woulda beat the brakes off that nigga and threw his ass out the window. Fuck if he had a gun or not, nigga. He would have had to kill my ass."

Zeek knew Lonzo was talking out the side of his mouth and wouldn't have done anything that he said. Although, he did wish he would have done something instead of leaving the way he had. He was now starting to feel like a straight sucker.

"So what you goin' to do now?" Lonzo was curious to find out.

Zeek rubbed his hands together while he looked off. "I've been thinkin' 'bout that a whole lot lately." Zeek paused before speaking again. "I'm goin' to start hustlin'."

Lonzo gave him the sideways look. "What? You can't be serious?"

"Yeah. I am. I'm tired of this 'lookin' for a job' shit. I can't take it no more."

"Come on, man. It ain't even been that long. Have you even really been lookin'?"

"Hell yeah, I've really been lookin'. I even had an interview a minute ago and I still ain't heard shit yet. I can't wait around for them no more. I holla'd at my cousin, Maurice, from Pittsburgh. He said he got the streets on lock up there. I'm gonna go check 'em out in a couple days."

"Well, he must only got the keys to about four or five streets, 'cause I heard Pittsburgh was small as hell," Lonzo stated, trying to demean the city.

"I don't know about that. All I know is that he said he was the man."

"I doubt that. Pittsburgh is only known for dirty-ass steel mills and ketchup. I ain't never heard of no big-time hustlers comin' out of there. I think ya cuz is fakin', but I could be wrong. But you hustlin'. You lunchin', young. Me and you both know neither one of us is built to hustle like dat. If you really want to hustle, then me and you need to start our own business. I got this idea for a cleanin' company. It's goin' to be hard work, but we can do it."

Zeek liked the idea of having his own company, but it wasn't going to give him the type of money he wanted to have right away. By the time he got rich doing that, Chelsea would be well into her thirties. He needed her to respect him way sooner than that. Zeek wanted Chelsea to see what he could really become: a hustler.

"I feel what you sayin', yo. I really like the idea but I need money now. Chelsea needs to regret she ever played me like that."

Lonzo was disappointed with his friend's reasoning. "You mean to tell me you want to sell drugs all because of a woman? My fault. I mean, bitch, 'cause that's what she is. I can't let you go down for somebody like her."

"Goin' down? Look at me, man. I ain't got shit. Everything is real fucked up for me now, cuz. I got to get some paper, and I got to get it now."

"If that's what you think you need, then go 'head and do it, but you goin' to see in the end. You gonna end up dead or in jail. Only a few make it to the top, Zeek. You hear me…only a few. I'll holla at you later, young." Lonzo left without even dapping Zeek up.

Zeek could tell his friend was upset with his decision by the way he rolled out. Zeek only cared halfway because Lonzo had money, and he didn't. That was something Lonzo wouldn't be able to understand.

Zeek arrived at the Pittsburgh Greyhound station at 10:45 Thursday morning. He was greeted by one of Maurice's friends he remembered playing with as a child.

"Damn, Zeek. After ten years, ya ass still look the same." The young man smiled.

Zeek couldn't believe who it was. "Oh shit! What's up, Wilk!" Zeek smiled, then dapped him up.

Zeek hadn't seen Wilk since he was eleven years old. He looked the same as well, except he was taller and more muscular than Zeek. Wilk was six-two, with a pitchy-black complexion and wore his hair cut low.

He was a pretty thug who wore a lot of platinum jewelry and loved to showcase all the tattoos that covered his upper torso.

"Damn, nigga. You got big as shit. You been doin' time?" Zeek asked.

"Yeah. I did a couple years. I've been out for about a year now."

Zeek was so surprised by Wilk's appearance. He used to be so short and skinny, but these days, he was the exact opposite.

Wilk and Zeek walked outside where Maurice and another kid named Jidder were waiting for them. Maurice was reddish-brown, about five-five, and kept his hair cut down to a Caesar. Jidder was slightly more bronzed than Maurice, but wore his hair in cornrows, and was a little on the thick side. They were leaning up against a black Lincoln Navigator that was sitting on chrome 24s. Maurice was happy to finally see his cousin.

"Yo, what up, Ike?" Maurice yelled out to Zeek with his local slang as they walked closer to each other.

"What up, young?" Zeek responded.

They dapped each other up and embraced with a hug.

"Long time no see," Zeek said as they broke their embrace.

"I know, Ike. Damn, you got big. I remember when we was little. I used to be taller than ya ass. Now look at you. And you got bulky too. You been locked up, huh, Ike?" Maurice asked.

"Nah. I ain't never do no time." Zeek noticed that Maurice was a little cut up himself.

"Yeah. Me neither," Maurice responded with a grin.

Zeek could tell by the way Maurice and his people were rolling that they were major players. The shiny black SUV and jewelry said it all.

Maurice peeped out his cousin's gear and knew he was in need of an upgrade. "While you here, Zeek, everything's on me, Ike. You ain't got to pay for shit. We gonna show you how we do it in the Burgh. For real, Ike. But first I'ma take you to the mall to get you some hot shit. We gonna do it up tonight. Let's roll out."

Zeek got in the backseat with Maurice, while Wilk rode shotgun. They rode out to Century III Mall to get some new clothes from Mo-Gear. Mo-Gear had all the latest fashions and it was one of Maurice's favorite stores. Maurice led Zeek to a table that had a new display of leather shorts. Maurice told Zeek that everybody who had money wore those, and no other city had them. At $120 a pair, Zeek didn't know too many people who would buy them where he was from. He got a black pair and some burgundy ones, and later got authentic Steelers and Redskins jerseys to go with them.

He then went to Foot Locker and got two pair of Air Force Ones. Zeek was almost complete, and all he needed to do now was get some jewelry. Maurice got him a thirty-inch, fourteen-carat white gold chain with a Jesus piece and a pair of half-carat diamond earrings. Zeek never got the hookup like this before. He was guaranteed to be stunning when he stepped out tonight for sure. After they were done shopping, Zeek was curious to see how big the Burgh was and wanted to be shown around. Maurice figured he was talking about going to see all the hoods; that's where he was going to take him anyway.

There were people hanging out on corners and tons of project buildings all over town. Zeek thought all the hoods they drove through looked grimy and run-down like the ones he was used to seeing around his way, except there was something strange about all the people. Everybody saluted Maurice when he came through and were calling him Catch'em.

"Hey, young, these Burgh niggas is cool as hell. Everybody knows you n'shit. It ain't like this in D.C."

That's when Maurice gave him a firm look. "Look around, Zeek. It ain't Sesame Street around this mothafucka, Ike. These niggas ain't cool. I had to earn my respect."

"They call you Catch'em. What that mean?"

"It means I've been runnin' shit for years, and I ain't never been caught. I ain't never gonna get caught either, Ike," Catch'em stated with assurance.

As they continued to drive, Zeek realized his cousin Maurice, or Catch'em, was not to be played with.

Catch'em really did have shit on lock. He controlled the whole East side, the St. Clair Village projects on the South side, and all of Uptown, which was called The Hill, or the H-I-Double. The Hill was where Maurice and Wilk were from. They started supplying the entire area by the time they were seventeen and never looked back.

Jidder pulled into the Francis projects when they got on The Hill and dropped everybody off, then peeled out.

"Yo, Zeek, you remember this shit here, Ike? We used to live on the second floor of that building there." Catch'em pointed at the building gathering up memories.

Zeek did remember coming to visit him here, but everything looked so run-down. It was hard to imagine it was the same place.

"Yo, Ike. I'll get up wit' y'all later. I got to make moves," Wilk intervened. He gave them both a head nod and drove away in a silver BMW 745 on 20s, while Catch'em and Zeek left in an old beat-up Nissan Sentra.

Catch'em had Zeek really confused. He didn't understand why all of his boys were pushing fly rides and he, being on top of the game, was driving a hooptie.

"Hey, young. How come you don't drive a nice whip?"

"I do. But not in the hood."

"Why not?"

"No point. All it's goin' to do is make me hot. I only drive shit like that if I'm goin' out to dinner or to a club or somethin'. That shit ain't for every day."

"Then why do Jidder and Wilk do it?"

"They only let their discipline take them so far. I used to tell 'em all the time that even if you ain't ridin' dirty, don't mean you still got to scream for attention."

Zeek was still confused. "But, I thought that was what the game was all about? Havin' fly whips, flossin' through the hood, and gettin' rich."

Catch'em shook his head. "You and everybody else got the game twisted. It's all about longevity. Sellin' drugs ain't legal, Zeek. You're supposed to move like the mob, in silence. That's the only way you goin' to win out here." Catch'em paused and looked back over at

Zeek. "Cuz, picture this shit like a card game: the day you decide to throw ya hand in, make sure you got enough money to walk away from the table. Most niggas don't. They play they hand until they broke, and then look for help to get fronted some chips. As long as you play this game right, you gonna walk away a millionaire and the feds won't even know."

It was all clear to Zeek now. If he wanted to learn how to hustle the right way, he had to watch Catch'em.

Zeek couldn't wait to see his Aunt Maddy. Catch'em and Zeek were on their way to her house, which was thirty-five minutes out-side the city, in Cranberry Township. Zeek couldn't believe his eyes when they pulled into the driveway of the biggest house he had ever seen.

"Yo, where we at?" Zeek questioned.

"This Mom's crib."

Zeek was amazed that his Aunt Maddy had such a huge house. In the driveway she had two vehicles, a gray Lexus GX truck and a white S550 Mercedes-Benz.

Maddy noticed them coming up the walkway from the window, and ran outside to give her nephew a big hug. "Oh my God! It's Zeeky. Just look at you, boy. You got so big. Damn, you look like Donna. It's like she spit you right out."

"Yeah, everybody says that. Wow, Auntie, you got a big house."

"Thank you, baby. Here, come on in so I can show you around."

Maddy gave Zeek the grand tour. She walked him through four bedrooms and the master bedroom, all on the top floor. There were six complete bathrooms, two living rooms, and an Olympic-sized pool in the backyard. After Zeek saw the entire house, Maddy took him into the kitchen so they could talk. When they sat down at the table, Zeek noticed a big white dish filled with marijuana in the center of the table.

"Dag, Aunt Maddy. You got a lot of weed in there."

"Yep. You know I got to get my smoke on. You still smoke?"

"Yeah, I smoke."

"Come on and smoke wit' me and your cousin. We ain't smoked wit' you in a long time."

Maddy lifted up the dish to reveal eight blunts already rolled underneath. She grabbed three of them and let Zeek light up the first one. As Zeek smoked, he reflected back to when Maddy had handed him his first joint. He was ten years old, and since then, he always kept that secret from his mother.

Aunt Maddy was so pretty to Zeek. In fact, she was a spitting image of his mother, except Maddy had more style and personality than her older sister. Tonya was the youngest of four children and got the name Maddy from not being able to say "daddy" as a baby. She looked like the Whitney Houston from the '90s and wore her hair in microbraids. Maddy was still a hot mama even at age forty-two.

They all sat around the table and continued to smoke and talk about old times. Zeek was happy to be reunited with his family, but he had questions that long needed answers.

"Aunt Maddy. Who else in the family know y'all are livin' like this?"

Maddy dusted the ashes from the blunt and blew the smoke. "None of them do. They wouldn't be able to handle it."

Zeek was confused. "What do you mean?"

"Come on, Zeeky. You know how your mother and 'em are, how they feel about drugs and what they can do to you. Shit. They would disown my ass if they knew I went down the same road as our father did."

"Wait a minute. You mean to tell me Granddad hustled?"

"Yeah. I guess your mother never told you. He even went to prison 'cause of that shit, too. When he came out, the family wasn't the same no more. Your mom was pregnant wit' you at the time, and I found out I was, too, shortly after. Dad felt like he failed us and didn't want any of us to disgrace the family name ever again. That's why I got to live a double life, Zeek. They wouldn't understand the one I chose."

Zeek was unprepared to find out the secret past that his mother purposely hid from him about his family. All throughout Zeek's upbringing, his mother had done a good job keeping him out of the streets and teaching him how to live life honestly, but when Zeek felt he was backed into a corner, being honest or staying out of the streets didn't work for him anymore. He wanted his cousin to teach him everything he knew about the drug game.

Catch's house wasn't as big as Maddy's, but he had a theater room and more cars out front. He had a CLS 500 Mercedes-Benz, Corvette, Range Rover, and an Escalade. Catch'em gave Zeek the option of picking what he wanted to ride in for the night. Zeek was leaning toward the Escalade since Rodney had one, but he still wasn't sure.

"Which one is better between a Range Rover or Escalade?"

Catch'em shrugged. "I like 'em both. But the Range will get you more bitches, and it cost more too."

Zeek wanted to be on a different level than Rodney anyway, so the Range Rover was his choice.

Later that night, they went out to Chauncy's, which was the best club to go to on a Thursday night. Zeek didn't go out much and this was his chance to do it in style. As soon as they hit the entrance, everybody was showing Catch'em mad love. Zeek felt privileged to be related to a ghetto superstar. Catch'em got a booth and ordered two bottles of Cristal. The club didn't even stock that type of champagne, but they always had some available for Catch'em.

As the night went on, Zeek got more attention from the ladies than he knew what to do with. His close association with Catch'em made him a wanted man. The longer Zeek talked to girls, the more he noticed that they all used different slang. "Yo, cuz, these two chicks I was just rappin' to ain't believe me when I told them I was your cousin. One of them said, 'say nephs' and the other one said, 'who's grave.' What's that all about?"

"Almost every hood say shit that only they say. That lets you know where they from. Nephs and who's grave is like sayin' swear to God. Us Hill mothafuckas say nephs and mothafuckas from out Duquesne say who's grave."

Zeek wasn't used to this because everybody in D.C. all used the same words. Pittsburgh was more "*hood*" than he thought.

Catch'em had a surprise waiting for Zeek when they left the club. He arranged for two freaks to go back to the house with them and do whatever they wanted. Melli and Jayla were lady hustlers and loved to get down with Catch'em any time they could. The girls got into a pink Porsche Cayman and followed Catch'em to his condo in the Waterfront area of Homestead. Catch'em had spots all over the city, but never took anybody to his main house, except for Wilk.

Catch'em's condo's interior walls were all painted black. He had two long sectional black leather sofas, thick black carpeting, and all black counter tops and appliances. Catch'em even had everything black in his bathrooms, including his toilets. Black was his favorite color and he wanted to express that in at least one of his homes. Catch'em called this house "the black hole."

Melli and Jayla were so sexy to Zeek that he couldn't stop looking at them. Melli was five-seven, weighed about 135 pounds, and had skin the color of sand. She lay across Catch's lap eating all the cherries out of her cocktail. Jayla sat on Zeek's lap while they sipped Moët from the same glass. Jayla was about the same height as Melli, but was a little thicker. She had bronze skin, full lips, and wore her hair in cornrows with long tails that swooped over her right shoulder.

Both girls looked so good in their short flowing dresses that Zeek couldn't keep the blood from circulating to a certain part of his body. Jayla felt the lump under her thigh and wanted to do something about it quickly. She stood up and let her dress fall to the floor, exposing her naked ripe body. While Jayla helped Zeek remove his clothes, he glanced over at Melli giving Catch'em head.

Damn, this nigga's a pimp, Zeek thought as he admired how much control Catch'em had over women. Jayla pulled Zeek onto the floor and grabbed a condom off of the glass table.

Jayla rolled it onto Zeek's throbbing package and started to ride him slow as she sunk her nails into his chest. Zeek positioned his hands on her firm backside as she rotated her hips in a circular motion. Zeek couldn't help but to stare up at the beautiful vixen as light moans expelled from her lips. Jayla was exactly what Zeek needed to take his mind off of Chelsea. *Only if that bitch could see what I was doing right now*, he thought as a menacing smile appeared on his face.

Zeek hadn't had sex with another girl other than Chelsea in a very long time and prayed he didn't cum prematurely. That was the last thing he needed was to look bad in front of his cousin. Zeek tried his best to think about something else so he wouldn't be overwhelmed by the pleasure. He was doing well until Jayla started grinding harder, causing him to go deeper inside her wetness. Zeek lost his focus and couldn't hold it in anymore. His face tightened as he firmly grabbed down on her waist and enjoyed the last few seconds that still remained.

Jayla smiled when she felt Zeek go limp and then lay on top of him. "Aww shit, baby. That's all you got for me?" she asked, whispering into his ear.

"I got more. That was round one," Zeek said halfway out of breath.

"Are you sure you gonna be able to go again? It sounds like I got you worn out," she joked.

"Don't let her talk slick, Zeek. You better tear her ass up on the next one," Catch'em smiled as he instigated while still getting head from Melli.

"I got her, cuz. I'ma make her feel it on the next one. The shit ain't gonna be funny to her then," Zeek assured him.

Jayla laughed as she sashayed her naked body across the room and pulled a blunt out of her purse. She lit it up and took a couple strong pulls from the thick blunt and gave it to Zeek. They continued to pass the blunt around the room until there was no more left. Jayla was now high, drunk, and wanted some more of Zeek. She grabbed everything she felt between his legs and put it in her mouth. While Jayla had her head sunk heavily into Zeek's lap, Catch'em quietly left the room, but not before commanding Melli to join them. Melli crawled across the couch on the other side of Jayla and got her to share what was in her mouth. Zeek couldn't believe he was getting head from two girls at the same time. He always wanted to have a ménage, but never imagined ever having one. After that night, Zeek wanted to be like his cousin even more.

CHAPTER FIFTEEN

The two weeks that followed were all aimed toward Catch'em helping Zeek learn the drug trade. He wanted to know all of the dos and don'ts about being a hustler. Catch'em showed him how to cut, cook, and bag up cocaine. Zeek observed how Catch'em had his corners set up and liked how quick and smooth transactions went. Catch'em constantly cautioned Zeek that if he wanted to be like him, there were certain rules he had to follow.

Rule #1: Keep the streets happy.

Rule #2: Family comes first. Money comes second.

Rule #3: Stay above the law.

Rule #4: Never take risks.

Rule #5: Trust no one.

Rule #6: Don't let a woman be your downfall.

Catch'em specified that these rules didn't have to be followed in that order; they all were equally important.

Zeek never told Catch'em about Chelsea and felt ashamed that she was his main reason for wanting to sell drugs. Zeek was already breaking rules because Chelsea was indeed his downfall. As the days went on, Zeek had progressed faster than anyone Catch'em had ever seen. Zeek did everything well. He was good at being a lookout, could work the corners, count money quick, and successfully ran the stash houses. Zeek was a natural.

Zeek never had held a gun, but if he wanted to protect himself on the streets, he needed to learn how to shoot. Catch'em took him to a gun range, so he could fire off any gun he wanted. At the end of the day, Zeek learned he could shoot best with a 9mm than he did with a .45 caliber or a .357 Magnum. After a couple days of practice, he felt like he was a definite sure shot. *With an aim like mine, niggas betta watch out*, he thought while still holding the gun sideways, after ripping apart his target. Zeek was slowly becoming a savage.

Chelsea had yet to fully recover from her embarrassing incident with Rodney. She had been keeping a low profile lately, not wanting to take any chances being seen by Zeek. She still couldn't face him after being caught between the sheets with Rodney. Yet, the sex she continued to have with Rodney was the bomb.

She was able to escape from her harsh reality until their act was over. Afterward, she fell right back into her depressing slump. *How could I make such a horrible mistake like this*, she thought, sobbing. Chelsea felt like running away.

Rodney wasn't feeling at his best, either. He had ninety pounds of marijuana left and his supplier's phone was disconnected. He was most likely to run out of weed in about three weeks and wanted his next batch of Northern Lights on its way. While it only took two days for his shipment of 300 pounds to arrive from Chicago, he still was a little nervous. It was unlike his connect to get a new number and not call him with it. *Maybe I'm overreacting*, he thought. Rodney decided to wait a little while longer before he really started to panic. He only hoped that Lunchmeat would give him a call soon.

❖ ❖ ❖

Zeek was having so much fun in Pittsburgh that he had little time to think about Chelsea. He went out every night, having sex with different girls, and learning how to make money. Zeek never wanted to go home. If he stayed in the Burgh, he had everything he wanted to become a baller, except for Chelsea noticing his come-up. He had to learn everything he could and take it back to D.C. with him. That's where he would devise a plan to get his own operation going. Catch'em felt it would be good for Zeek to see how other hustlers handled their business. He wanted to show Zeek the difference between his setup and theirs.

Zeek rode around with Jayla in her black Porsche Boxster all day long while she made money pick-ups and package drop-offs. It was strange for Zeek to see a girl knee deep in the game doing her own thing. Jayla only sold dope, while Catch'em sold it all: heroin, cocaine, crack, marijuana, ecstasy pills, and LSD. She didn't want to be known for pushing all types of narcotics; she only wanted to be infamous for heroin. Liberty Bell was the most potent dope found on the North Side, and Jayla was the only one who had it.

Catch'em later had Zeek hook up with Wilk and Jidder. Wilk was second in command of Catch's whole enterprise, while Jidder only handled crack and ecstasy pills. Unlike Jayla, Wilk and Jidder didn't ride around collecting money or delivering packages. They only arranged for transactions to be made and never put their hands on the product. Melli, on the other hand, only sold kilos of cocaine, and buyers had to come to her if they needed something. Melli moved on average four kilos a week, making $5,000 off each one of them. Melli could sell way more, but she wasn't trying to be greedy.

Zeek understood now why Catch'em wanted him to pay attention to so many hustlers. He wanted him to find his own identity. Everybody did it differently, but he needed to do what worked best for him. However, Zeek didn't care much about identity; as long as he was making money, it didn't matter to him. Zeek wanted to jump in the game, head-first, without even knowing how to swim.

"Aight, young. Thanks for everythang. I'll never forget it," Zeek said as he exited the Range Rover, looking ahead at the Greyhound bus. It was time for him to go and money to be made.

"Don't worry 'bout it, Ike. Just make me proud. If you get rid of those two ounces quick, I'll have more on the way."

Zeek dapped his cousin up and got on the bus headed back to D.C. It was time for Zeek to start up his own empire back home and apply everything he had learned from Catch'em. Catch'em gave him a scale, $2,000, and two ounces of crack to start off. If he was able to move that with ease, Catch'em would send him whatever he needed. Zeek was up for the challenge.

There was only one seat left on the 12:23 a.m. bus, and Zeek had to go all the way to the last row to get it. The seat was already occupied by a pretty, dark-skinned girl, whom he wouldn't have a problem sitting with anyway.

He cleared his throat. "Excuse me. Can I sit here?" he asked her while she was all into a *Vibe* magazine.

"Sure, cutie. Why not." She smiled and moved over to make room for him.

Zeek was feeling this girl and hoped she was feeling him, too. He hoped during the bus ride, they would get to know each other better, and he hoped she wanted the same.

During the short distance they had traveled, Zeek and Makeffa found out a lot about each other. Makeffa was from Youngstown, Ohio, and was on her way to New York to do a photo shoot for *XXL* magazine. She had been trying to get in the magazine for over two years and finally landed the gig. Makeffa had Hershey chocolate skin, a Halle Berry hairstyle, and a banging body.

"Damn, girl. This is you?" Zeek's eyes were wide open looking at her portfolio under the overhead lights.

"Yep. Every picture in this album was taken four months ago."

Zeek was mesmerized by how fine she looked in her photos. Zeek became aroused as he examined all of her pictures. *Some of these should be in* Playboy.

Makeffa found herself getting close to Zeek in the little amount of time they shared. She liked that he listened to her problems and gave her confidence about herself she needed to hear. She could tell Zeek was special and didn't want to forget about him after their trip was over. Halfway through the bus ride, Makeffa wanted to give Zeek something in case they never saw each other again. She couldn't wait until they got off the bus. She had to do it now, while it was dark and everyone was asleep. She shut off the overhead lights to make them even harder to see. She pulled her velour jacket over her head and lay on Zeek's lap.

Makeffa let a few minutes pass by before she went for his zipper. She pulled out his semi-hard package and rubbed it in between her fingers until it was completely hard. She then massaged his piece with her mouth slowly, so she wouldn't show too much head movement.

Zeek's mind was now in a happy place. He was feeling more confident about himself than he ever had as girls wanted him now without the help from his cousin. He had Makeffa to thank for that. Zeek also felt Makeffa liked him so much as she knew he would be the man one day.

CHAPTER SIXTEEN

"**D**amn! Ain't no money down this shit! Marcus don't know what he talkin' 'bout." Zeek had been posted up in an alleyway behind Florida Avenue for two days now. Still, no fiends had passed through. His friend Marcus, who also hustled, had told Zeek the area was an open market and a good place for him to start. This was far different from what Catch'em had going on. But, if he wanted to move up, he would have to make something out of nothing. He told himself he would stick it out for a few more days to see if anything changed.

Out of nowhere, Zeek noticed a man walk through the alley. "Aye, you holdin'?" he asked.

"Yeah. What you need?"

"Whateva I can get for fifty, young boy."

Zeek didn't bag up any fifties. He only made up twenties. Not knowing any better, he had to give the man three of them.

"Good lookin', young boy. If this shit is like that, I'll tell my people 'bout you," the man said as he walked back up the alley.

Zeek was so happy he'd made his first sale. Even though he took a $10 loss, he remembered Catch's rule to keep the streets happy. No more than thirty minutes later, the man brought two more fiends back with him. Zeek ended up making over $600 before the night was over.

For the next few days, things were running pretty smooth for Zeek. He had regular customers and he went through his first ounce. Everything was going fine, until an unfamiliar face came up to him. "Yo, young. You hustlin'?" the short dark-skinned thug asked.

"Yeah. What you need?"

The boy didn't dress like a fiend to Zeek, but he still had to ask. You never could tell.

"I need you to bump, mothafucka. Ain't no hustlin' here."

Zeek was confused. "What?"

"You heard what I said, nigga. Ain't no hustlin' here."

"How come I been here for a week and I ain't never seen you?"

"Slim, I ain't here to answer no fuckin' questions. I don't give a fuck how long you been here, young. You gotta go."

Zeek wasn't sure how serious the boy was about getting him to leave the alley. He figured he might have been trying to punk him, and he wasn't ready to leave yet.

The boy lost his patience. "Oh, you ain't movin'?" he asked as he pulled a gun from his waist.

Zeek knew he meant what he said, so he decided to move. That's when the boy pistol-whipped him with the butt of the gun.

"And don't come back. If you do, you gonna be sorry."

Zeek held the back of his head as he rolled up out the alley. Zeek had been humiliated and kicked out of his spot. He didn't want to, but he had to tell Marcus what had happened.

"Who pistol whipped you, young? What did they look like?" a concerned Marcus asked.

"I don't know, young. I know that this nigga was black as hell and had little twisties in his head."

"That sound like that nigga, Durty."

"Durty?"

"Yeah. Him and his boys got ran out of Trinidad and they tryin' to take over any spot they can. I guess they heard where you at was sweet."

Zeek was pissed. "I got to get that spot back," he said, thinking about all the money he was missing out on.

Marcus had an offer. "If you can get some more of that crack you got, I can get it back for you."

"Yeah, I can get as much as I want. But how you gonna get it back?"

"Let me worry 'bout that." Marcus let Zeek in on his plan. "Young, if ya cousin hook us up wit' dat' shit there, we can run this damn city."

Zeek didn't have to think long about it. The city was what he wanted. He was going to make it happen.

Marcus had known Zeek ever since he was in the tenth grade. Zeek transferred to his school, and he was the first one to become friends with him. Marcus thought it was funny for he and Zeek to be hustling together, especially after they were on the right track back in high school. Marcus was five-eleven, a solid 190 pounds and had received a full scholarship to Virginia Tech to play basketball. Unfortunately, he had to drop out of school after a year so he could support his family. That's when he turned to the streets. Zeek wanted to go to Duke University to become a doctor, but couldn't score high enough on his SAT. Ever since, he became discouraged and took regular jobs after he got out of high school.

Later that evening, Zeek called Catch'em to tell him he was out of crack. Catch'em was impressed at how fast Zeek had gotten rid of the two ounces. Zeek told him he needed a lot more, but didn't explain why because the phone may have been tapped, but Catch'em caught on to what he wanted. Catch'em told him he would be cool by tomorrow, and that's what he meant. The next morning, Zeek got a call from Goose. Goose was Catch'em's out-of-town delivery driver. He got Zeek's address and was at his house in ten minutes.

Goose pulled up to his house in a blue Audi A8, and hopped out wearing a three-piece Ralph Lauren suit. Goose was brown, tall, and slender. He always dressed up when he went on the road, so he wouldn't look suspicious to police.

"Is anybody else here?" Goose asked as he entered the house.

"Nope, I'm the only one here."

Goose handed him the laptop bag that he'd carried in on his shoulder. When Zeek opened it, he was surprised at what he saw.

"How much is this?

"A half-key. That's eighteen ounces."

Zeek had wanted more, but didn't think he would get that much. He didn't know what he would do with that much crack.

"Now ya cousin gave me specific instructions to tell you. He wants you to find a good stash spot where you can keep this. When it comes to your crew, don't tell them how much you got. Assure them that they will never run out. Most importantly, they got to know you're the connect; you control this shit, not them. Catch only wants you to get him back ten gees and call him when you get down to five ounces."

Goose spoke very firm, and Zeek took him seriously. When Goose left, Zeek jumped on the phone to tell Marcus he was straight. Once he ended the call, he took out what he needed and stashed the laptop bag under his bed. He was now ready to meet up with Marcus.

"Here, young. This is four and a half. I need three gees back off this."

"That's easy. I got you, young. We gonna make this shit happen."

Zeek handed him the package, and they dapped each other up. But before Zeek could walk away, Marcus spoke. "Oh yeah, young. You can go back to that spot now. I took care of that problem for you."

Zeek was confused. "How you do that?"

"I had Cook put a few hot ones in 'em. That nigga gone."

Zeek didn't know how to feel about Marcus getting Durty killed for him. He did indeed want his spot back, but he wasn't sure if it was worth killing someone over. *The game was getting real.*

"There's a key of crack and an eighth of a key of heroin in there, per your order," Goose said as he handed Zeek the laptop bag. "Make sure you keep that shit in rice, man. You don't want that dope to get moisture in it."

In a month's time, Goose had seen Zeek three times already. He had literally blown up overnight. Zeek kept making more money and didn't care where it was coming from. He had a group of young hungry soldiers that were always on the grind. Zeek gave his click the name U.B.N., or the U-Haul Boy Network, since they kept moving crack for him. Now that U.B.N. had the chance to push heroin, money would pile up a lot quicker.

It was now July, and Zeek's hope of getting a car by September looked better than ever. Yet, Zeek didn't want any car anymore. He wanted a Range Rover. Zeek wanted to surpass Rodney by getting the ultimate sports utility vehicle, and a Range Rover was it. Zeek would have to get in the field and off the sideline, in order to get one. Zeek was only supplying his clique with weight and didn't work the corners anymore. But, now he would have to go back on the block. He had guns now that Goose had brought them and was ready to protect himself, if needed.

Zeek was determined to stay out all night, until all his vials were gone. By about three a.m., he had two grand in his pocket and only five vials left. He was getting tired and wanted to get rid of all the vials to the first fiend he saw. That's when a lady made her way up the street toward him.

"Ezeekiel, I know you ain't out here hustlin' now?" the woman asked once she got up on him.

No one has called me Ezeekiel in a long time, he thought. Whoever it was definitely knew him well. Zeek stared at the lady. Yet, he still wasn't able to make the connection. "Are you a friend of my mom's?" He took a wild guess but was afraid to ask.

"No. I went to school wit' you." Zeek was really puzzled now. "I can't believe you don't remember me," the lady said while putting her hands on her waist. By the way the lady moved, Zeek knew exactly who she was.

"Shawnna?"

"Yeah, baby. It took you long enough. How you been?" she said with her groggy voice from all the years of being on drugs.

"I'm good."

Zeek didn't have to ask her how she was doing. It was obvious because of her gruff and emaciated appearance. The beautiful, brown sugar-skinned princess Zeek remembered was no more. Shawnna had lost weight since high school and had a lot of markings all over her face. Life had really gotten the best of her. This was the same girl Rodney used to beat him up over. They both reminisced briefly about the last time they had seen each other, but Shawnna was ready to leave after she got her drugs.

Shawnna wanted to have lunch with Zeek to catch up on old times. Even though she was on that "shit," Zeek still accepted. Zeek had a soft spot for Shawnna even if she was on drugs. That's why he gave her all the vials he had left for free. She needed the drugs more than he needed the money. He really felt sorry for her.

For days now, Rodney had been hearing Zeek's name come up constantly in the streets. He'd been steady trying to ignore it. Zeek was quickly rising to the top in the game, while Rodney was facing an all-time low. Once he got word that Lunchmeat was killed and Poundcake was on the run, he faced the fact he would have to search for another connect. With shady connects around and potent weed hard to come by, Rodney had to ration out the few pounds he had left. All of his re-up money had gone to splurging on Chelsea.

In the short period of time he'd known her, they'd been to Belize, Jamaica, and Aruba. Rodney was so into impressing Chelsea that he didn't watch how much money he was spending. Now, he was almost broke.

Rodney needed a quick come-up and selling weed wasn't it. Zeek was supposed to have the best product in Northeast, but Rodney knew Zeek wouldn't deal with him. Rodney wanted to stick to his guns and tough it out. That's all he could do until the hard times passed.

CHAPTER SEVENTEEN

"Can I have a seafood platter and a catfish dinner?" Zeek said, as he ordered him and Shawnna food from The Shrimp Boat. They sat on the hood of Shawnna's Mercury Sable where they ate and talked about old times.

"So what made you start hustlin', Zeek? Last I knew, you were tryna go to school to be a doctor or some shit. Whatchu doin' out here?"

"I ain't make it into the school I wanted. Now I'm out here gettin' my paper up, so I can start a business."

"Oh yeah. What kind of business?"

"A cleaning company. You remember Alonzo, right?"

"Yeah. Youngin' you was always wit'?"

"Yeah. Well, it was his idea. But we gonna to do it together. Hopefully, it will blow up."

"That's what's up, Zeek. Y'all idea is good. I'm glad you ain't like some of these other niggas out here. Just hustlin' to impress bitches n'shit."

Zeek was so uneasy by her comment that he changed the subject.

"So, what happened to you? How you get on drugs anyway?"

Thinking about what happened to her made her stomach turn. "Because of that nigga, Rodney."

"Rodney?" Zeek asked in total astonishment.

"Yeah. You remember that nigga, don't you?"

Zeek was shocked to hear his name of all people to come out her mouth. "What happened?"

Shawnna took a deep breath before telling the story. "That nigga was comin' over my house to smoke. Supposedly on some 'I'm just tryin' to be cool' type shit. You know how y'all niggas do. Everything was all to the good, until one day he started touchin' on me and I told him to leave. Well, a few days later, he came back wantin' to apologize n'shit, and had some dro and Henny wit'em. I thought it was funny that he said he stopped smokin' and let me face the blunt by myself.

"After that, he came over and let me smoke a couple more times by myself still. Then, he stopped coming by for a few days. The next time I saw him he offered me some crack, and I took it. That's when I knew I was hooked. That mothafucka was lacin' his shit, and now I'm all fucked up."

Zeek was hurt that Rodney had harmed his childhood sweetheart. Just like Chelsea, Zeek now felt Rodney was out to get every girl he ever loved. Zeek wanted revenge, but wasn't sure how to go about it yet. The thing he had to do first was get Shawnna some help.

"Is that all he did to you?" Zeek asked with a sad look on his face.

"If you're askin' if he ever fucked me, then the answer's yes." Shawnna felt ashamed. "I was fuckin' him and suckin' his dick, but it was only 'cause he had that shit, you know what I'm sayin'?"

"When was the last time you've seen him?"

"About eight months ago. He just all of a sudden stopped comin' to see me. That's when I went out to look for him, but I ended up finding dope instead."

In the morning, Shawnna agreed to let Zeek check her into a

rehab center. They both hoped when she came out of the program, she would stay clean. In exchange for Zeek helping her get right, she put him in touch with every user she knew. Soon, Zeek would have nineteen new fiends coming to him on the regular. Business for him was looking good, especially when Marcus continued to grab weight off him. Marcus was copping a half a key a week and Zeek had no problem keeping up with him. He wondered how he was moving so much, so fast.

Zeek was tired of walking and was ready to buy a car now. Catch'em told him to wait until next spring to get a Range Rover since the new '05s would be cheaper then. Zeek listened and settled for a new Chrysler 300M. He'd never had a car and driving around in his gold 300 was a thrill. The first thing he did was take his mom out to one of D.C.'s finest restaurants, Oceanaire. He wanted to celebrate his first two months of consistent work. His mom was led to believe he had a good job doing construction.

Later that night, Zeek picked up Lonzo and went down to Dream nightclub. Dream was the number one hot spot in the country on Friday nights, and Zeek wanted to see what it was all about.

"What's up, Zeek?" was all he heard when they walked through the club. People were speaking to him he didn't even know. That gave Zeek a nice feeling knowing the streets only had good things to say about him. Zeek went to the bar and ordered two bottles of Moët for him and Lonzo.

"You sure you ain't tryna get in the game, young?" Zeek asked Lonzo as he popped his bottle, trying to impress him with his lifestyle.

"Nah. You got it, young. My cleaning contract is about to start soon. I'm goin' to live off that."

Zeek shrugged. "That's cool. You know the door's always open?"

"Yeah, I feel you," Lonzo said, looking disinterested.

"Well, good luck wit' ya business. I'm proud of you, bro. Let's make a toast." They both lifted up their glasses.

"Damn, that nigga's fine. Look at him over there poppin' Mo. They was right. He is doin' his thing," the girl said, admiring the man with the fly outfit and matching gators. "I'm gonna go holla at my boy," she continued.

"Now, you know Chelsea wouldn't be feelin' that," the other girl gestured.

"He don't belong to her no more. She lost that. Besides, you know I've been wantin' that nigga way before they got together anyway. I'm sorry, but she's short."

"Girl, you are crazy," the other girl stated.

She gave her friend a serious look. "So, if I go holla, you gonna tell Chelsea?"

Her friend raised her hands. "That's between you and her. I ain't sayin' shit."

"Cool."

"Where is Chelsea at anyway?" the other girl wondered.

"Her and Dya went to Juste Lounge."

"Oh. Okay."

"Aight. I'm gonna go say what's up," she said as she made her way over to the bar. Her friend simply looked at her walk away, hoping she knew what she was doing.

Zeek was trying to ask Lonzo what else he wanted to drink, when a pair of hands covered his eyes. "Guess who?"

Zeek couldn't really make out the voice, but the only person he kept thinking about was Chelsea. He was eager to run into her so she could see his new status. When he lifted the soft hands from his eyes and turned around, he was thrown off by who it was.

"Qwanda?" he said with a puzzled look on his face.

"You didn't know, did you?"

"Nah. I didn't know who it was."

Qwanda started to make her move. "I know you might find this strange, but I wanted to buy you a drink."

Zeek felt there was a setup coming. "Is Chelsea wit' you?" he asked as he looked around for her.

"No, she's out somewhere else. So, what can I get you to drink?"

Seeing the sweet look in her eyes, Zeek still had to test her. "Get me a double Remy on ice."

Qwanda ordered him and her both doubles and gave the bartender a fifty-dollar bill. Zeek was impressed.

"I'm gonna let you and Lonzo finish rappin', but I want you to call me when the club let out." She wrote her number on a table napkin, and then put it in his hand. "Don't be fakin', either," she said as she winked and walked away.

Zeek was at a loss for words about what had happened. Qwanda was wearing a shirt that exposed most of her back and that didn't help, either. She was looking too damn sexy and Zeek still thought he might be in a trap. Zeek tried to avoid Qwanda on his way out of the club, but she was standing by the door when he got there.

"I know you ain't tryna leave wit' out gettin' at me?" she asked with her hands on her hips.

"Nah. I was gonna call when I got outside."

Qwanda didn't believe him. "Look. I know you don't trust me yet, but I want to go somewhere, so we can talk."

Still leery, Zeek agreed. He wondered what she was up to. They took Fawn and Lonzo home, and then Zeek followed Qwanda to the Best Western hotel on Oxon Hill Road. Since it was Qwanda's idea to go there, she paid for the room. Zeek had only been to a hotel once or twice with Chelsea, but it wasn't to go "talk." He figured Qwanda had ulterior motives.

"So what you want to talk about?" Zeek asked while facing her on the bed.

Qwanda began to blush from embarrassment. "I don't know how I want to say this, but…did you know I always liked you?"

Zeek was surprised. "Fo' real? Since when?"

"Since I was thirteen; I always had the biggest crush on you," she said, looking off, still feeling silly for even telling him.

"Oh yeah? How come you never said nothin'?"

She tilted her head to the side. "You know why. 'Cause you was wit' Chelsea. Besides…you wouldn't of looked at me like that anyway."

She was right. Qwanda wasn't very cute at a young age, and Zeek would've never talked to her, with her pimpled-up face and big glasses.

"Chelsea even knew I wanted to go wit' you, but she stepped to you first."

Qwanda continued to go on and on about all the things she remembered and liked about Zeek. He couldn't believe she used to do so many things to get his attention, but he never noticed. It was clear to Zeek now that Qwanda wanted to fill in the space Chelsea held for so long. Qwanda knew it was a gamble, but she had to take a chance. She moved in closer to him and gave him a kiss on his forehead, followed by a kiss on his nose, advancing with a kiss on his lips. The scene that she was creating was sure to be her best experience yet, one that she had been waiting to have for almost a decade.

Qwanda slowly undressed him, and he did the same to her. They passionately kissed on each other's bodies under the dim light. Qwanda's insides were as wet as morning dew. She was ready for insertion. What seemed like eternity for Qwanda only lasted about five minutes when Zeek came. She'd already climaxed a couple of times, grinning at her conquest.

Qwanda was pleased by what had taken place, even if it would never happen again. From that moment on, she would still be in pursuit of him. Zeek adored the sex they had also, and wanted to do it again. Whether it was revenge or lust that brought them together that night, they had started something neither one of them would be able to handle.

Qwanda stared into his eyes and saw someone that didn't deserve to be hurt the way he'd been. She wanted to be the only woman in his life. The crushing she'd done when she was younger had flourished; Qwanda had fallen in love. Zeek stared back at her, looking at the once-ugly duckling, which she somehow, miraculously, had turned into a beautiful swan.

I wish I could have been wit' this girl all along, he thought. *I would have been happier not ever knowin' Chelsea's name.*

"That's that nigga Poonie right there, huh?" Marcus asked Cook, as they sat in a black Denali across the street from all the action.

"Yeah, that's him," Cook responded.

"So, how many strips this nigga got?"

"I hear he got four, but this is the busiest one, though."

"We got to take this one first. We'll get the other ones later. Call that nigga over here."

Cook beeped the horn a few times to get Poonie's attention. When Poonie noticed the two guys in the truck, Cook signaled him to come over to them. Poonie was a straight gangster. He had a big section of Southwest under his belt and had the best coke in the area. He saw the truck pull up and wondered who was inside until he was signaled over. He went over to see what they wanted as his homies looked on. They had their heat cocked, ready for something to go wrong.

"What's the deal, son?" Poonie asked as he looked in the truck.

"Aye, young. You ever hear about a nigga named Marcus from over Northeast?" Marcus asked.

"Yeah. That's you, right?" Poonie responded.

Marcus laughed. "Damn. I didn't think y'all Southwest boys heard of me over here. That's crazy, young."

Poonie was getting irritated. "So, what is it that y'all want? Y'all on my time."

"Okay, businessman. I ain't gonna take up too much of ya time. I see ya block is makin' money, but I feel if you was movin' my product, you'd be makin' a lot more."

"I doubt that. I ain't fuckin' wit' y'all, so y'all can be on ya'll way."

Marcus wasn't feeling it. "Look, nigga. I'm tryna be nice about this shit. Now, you got three choices: you can buy my shit, sell my shit, or y'all niggas can fuckin' bump."

Poonie got angry. "What, nigga? Do you know who the fuck you're talkin' to?"

"Yeah, but do you? Y'all Southwest niggas heard about me. Y'all know I don't do no mothafuckin' fakin'. You got three days, nigga." Cook dropped a card out the window and drove off.

Poonie never called the number on the card. Marcus had to send him a message to prove he meant business. Within the next six days, Poonie and half of his crew were found laid out all over the Southwest area. Poonie's remaining soldiers got down with Marcus soon after, and U.B.N. became ever stronger.

CHAPTER EIGHTEEN

"Could you please call that nigga for me?" Rodney begged.

"Sorry, boo. I know he won't talk to me," Chelsea advised.

"Well, what's his number? I'll call him myself."

"If he won't talk to me, why would you think he'd talk to you?"

"I don't, but I gotta try."

"Why can't you cop from somebody else?"

"All these niggas out here got garbage. Zeek got that pure shit. Could you call him, please?"

Chelsea rolled her eyes. "I'll dial the number for you, but you gotta holla at him ya self."

Rodney was now damn near broke. He had forty-seven hundred and only one ounce of weed left to his name. He'd been smoking blunt after blunt trying to deal with all the stress. Rodney had tried to cop from other dealers, but ended up getting beat several times. Chelsea was never aware of his shortcomings and didn't know Zeek was his last option.

Zeek heard his phone ring and saw the call came up "private." He still decided to answer it.

"Hello."

"Is this Zeek?"

"Yeah. Who dis?"

"Rodney."

Zeek got heated. "How the fuck did you get my number?"

"I didn't. Chelsea called you for me."

"What the fuck you want?" Zeek barked.

"Chill, young, chill. It ain't like that. I got to holla at you about somethin'. I need you to meet me out front of RFK Stadium."

Zeek didn't know what he wanted, but agreed to meet him anyway. He knew it was time they finally met face to face. "I'll see you in twenty minutes, and don't bring that bitch." *Click!*

"Who was you talkin' to like that?" Qwanda asked while coming out of the bathroom wearing just a towel.

Zeek was still mad. "Fuckin' Rodney's gay ass."

"Rodney? What that bama want?"

"He wants me to meet 'em. He say he wanna rap about somethin'."

Qwanda sucked her teeth. "He probably wants you to help his broke ass get back on."

Zeek was surprised. "Rodney's broke? How you know?"

"Dya told me that his uncle from Chicago got killed. That's who he was gettin his weight from. She also said he spent all his money on Chelsea, and now he ain't got shit."

Zeek couldn't wait to see if what Qwanda was saying was really true. "I'll go see what he wants, but I doubt if I'll fuck wit' him, though."

"Boy, you betta take that nigga's money. Remember, he needs you more than you need him."

"I'm feelin' that. I'll be back in a minute," Zeek said as he tried to roll off the bed.

"You can't leave until you hit me off first." Qwanda smiled as she dropped her towel to expose her naked body. "It's only going to take you a minute to fuck me anyway," she teased.

"Come here and get your sixty seconds, girl." Zeek smiled and pulled her down on the bed so he could give her what she wanted.

Zeek liked that Qwanda never complained about how long he could perform with her. It didn't matter to her. All she cared about was being with Zeek.

Rodney had been waiting for Zeek for almost forty minutes. He looked up and down the street to see if he was coming. *I think this nigga's tryna play me*, he thought before he saw a gold 300M pull up behind him.

Rodney was standing up against his truck when Zeek walked over to him. "What up, young?" Rodney said.

"What up?" Zeek coldly responded.

"Yo, how that 300 ride?" Rodney asked, trying to make small talk.

"It's a'ight. It's somethin' to push until I get my Range Rover next spring." Zeek wanted Rodney to show an expression of disbelief, so he could get his Range the next day, but Rodney believed him. Rodney knew Zeek was playing with big money.

"That's what's up," Rodney said nonchalantly, as Zeek was getting impatient.

"So what you want to holla 'bout?"

Rodney scratched his head. "I didn't mean for it to go down the way it did wit' Chelsea. She came after me, young. She told me she wasn't fuckin' wit' you and I believed her. But I'm sure…if you were me, you would have done the same thing."

Zeek wasn't feeling that shit at all. "If that's your apology, then whatever, Joe. So, we done?"

"Not really. I heard you got that melt. What can I get wit' four stacks?"

"You can get four and a half for forty-two."

"Forty-two? That's more than what I thought it would be."

"If you want the best, that's what it cost. But, if you don't want it—"

"Nah. That's cool," Rodney interrupted. "When can I get it?"

"You got that on you?"

"Yeah," Rodney eagerly responded.

Zeek got on his phone and called up one of his runners. Within three minutes, a car pulled up, and Zeek directed Rodney over to it. They made the exchange, and the car drove off. Rodney thanked Zeek for the hook-up. He got in his truck, gazing happily at his purchase. Little did he know Zeek had overcharged him by at least $700. Rodney now only had five hundred left in his pocket. He would really have to grind it out, if he wanted to get back to the top.

Chelsea waited for Rodney to return while thinking about everything that had happened between her and Zeek. She felt foolish. Zeek had become someone she never thought he would be, and now he wasn't hers anymore. If she would have known Zeek would've made such a transformation, she could've stuck it out with him for the long run. *He'll never take me back*, she thought. As Chelsea sat on the couch drowning in her own sorrow, she heard the mailman drop something in the mailbox. She hoped it was a letter from Wheelz, since he hadn't written her in a while.

Citywide Insurance? Why am I getting somethin' from there? But I have car insurance through Piedmont. She was so confused. When she opened the envelope, she found out that the BMW truck was in her name.

Lunchmeat bought that truck for me? She couldn't believe it. Chelsea was so happy the truck was really hers after all. She wasn't sure how she would feel if Lunchmeat were still alive. Lunchmeat was Rodney's uncle, and since having had sex with both of them, she would have really looked like a hoe. *If I would have stayed true to Zeek, none of that would've ever happened,* she thought. She wouldn't have a nice truck, but at least she would have a good boyfriend.

CHAPTER NINETEEN

oday may be the day that Wheelz could finally go home. Wheelz had been in Detroit for over three months now. He had been holding Mary Ramsey hostage in an undisclosed location. Mary Ramsey was the mother of Devon Ramsey, the man who could clear RoRo of all charges today in court. Mary was hiding out of town in protective custody from people like Wheelz, but when your daughter was on dope, it was easy for someone to find you. Wheelz gave Mary's daughter, Carol, a brick of heroin, and Carol gave up her mother's location without a second thought.

"When are you goin' to let me go?" Mary asked angrily while being tied to a chair.

Wheelz gave her another cold stare, one colder than the one he'd given her a few minutes ago. "You keep askin' the same question and I keep givin' you the same fuckin' answer. When I get the call that my boy is comin' home, I'll let ya old ass go. A'ight?"

"You guys are some animals! What if someone had your mother tied up somewhere?" Mary snarled.

"That would never fuckin' happen. I got too much power in the streets, but ya bitch-ass son don't."

"How do I know you're not goin' to kill me even if your friend is set free?" Mary was concerned.

Wheelz got frustrated all over again. "Look, bitch! I told you I would let ya scary ass go, didn't I?"

Mary took a hard swallow. "What if he's found guilty?"

Wheelz gave her another evil look. "Then your soul is goin' to heaven."

Mary started crying, fearing what her fate would be in the short hours to come. She was petrified and had no hope that she would live to see another day. She closed her eyes and started to say a prayer trying to find a safe place in her mind. She repeated to call upon the Lord in a hushed tone as tears met her crusted lips.

Mary had somehow managed to cry herself to sleep. She was enjoying her peaceful nap until she was awakened by the uncomfortable sound of a ringing cell phone. Her heart dropped to her stomach. This might be the call that Wheelz was waiting for. This also might be the call that determined whether she lived or died. Mary's lips quivered as Wheelz reached for his cell phone.

Wheelz stared into Mary's scared eyes as he answered the phone. "Yeah. What? Are you sure? Cool." *Click!* Wheelz looked pissed as he walked over to Mary while she started to fear for her life. "Fuck. I wanted to kill ya ass. Today is ya lucky day, bitch. I gotta let you go."

Mary was so relieved her life was spared, even if justice wasn't served. Today, Rodell "RoRo" Rogers was cleared of two counts of first-degree murder and one count of attempted murder. RoRo didn't beat trial because he had a bad-ass lawyer. It was because Devon Ramsey was the only testifying witness that could put RoRo away for the rest of his life, but didn't. Instead, he told the courtroom that RoRo wasn't the one who had shot him, or two others, and couldn't place him at the scene of the crime, either. With his mother's life in the hands of a killer, he had to follow the code of the streets, and not the laws of the judicial system. *Another guilty man had been set free.*

CHAPTER TWENTY

"I thought Qwanda was comin' wit' you?" Chelsea asked.

"I thought she was, too, but she ain't been answerin' her phone," Fawn responded.

"Yeah. What's been up wit' her lately? I asked her to go out the last three nights, and she carried us. What's that all about?" Dya added.

Chelsea and Dya were clueless about Qwanda, and Fawn wanted to keep it that way, so she changed the subject. "I don't know y'all, but I'm tryna sip on somethin'. Can we go in now?"

For the moment, Qwanda's actions would be put to the side and they all went into Club U to try and have a good time.

Club U was one of the well-known nuisance clubs in D.C. Besides the Rare Essence go-go band playing there on Saturday nights, the girls went there for the stiff drinks and free buffet. Chelsea had been going out a lot lately trying to keep her mind off the Zeek and Rodney situation. When they got to the bar, Chelsea was surprised by who she saw. It was Wheelz and RoRo.

"Ro. Wheelz. What y'all doin' here? I thought you was supposed to be down in the ATL?" Chelsea said to Wheelz, then looked at RoRo. "And I thought you was locked up?" Chelsea was highly confused and wanted answers.

"I got back from the A this mornin'," Wheelz answered.

Chelsea shifted her attention back to RoRo. "And what about you? When did you get out?"

"I've been out a couple days now."

Chelsea sucked her teeth. "Why ain't you hit me up then?"

"My bad, boo. But real shit started happenin', and I been tryna get it straight."

"Yeah, a'ight," Chelsea said with an attitude.

RoRo held his arms out. "Come on, boo. You can't be that mad at me. Come give ya boy a hug. I missed you."

Chelsea smiled and gave him a hug. She missed him, too. She hadn't seen him in over a year, and he was still looking fine as always. RoRo was tall with bronze-colored skin and had his hair cut low. He wore a blue Polo button-up with some denim Sean John jeans and a pair of tan Timberlands. He was blinging from ear to ear and wore a rose gold chain that hung down to his stomach.

"Damn, boy. You lookin' good. I see you was gettin' ya weight up in there," Chelsea said, looking at his muscular forearms.

"Yeah, I was doin' a little somethin' to keep the time goin' by. What about you. It looks like you done thickened up, too. Turn around for me."

Chelsea did a little cute turn in her cut up light denim Forever 21 jeans.

RoRo nodded. "Yeah, that ass is fat. Some other nigga got it like that, huh?"

"Yeah, right, I been eatin' right."

"Well, it don't matter who been hittin' my kitty, daddy's home now. Them other niggas gotta bump."

"Well, daddy needs to buy his girl a drink."

"I can do betta than that. I'll buy all y'all drinks. Tell ya girls to get whateva they want." RoRo wanted to celebrate with everybody because he was home now. Hopefully, he would be there to stay.

Chelsea stood with RoRo the whole time she was at the club. She had so much to talk to him about, but it seemed like he wasn't listening to her. He kept getting lost with what was going on in the crowd.

"Are you lookin' for someone?"

"What?" he asked, still not looking at her.

"Are you lookin' for someone? You keep starin' into the crowd like you tryna find somebody."

"Nah. I'm chillin'," he said, giving her his full attention.

"Well, I'm tryna talk to you, but you're not listenin'."

"My bad, boo. Let's get out of here, so we can talk somewhere else."

"Like where?"

"The telly," RoRo said, giving her a wink.

Chelsea smiled. "That's fine wit' me."

Dya and Fawn knew what it was when Chelsea and RoRo left, but they didn't care because they had plans of their own. Dya left with Wheelz to get something to eat, while Fawn left with someone she met on the dance floor.

Chelsea and RoRo went to the Hampton Inn on Sixth Street to have wild animal sex. They hadn't been with each other for over a year and went at it like they would never get another chance in life. RoRo was putting Chelsea in every position he knew, and she climaxed so many times she lost count. She hasn't had sex like that in almost two months and wished she could get it like that every day. The night was going so good for her until RoRo was ready to leave.

She was confused. "What you mean am I ready? You ain't tryna stay?"

"Nah. You can stay, but I gotta go. I got things to do."

"If I stay, will you come back?"

"No. I can't. I gotta go. I'll holla later, baby." He gave her a kiss and left out the door.

His actions caught Chelsea totally off-guard. Any other time RoRo would have stayed the night with her. For some reason, this time was different. *Why was he at Club U if he didn't like listenin' to go-go? And why was he in such a hurry to leave,* she thought. This wasn't the RoRo she used to know.

For the next couple of days Chelsea and RoRo continued having sex with each other. They did it anywhere they could. They did it at hotels, her house, in Wheelz's basement, and in the backseat of her truck. They couldn't get enough of each other. Yet, Chelsea was irritated by RoRo's hit-and-run routine. She continued to ask him what the problem was, but he kept playing it off like it was no big deal. She couldn't call it, but something was definitely wrong with him.

The girls had so much fun last Saturday at Club U that they wanted to do it again. This time, Qwanda would be in attendance. Even though Qwanda came, the girls noticed that she was acting different.

"Hey, why you carry ol'boy like that? He was only tryna holla at you," asked Dya.

Qwanda shrugged. "I wasn't feelin' him."

"But, that nigga was fine as hell, and it looked like he had big paper, too," Chelsea added.

"True indeed, but I wasn't feelin' him like that."

"You weren't feelin' him or the youngin' I met here for you from last week, either," Fawn said, while Qwanda gave her a look like she was giving away too much information.

Fawn then remembered that Qwanda was all into Zeek and nobody else mattered. Qwanda wished she could tell her friends about her newfound love, but her friendship with Chelsea would be put in jeopardy.

The club was packed, and the girls were on the dance floor getting their groove on, while Rare Essence was ripping it up on the stage. They really had it cranking. Everyone started beating their feet when "Overnight Scenario" came on, and the night seemed like it was getting started. Chelsea happened to glance over at the bar, when she saw RoRo leaning up against the counter. *What the hell is he doin' in here again*, she thought. She had to go find out what was up with him.

Wheelz was standing right beside RoRo looking at the same thing. Wheelz saw RoRo was about to go crazy. "Is you goin' to be a'ight, young?"

"I'm goin' to kill that nigga and that bitch," RoRo grunted.

"Be easy, young," Wheelz tried to calm RoRo down. "We'll see that nigga outside. Don't do shit up in here. There's too many people, a'ight?" RoRo didn't respond. "Come on, Ro. Don't lose focus. Let 'em do what they do, until we get outside. Remember, nigga, you got out days ago, and I did all that work so you could beat that case. I hope it wasn't for nothin'. You feel what I'm sayin'?"

RoRo was slow to respond. He twisted up his face. "Yeah. I feel you."

"Shit. Here comes Chelsea," Wheelz alerted him. "I'm goin' to go take a piss. Don't do shit." Wheelz stopped Chelsea in passing. "Aye, watch that nigga 'til I get back, a'ight?"

"Why? What's goin' on?"

"Nothin'. Just watch 'em for me. I'll be back in a minute." Wheelz walked off while Chelsea was left standing there looking confused.

RoRo continued to keep his eyes on one particular couple that made their way to the dance floor.

Chelsea walked over to him. "Ro. What's goin' on wit' you?"

"Nothin'," he responded without even looking at her. RoRo had never given her the cold shoulder and had promised he never would. Chelsea feared that things between them had changed. She continued to ask him questions until he completely blocked out her words.

His heart began to race, and his eyes started to water. RoRo didn't like what he was seeing at all. The couple he had been following all night started kissing and grinding on each other. Now, enough was enough. RoRo was sweating heavily while his body continued to quiver. He couldn't take seeing his wife being intimate with another man. Not any man, but the same man he went to jail for. Also, the same man that was about to have a baby with his wife. RoRo could have waited until he got outside to handle his business, but he didn't. He had to end that shit right then.

RoRo walked away from the bar while Chelsea was still talking to him. Chelsea wondered where the hell he was going in a rush. When he got on the dance floor, he pulled a chrome .45 from his waist and proceeded over to where his wife had been dancing. One of the bartenders had been watching RoRo all night and knew he was acting strange. When he saw the glare from RoRo's gun, he rushed to get security right away.

RoRo walked up on his wife and poked the man she was kissing in the back of his head with the gun. When the man turned around, RoRo fired a shot that blew off part of his face. He stood as he watched the man's body hit the floor. The crowd started screaming and running while RoRo continued to fire shots into the fallen man's chest.

After shooting the man four more times, RoRo raised his gun and pointed it at his terrified wife, who had blood splattered all over her. "This ain't all your fault," he uttered as a single tear fell from his eye. In the next moment, he was tackled to the ground by the police.

Wheelz had come back to the bar when he had heard the first gunshot go off. Wheelz and Chelsea couldn't believe what had taken place. RoRo was handcuffed and immediately removed from the club. RoRo's wife fell to her knees and cried over her boyfriend's bloody body, praying, thankful to still be alive.

The police were able to respond as quickly as they did because they were about to raid the club anyway. The heavily troubled club was under investigation for underage drinking and drug trafficking. The police got more than a few drug possession rips that night. They got a murder, as well.

Wheelz made sure he got Chelsea and the rest of the girls out of there before IDs started being checked. "Are y'all a'ight?" Wheelz asked when they got across the street from the club.

"What the fuck happened in there?" Chelsea cried. The other girls were emotional, too.

"Look, I'll explain everything, but you need to get me the fuck out of here first! Ro is the one who drove, and he got the fuckin' keys!"

Chelsea and Wheelz ran to her truck, while Dya and the others ran to their cars. They all dipped out of the parking lot and followed Chelsea to wherever she and Wheelz were going.

"Fuck, Ro! Why couldn't you wait?" Wheelz shouted.

"Why did he do that?" Chelsea was eager to know as Wheelz stared up into the ceiling, until he was ready to explain.

"The reason he killed slim was because he was fuckin' wit' his wifey."

Chelsea couldn't believe what she heard. "What you mean wifey?"

"That nigga married, Chelsea."

Chelsea was so pissed. "How long has his ass been married? And how come I didn't know nuttin' 'bout the shit?"

"He's been married way before he knew you, but I don't know why he didn't tell you himself."

"Then, why didn't you say shit, nigga? You could've told me in one of those letters you wrote me ya damn self."

"That would have been breakin' codes. You know how the game goes."

Chelsea knew Wheelz was right. She never would've put any of her friends' biz out there like that and her friends wouldn't do that to her, either. For whatever it was worth, she still wanted to know what had led up to the murder. Wheelz's feelings were hurt that RoRo had him do so much to keep him out of prison, and he didn't appreciate it. Wheelz was now ready to confess to Chelsea, and this would be the only time he would ever tell this story, ever.

It all began when RoRo's wife, Paris, was fed up with his cheating ways. After she caught him in bed with another woman for the third time, she had to get a little plaything of her own. Paris was kind of tall with a thin curvaceous body. She was a beautiful redbone with long black hair and full lips. She had met RoRo at a citywide fashion show that was held every year in Philly.

Paris always had dreams of becoming a runway model, but ended up getting married at the tender age of eighteen. RoRo influenced her to fall back on her dreams and live the life of a hustler's wife instead. Paris had sacrificed her career for love. It wasn't only RoRo she was in love with; she was in love with his money, too.

RoRo took Paris from rags to riches. He gave her anything she ever needed. There was no way she could leave him, even though he messed around on her. That's why she found someone to creep with. When RoRo found out Paris had somebody on the side, he had to end it the best way he knew how: murder. Though he cheated on her many times, he didn't want anyone to touch his priceless jewel.

RoRo and Wheelz had committed a home invasion on the man he thought was messing with Paris. The three men in the house were robbed of six kilos of coke, leaving two of them dead and one fatally wounded. That wounded victim was Devon Ramsey. The man they really were after, Boney J, had left the house minutes before the robbery had taken place. Since Wheelz was smart enough to keep his mask on, RoRo was the only one that caught a case.

While RoRo was in jail, he got word that he didn't kill Paris's boyfriend, and they were still together. That meant RoRo had to get out of jail somehow and kill Boney J. For this to happen, Wheelz had to kidnap Devon's mother and hold her until the trial was over.

Devon was the only witness who could testify against RoRo. When RoRo was finally freed, Paris promised to get an abortion and never see Boney J again. Yet, when RoRo found out she was still sneaking around with him and wanted to keep her baby, he decided to make her pay the price for being disloyal to him. RoRo had to hang out at Paris's favorite club to catch them both in the act. He planned to wait until they left the club and kill them on the way to their car.

The night RoRo planned to kill Paris and her boyfriend he had been high on ecstasy and wet. The combination of E pills and

PCP made RoRo more violent than he already was. If he would've waited until they both got outside of the club, he would've gotten away with killing them both. Since he couldn't control his jealous rage, he would go to prison for the rest of his life. Chelsea now knew the truth.

CHAPTER TWENTY-ONE

Goose entered into Zeek's house again with his re-up. He walked into the living and set the bag down on the coffee table. This time he brought with him three kilos of cocaine, a half-kilo of heroine, and a little something else Zeek requested.

"Did you bring that other shit?" Zeek asked.

"Yeah, I got it. I still don't know why you want to fuck wit' this shit, though. It's a body dropper."

"I know. I ain't sellin' the shit myself. Somebody else want it."

Goose was confused. "Somebody want fentanyl?"

Zeek shrugged his shoulders. "Yeah, believe it or not."

Goose knew fentanyl was fifty times more potent than morphine. Anybody wanting that was asking for trouble.

Rodney needed more supply and was ready to see Zeek again. Crack money wasn't coming fast enough for him, so he wanted to change over to dope. Once Rodney found himself a few dope heads over in Southeast, he went to Zeek to cop five bricks of heroin; although what Zeek had given him wasn't heroin at all. It was fentanyl. Zeek had cleverly started his revenge. He would pay Rodney back for what he'd done to Shawnna and stealing Chelsea from him at the same time.

❖ ❖ ❖

For the next couple of weeks, Rodney and other dealers' fiends were dropping dead like flies. One particular hustler named Glimpse quickly took notice. Glimpse was a tall, brown-skinned man with a husky frame and a pretty-boy thug look. Glimpse controlled half of Southeast and several parts of Maryland. He knew that dead fiends wouldn't bring him any money, and he had to find out who was responsible for all the deaths. When word got back to him that someone was selling dope, and fiends were dying from it, he had to put an end to it. Southeast was getting hot from the high body count, so he needed to calm things down.

Rodney was unaware of all the overdose deaths he was committing and continued to distribute his product. It was a little after eleven one night when a young girl approached him. *She don't look like a user, but you can't really tell,* he thought as she got closer.

The girl had lemon highlighted skin with a short-length ponytail. She was medium height and thinly built. She wore a gray hoodie, black shorts, and black Timbs. Rodney thought her looks were average, but could've looked better if she wore some makeup and did her hair.

"Aye, young. You dealin'?" she asked.

"Yeah. What can I do you for?"

"Depends on what you got."

"I got that, boy. Since you new I'll give you three dimes for twenty."

The girl got irate. "Dope? Do it look like I'm on drugs, nigga?" she said after taking the blue raspberry Blow Pop out of her mouth.

Rodney took a step back. "My fault, boo. What you need, a brick or something?"

The girl shook her head. "Don't nobody want dope over here, man. Niggas want that water. I can't make no money off that shit."

Rodney thought about it. "Yeah, you might be right about that.

Almost everybody I sold to ain't never come back. I thought it was me."

Once Rodney responded, the girl changed her mind. "You know what, man? Let me get a bundle off you. I think I know somebody who might want it."

Rodney was happy he was about to make his first big sale. He looked to his left, then right. "Aight. Walk to the cut wit' me." Rodney took his first step and the girl followed.

"What's ya name anyway?" Rodney asked as they walked in between two abandoned houses.

"Trish," she answered with a groggy tone.

"Aight, Trish, wait here."

Right when Rodney turned his back to get his stash, Trish shot him in the back with a black 9mm. After he was down, she shot him twice in the head. She reached in his pocket to get his stash, and then stood over his body. She looked at the name "King Kong" imprinted on the stamp bags. "You ain't gonna be sellin' no more of this shit over here, mothafucka."

Trish tucked her gun in her waist, put the stamped bags and all the money he had in her pocket, and then threw the bags in a sewer on her way down the street. That was the end of Rodney.

Trish was no ordinary chick. She was the one Glimpse sent to kill whoever was flooding his area with dope. When Rodney told her his fiends never came back, she knew he was the one behind the deaths. Glimpse didn't know that fentanyl was the cause of the overdose deaths. As long as the bad product was off his streets, he could give a damn what it was.

When Zeek found out Rodney had been killed, he was happy his plan had worked. Zeek knew Rodney was hustling in the part of Southeast where nobody sold dope. He remembered reading about fentanyl in high school and that whoever took it could easily die from an overdose. Rodney was so inexperienced with dope that he didn't even know what he had. His only concern was getting back to the top. Rodney's death didn't only get the revenge Zeek wanted for himself, but he also got it for Shawnna, too. Yet, Zeek didn't realize he had successfully orchestrated a murder and was changing into somebody he wasn't.

He was somebody that was slipping farther into a world where there was little chance of return. A world that transitioned innocent boys into cold-hearted killers, and Zeek was now halfway there. His moral goodness was on the verge of perishing. Now Zeek's harbored emotions about Rodney and Chelsea would fuel his course of destruction. This marked the end of the good old Zeek.

Shawnna had successfully completed her drug program and had been clean for over a month now. Zeek was proud of her and couldn't wait to see her. He waited in the car until Shawnna came out of the Pathways Alcohol & Drug Rehabilitation Center in Annapolis, Maryland. When he saw her for the first time in two months, he couldn't believe his eyes. Shawnna was so beautiful to him. The way she looked now took Zeek back to how he remembered her in high school.

Zeek got out the car and hugged her, not wanting to let her go. He owed her so much. Shawnna was the reason he was in the game, and Shawnna felt the same way about him getting her off of drugs. She smelled so good too. He wondered what fragrance she was wearing, but it really wasn't that important now. He was so glad to have her back to her old self.

Zeek took her to Morton's The Steakhouse to celebrate her victory. She kept telling him that she never tasted a more tender steak in her life. Zeek assured her this was only the beginning of good eating for her. There was so much he wanted her to do and things he wanted her to have. On the way to her house they stopped at the dealership and picked up the new Acura TL he had bought her. Shawnna was so happy when she saw the car that it brought tears to her eyes.

No one had ever done anything like that for her and she was overwhelmed with joy. *It sure as hell is better than the beat-up Sable I got*, she thought as she hugged Zeek with all her might. Without words, Zeek understood how appreciative Shawnna was to have the car. This was only the start of gifts from him. Shawnna wanted to pay Zeek back the only way she could by becoming one of his top drug lieutenants. With her experience, she would turn out well and help move Zeek into a closer position to be king.

"Fuck me, daddy! Fuck me! Oh shit, right there! Fuck me harder! I wanna feel that shit in my stomach!" Shawnna commanded, as Zeek had her face-down on her couch while he rapidly stroked her from behind.

Zeek couldn't believe he was having sex with his childhood girl-friend. It was still all too strange to him how they'd reconnected after so many years. The little shy Shawnna was now a grown woman who wasn't afraid to speak her mind anymore, especially during sex. Her dirty talk was new to Zeek. Shawnna's raunchy mouth turned him on like nothing had before. The more, she talked the closer Zeek felt like he had to let go. Her foul chatter continued to toy with his mind and he couldn't take it anymore. "Oh shit," Zeek said as his calves locked up when he shot out his heavy load.

Zeek fell back on the couch trying to catch his breath as the tip of the condom stuck to the leather seat between his legs. He looked over at Shawnna and smiled. "It's gonna be hard to keep up with you, girl. I can already see it."

"You're bullshittin', right? Zeek, that was only like ten minutes and I ain't even do nothin' to you yet," Shawnna said, giving him a puzzled look. "I'ma really need you to step it up on the next one, okay?"

"Uhh, not you, too. You sound like Chelsea with that shit. Always wanting me to last long as shit. I can't help that I cum quick."

"Yes, you can. You're not trying."

"How you gonna tell me I'm not tryin'? Oh, I guess you know what it's like to have a dick."

"No, I don't, but I have fucked wit' niggas that couldn't handle pussy, until they met me."

"So are you supposed to be some type of dick doctor or somethin'?" Zeek asked as he scrunched up his face.

Shawnna had him irritated and he felt like leaving. Qwanda never once asked him to make miracles happen in bed and that's why he liked her so much. Zeek told himself that he would never cross the line with Shawnna again. He didn't like being pressured by Chelsea and he refused to let it happen again with Shawnna.

"Zeek, I'm not trying to carry you, okay. I'll be honest. If a nigga told me I had some wack-ass pussy I would be all in my feelings, too. But I would find out what he didn't like about it and try to work it out. And I'm not sayin' ya dick is whack by any means. You could actually be a pipe layer if you switched your shit up. I want to help you. Can I help you?" Shawnna asked as she grabbed his hand.

Shawnna's words and soft touch let Zeek know that she was being sincere. He couldn't help but to put down his guard and be open-minded. The fact that she thought he had great potential gave him another reason to hear her out.

"What can you do to help?"

"I can help you change the way you think about pussy. It might take a little time, but I can get you right," Shawnna said as she reached between his legs and pulled off the condom.

She tossed it in a small garbage can by the couch and then started to slowly stroke his soft package.

"I'm about to show you something. Let me know when you're about to cum, aight?"

"I will," Zeek said with convincing eyes.

"Aight, you better." She gave him a crooked eye before she took his jewel into her mouth.

Zeek was totally caught off-guard as he slowly started to swell up in Shawnna's warm mouth.

Shawnna's tongue swirled around along the tip of his head as she tickled the bottom of his shaft with her fingers. Zeek locked up his stomach as the sensation became overwhelming. Zeek knew he would bust soon from what Shawnna was doing and didn't see how she was helping. All she was doing was proving him right.

"Oh shit. Here it comes," Zeek said as the pressure in his crown reached the ultimate height.

Shawnna quickly pulled her mouth back and squeezed the base of his rod as hard as she could. "Hold it in," she commanded.

Zeek fought back the pain from Shawnna's tight grip as he strained to keep from exploding on her hand. He continued to fight the urge to release as the force in his cap mounted.

"Did it go back in yet?" Shawnna asked as she clenched down.

"A little bit. Wait...Okay. I feel it going away now."

Shawnna relaxed her hand and started to lightly rub his package again.

"Tell me when," she said before engulfing as much of Zeek in her mouth as she could. She then started to suck on his crown forcefully until Zeek felt like he was going to pop.

"Here it comes again," Zeek warned.

"Hold it in again," Shawnna said after she quickly removed him from her mouth and squeezed down on his base again. Zeek didn't feel as much throbbing as the first time, but Shawnna's grip was still as firm.

"Okay, it went back in," Zeek informed her.

Shawnna removed her hand and then reached in between the couch cushions and pulled out a condom. "Now it's time to fuck me again," she said, handing him the green-colored condom.

Zeek placed the condom over his rigid package while Shawnna got back into position. She then spread her cheeks to give Zeek a rearview shot of her slick pinkish-red gem. "Now that you know what to do, I want you to kill this pussy."

Zeek pushed himself back inside her and began to pump forcefully as he held her head down over the arm of the couch.

After twenty minutes of doing the repeated exercise, Zeek felt like he was a brand-new man. He had never imagined that Shawnna would be the one to provide a solution to his biggest problem. One that he was afraid to admit all these years: he was a minuteman.

Press and hold, press and hold. I could fuck forever if I keep doing this, he said to himself as he continued to drill Shawnna from the back.

Zeek wondered if he could perform the same way with anyone else. A devious grin came across his face as he thought of Qwanda. *Yeah, she's going to get it next.*

❖ ❖ ❖

Chelsea sat in her truck and felt eerie when she found out Rodney was killed. *First Lunchmeat, and now Rodney?* She was starting to think she was a curse or something. She never suspected Zeek had anything to do with his death and took it that Rodney had caught a bad one. This was a time in Chelsea's life that she really needed someone to talk to. She wanted it to be Zeek, but he'd be the wrong person to go to, especially if it had anything to do with Rodney.

Chelsea still couldn't help but feel that she needed Zeek by her side; not to comfort her, but to become his girlfriend again. "Look at the mess I made. I fucked everything up with Zeek. I had to get caught with Rodney of all fuckin' people. Zeek fuckin' hated him and now he fuckin' hates me. I'm such a bitch!" she cried out as tears dripped down her face. Chelsea felt so lost and didn't know what she would do from that point on. She dropped her head on the steering wheel and couldn't do anything else but cry.

"Are you sure we goin' to be straight?" Marcus asked.

"Yeah, young. My cuz say he never runs out. We'll be straight," Zeek assured him, as they sat on top of a wall and ate pistachios.

It was the beginning of drought season, and Marcus didn't know what the future would hold if they ran out of weight. He wanted to grow their empire into something that was larger than life, but needed to keep up with demand in order to do so. With Catch'em guaranteeing Zeek twenty-five kilos a week of cocaine alone, they would be able to regulate the drought. That meant they could charge whatever they wanted and still be able to move on new ground. They thought of all the possibilities as pistachio shells piled up below their feet. This was going to be a good winter.

CHAPTER TWENTY-TWO

It was the first day of spring, and it was safe to say the cold winter months were over. During the drought season, Zeek and Marcus strong-armed the game. Everybody had to come to them if they wanted weight at the best quality. Those who couldn't afford to keep up with the drought lost their strips to U.B.N. or other big-time dealers. Even though D.C. and Baltimore cats never got along, Zeek had gotten so big, he was even wholesaling to those out in B-More who were shying away from poor cocaine coming from New York. Hustlers in both cities put their beef to the side for the paper chase. When it came to making money, that was all anybody really cared about.

By December, Zeek was moving 200 kilos of cocaine a week and four kilos of heroin a month. He had quickly become a millionaire, and his soldiers were seeing money they never knew was possible. The drought also gave Zeek full advantage over the weed market, too. He had 450 pounds of three different types of super potent marijuana coming in once a month. If anyone smoked blueberry, bubba kush, or white widow in D.C. or Baltimore, there was a good chance it came from Zeek.

Zeek and Qwanda's relationship grew stronger over the cold winter months. Qwanda hardly went out with her friends anymore and chose not to mess with any other guys, either. She was always down for Zeek, even when he never requested anything from her. Getting with Zeek was one of the best things that ever had happened to her, and she wasn't ashamed for going behind Chelsea's back to get him. Qwanda had never been so drawn into a man; she was in love.

Zeek would buy Qwanda anything she wanted. Even though she always said, as long as she had him, she didn't need anything else; he still had to buy her things. He got her a new Jaguar S-Type and moved her into a two-bedroom townhouse in Largo, Maryland. He bought her all the clothes and jewelry a girl could want. Since Qwanda liked to travel, Zeek took her to Miami and on a seven-day Caribbean cruise. He was willing to give her anything she wanted, except love; he didn't love her. He had love for her, but wasn't *in love* with her. Zeek had a problem, and Qwanda was only part of it.

The things Zeek did for Qwanda was similar to the things he did for Shawnna, too. After expunging her strong addiction for heroin, Shawnna grew a stronger addiction for Zeek. What started off with Zeek becoming her lifeline accidentally turned into him becoming her lover.

It was easy for Zeek to get caught up with a girl like Shawnna. What man wouldn't? She was sexy, irresistible, and she had chinky eyes that complemented her radiant light-russet skin. Her body was shaped exceptionally well and had four tattoos all in the right places along her back and thighs that made her even more desirable. She was also a freak in the bed. Shawnna handled business for Zeek as Qwanda did. They did anything he asked of them. Both of these women loved him the same, but he loved neither one of them.

All throughout the fall season, Zeek thought the drought was what solely got him into the position he was in. Little did he know, Marcus and U.B.N. were seriously laying the murder game down. Marcus only targeted major dealers. Anybody known for holding five kilos of cocaine or better was on his list. He knew if he got rid of them, he would be able to move in and be the new connect. Once he carried out six murders all by himself, the streets started calling him Murda Marcus. Zeek naively thought he'd gotten the name because he was killing the crack game.

Chelsea was back at being herself once again. She was going out on the regular, getting numbers, and getting paid. All of her girls were doing the same thing, except for Qwanda. Qwanda wasn't doing anything. She wasn't checking for nobody or taking anybody's number. If and when she did go to the club, she didn't even dance with nobody. She would only drink and groove to the music all by herself.

Chelsea couldn't help but to worry about her friend. *Somethin' or someone caused Qwanda to change*, she thought. *What is causin' her to switch up? How did she get a new house and a Jaguar? Is she hustlin' her damn self, or is she messin' wit' a serious hustla I don't know about?*

These were all the questions she had for Qwanda, but Qwanda was always careful with her words. She didn't want Chelsea to find out about her secret boyfriend. Besides, it was none of her business anyway.

Chelsea messed with a few cats, but was most serious with Hummy and Shady. Chelsea really enjoyed being around the two of them. She knew them longer than anyone else she dealt with, and she liked how nice they treated her. From giving her money to taking her to expensive restaurants, Hummy and Shady did what was necessary to keep her interest. But they both stayed out of town a lot and weren't around half the time to keep track of her. Chelsea didn't want anyone knowing her every move. That's what made her like them even more.

Reminiscing on the chilly months that passed, Zeek thought about all the girls he'd been with in such a short amount of time. The player lifestyle was all so new to him since he had only been with one other girl before Chelsea. Now, he was known all over town and every gold-digging chick wanted to get at him. Even though he was occupied with Qwanda and Shawnna, he still made time to be with other girls. Zeek was sexing almost every day and still wanted more. He was getting so many women that he kept a garbage bag full of thongs and panties in his closet that he collected over the months. He even put in permanent marker who each one belonged to, so he would have something to remember each girl by. Out of all the lingerie he had in the bag, only about ten pieces belonged to the same girls.

Zeek rode in Cook's blue Denali on his way to pick up his Range Rover. He had bought it last week but hadn't driven it yet. He'd had it delivered to a detail shop to get leather seats put in and faux fur rugs. The Rover already had tan leather seats, but he wanted white ones instead. Zeek wanted his whole truck to be all white. Since he was the "coke man," he wanted his truck to really stand out.

As they continued to ride, Zeek asked Cook to pull over so he could holler at some girl who was coming out of a little mom-and-pop shop. He had seen the girl once, but was unable to talk to her because he was already with another girl at the time. He could've tried to talk to her anyway, but didn't know how she would perceive him, since he was with someone else. The girl he'd been hoping to see was once again in his sights. This time Zeek made sure he would talk to her before it was too late.

Zeek got out of the truck and walked up to the girl as she was putting a bag in her trunk.

"Excuse me," Zeek said, as the girl turned around. Zeek was so caught off-guard by her beauty, he almost forgot what he wanted to say to her.

"Yes," she replied, wondering why it was taking him so long to say something to her.

Zeek took a deep breath and finally got himself together. "I don't really do this, approachin' women, but I saw you before, and I didn't talk to you. I didn't want to make the same mistake twice."

The girl looked surprised. "You saw me? Where?"

"You were down at the 2K9 joint. Probably about two months ago."

"Yeah, I was there before," she answered quickly.

Zeek could sense she was in a hurry, so he had to make his move. "What's your name, ma?"

"Dora. What's yours?"

"Zeek."

"Well, it's nice to meet you, Zeek."

"Same here," he said, as he went into a daze.

Dora was superfly and extremely pretty. She was a half Black-half Brazilian mixed beauty. She was medium height with light-brown buttermilk skin, green eyes, and a beauty mark on the left side of her mouth. She wore a red mini dress that hugged her body well, with black and red stilettos. She wore her long curly hair in a ponytail that covered up a tattoo on the back of her neck. She had the body of Eva Mendes and the sexy look of a video vixen.

They ended up talking for only a quick minute, but were still able to exchange numbers. They promised to hook up later in the day, when they were both done handling their business. Zeek couldn't wait to pick her up in his new Rover, so he could floss her around. When she drove away in her black Corvette, Zeek hoped she was going to be someone special to him. He didn't want her panties to end up in his bunch.

CHAPTER TWENTY-THREE

For the last week, Zeek had been driving his Range Rover all over town. He was getting so much attention in his all-white ride and stopped driving his other cars for the time being. His twenty-two-inch spinning rims and mirror-tinted windows really stood out. Since he had the white faux fur rugs, he only let Qwanda, Shawnna, and Dora ride in his truck. For the exception, they had to remove their shoes before getting in and put on some slippers he kept for them to wear. He never would let any regular broad ride in the Rover with him. If he was out, he would go get another car first before picking any of them up. His Rover was his special truck for his special people.

Zeek had unconsciously started up a car collection. So far, he owned a S550 Mercedes-Benz, an H2 Hummer, a BMW 745, two Cadillacs, and his 300M. The Range Rover had become Zeek's favorite since it was his newest vehicle. It happened to be Dora's favorite, too, since she loved how comfortable the faux fur seats felt against her skin. Dora wanted to drive it, and Zeek would make sure she had her own set of keys…if they were together long enough.

Zeek and Dora had been on three dates since they'd met, and Zeek still didn't have sex with her. He hoped she would hold out as long as she could. He didn't want her to be easy because he wanted to keep her around. So far, she was special to him and he placed her on the highest pedestal. She deserved to be, too. Dora made her own money and didn't ask for any of his. She preferred to go on walks in the park instead of expensive dinner dates. She wanted to grab a bottle of liquor and chill rather than go out and buy several rounds of drinks at the bar. Zeek was convinced that Dora was a simple girl and that he didn't need to impress her with his money. Zeek felt Dora wanted him to be himself around her so she could learn everything about him. In return Zeek wanted her to do the same.

For the last few hours, Qwanda hadn't been able to get a hold of Zeek. She had gotten aroused after going to see some female strippers with Fawn and was in desperate need of his touch. It was strange for him not to answer her calls, so she went out looking for him. She drove past both of his houses in Bowie and Mitchell-ville, Maryland, but he wasn't at either one of them. Then, she drove back to D.C. to his hangout spot she had the key to. She pulled up to his row house on Q Street and saw that the light was on and his Hummer was out front. She parked behind it.

She was finally glad she had found him. She could feel herself getting more wet and couldn't wait to get in the house and perform a similar lap dance that one of the strippers had given her. Before she went in, she tried to call him again, but he still didn't answer his phone. She could only hope he wasn't depressed and would welcome her visit. Qwanda wanted to do anything to keep Zeek happy. She decided she was going to go in the house anyway to see what type of mood he was in.

When Qwanda got to the steps, she noticed another familiar car right in front of his. She suddenly grew suspicious. She quickly unlocked the door and heard loud music as she entered the house. Her suspicion grew stronger when the aroma of marijuana filled her nose and she heard the laughter of a woman coming from the kitchen. She walked slowly to the kitchen, not sure if she was ready for the awkward intrusion, but she shouldn't have felt strange at all, she thought. It was her right to see what was going on. Zeek was a part of her life, and she needed to see what he wasn't telling her.

As soon as she got in the kitchen, her body froze. She was right about who she thought it was: *Shawnna*. The sight of them together made Qwanda's eyes darken. Shawnna was sitting on Zeek's lap with her arm around him. She had a drink in her hand, while Zeek was holding a burning blunt in one of his and a drink in the other. There was a bottle of Remy, a fat bag of weed, and a large amount of money spread out on the table in front of them. Qwanda couldn't believe what she was seeing.

"What's up, boo?"

"Hey, Qwanda," they both said with a smile.

Qwanda looked at them like they were crazy.

"Have a seat. Get it in wit' us," Zeek suggested.

"Nah, I'm cool. I'll stand," she said with attitude. Qwanda stood against the wall with her arms crossed. She was pissed off, and Shawnna knew she had every right to be.

Shawnna didn't want to make a bad situation worse, so she decided to leave. "Aye, young. I'm gonna bump," she said to Zeek while rising off of his lap, and grabbing her purse out of another chair.

"Later, girl," she said to Qwanda after she patted Zeek on the shoulder and walked out of the kitchen.

"Humph," Qwanda gave as her only response, as if Shawnna should've known better than to say another word to her.

Shawnna didn't bother to respond and kept on walking. When

Shawnna got in her car, she thought about the predicament she was in. She knew Zeek was messing around with Qwanda and didn't mind sharing him. But Qwanda didn't know about her, which made their encounter seem so strange. Shawnna was okay with Qwanda being upset at what she saw because it could have been a lot worse. She reached in her purse, and pulled out a tampon.

"Woo!" She sighed, dangling it in her hand as if it was her life-saver. If she wasn't on her monthly, Qwanda would've caught them in bed together. She vowed from that day forth to never have sex with Zeek in that house again unless she would be prepared to fight. She now knew Qwanda had a key like she did. She threw the tampon back in her purse and drove off.

Back in the house, Qwanda stood up against the wall with her head down. Zeek really didn't know what her problem was, so he decided to ask. "What's wrong wit' you, girl?"

That's when Qwanda lifted her head and gave him an evil stare before she spoke. "What's wrong wit' me? No, nigga, what's wrong wit' you? I'm thinkin' you hurt or some shit 'cause you ain't an-swerin' ya phone! Then, I come up in here and you happily hugged up wit' that bitch!" she yelled, pointing at the door where Shawnna had left out.

"It wasn't what you thought you saw," he said as he stood in his defense.

"Then what the hell was it? The bitch was sittin' on your fuckin' lap, Zeek!"

Zeek knew she didn't believe him and had to think fast. "It wasn't like she was all over me or nothin'. She's like my sister, and I'm like her brother, you feel me? I would never mess wit' her like that."

"That's bullshit, yo! I know you fuckin' that bitch!"

Zeek knew he was cornered and had to come up with a different approach. "Then answer this. If we fuckin' around, then why did she leave?"

"Because the sneaky bitch was guilty, that's why!"

"No, because she didn't want you to think the wrong thing. Why would she stay and disrespect you?"

Qwanda didn't have an answer for that, but still needed something to come back at him with. "That still don't explain why you wasn't answerin' ya phone."

"I left that shit in the car, young. Go 'head. Call it. I bet you won't hear that shit ring in here."

Qwanda suddenly started not to care anymore. She realized she could be only but so mad, since Zeek wasn't her boyfriend *yet*. Zeek noticed she let down her guard and decided to move closer to her. He pinned her up against the wall and started kissing her all over her neck which helped her cares go away even faster. Her mind was warped and she anticipated how good the make-up sex would be.

Before she knew it, she was half naked with her bare ass on top of the counter. Zeek pounded away at her warm flesh, while she dug her nails into his butt checks, trying to moan over the loud music. When she finally busted, it was the hardest one she ever had. After she was done shaking and her breathing was back to normal, her lifeless body hunched over Zeek, like she was a baby falling asleep on her mother's arm. Her body was completely satisfied.

When Zeek carried her weak body over to the couch, he knew he was off the hook for now. He looked at her while she slept and wanted to tell Qwanda the truth, but knew she couldn't handle it. While he was penetrating her, he kept thinking that he shouldn't keep playing with her feelings. He had to decide to make her his girl or let her go.

CHAPTER TWENTY-FOUR

Qwanda had picked up all of her girls in her brand-new burgundy Escalade and were now headed to the club. Zeek had bought it after he'd messed up with her two weeks back. He felt guilty after the whole Shawnna situation. Fawn and Dya was happy for her getting the truck, but Chelsea was low-key hating on her. She didn't have the best car out of the click anymore and that bothered her. Yet, Qwanda was still her girl, so she tried her best to not let her jealousy show.

With Qwanda doing her thing at the club lately, Zeek was able to spend more time with Dora. He had been trying to have sex with Dora for almost two months now, and he still hadn't made any tangible progress. Hopefully tonight he could make it happen. They had dinner at Dora's favorite Thai restaurant, Mai Thai, and then went back to her place, so he could give her a massage. Zeek waited on the sofa while she took a shower. This was the first time he'd been to her apartment and noticed it was kind of empty like she'd recently moved in. Besides the sofa, there was a forty-two-inch television on a stand and a long lamp that stood in the corner on the floor. Zeek wanted her apartment to be more comfortable for him when he was over, so he planned to have Marlo Furniture deliver a few items, whether she liked it or not. He soon heard the water shut off and knew it wouldn't be long before his hands finally met Dora's body.

When Dora came out of the bathroom, she was wearing nothing but a thin, terrycloth robe. She signaled for Zeek to follow her into her bedroom and he wasted no time getting off the couch. Zeek thought she looked so sexy and exotic with some of her wet hair lying along her moist face. Zeek walked into her room and saw it was as bare as her living room. He definitely felt he had to do something for her quick.

She picked up a bottle of baby oil that was on the dresser and handed it to Zeek while he stood in the doorway. Dora situated herself on the bed while Zeek got the oil warmed up in the bathroom sink. He was confident about giving her a massage because he knew what he was doing. Qwanda had put him up on his massage game since hers was the bomb.

Zeek stood over top of Dora waiting for her to take off her robe. When she began removing her garment and exposed her shoulder, he was instantly aroused. Things got worse for him when she completely took off her robe and dropped it on the floor. His mouth began to water. He wanted to skip the massage and dig into her ass. He slowly poured oil from the top of her neck to the small of her back. The oil rolled down her spine, as he admired the tattoo on the nape of her neck.

Dora's tattoo was a black hourglass with the words, *Only Time Will Tell*, in cursive arched around it.

"I like ya tat. What made you get it?" Zeek asked as he rubbed her down with oil.

"It has a lot of meaning to it. Everything about life is built around the phrase."

Zeek could easily agree with that. Time would only tell if he would tear her up in bed or not as he greased up her fat rump. Dora's body was so soft it seemed like his hands were sinking into her. He wanted her badly.

He commanded her to turn over so he could oil the front part of her body. The cool breeze in the room caused her nipples to harden. Zeek started rolling them inbetween his fingers. That's when he got a reaction from her that he had never seen before. Dora started to breathe heavy and bit down on her bottom lip. It'd been months since she'd let anyone stir her coffee, and there was something about Zeek that made her want his spoon dipped inside of her. She unexpectedly pulled Zeek on top of her and started kissing him. Zeek couldn't believe what was happening as their lips met. His heart raced as he grinded on her, while kissing and biting down gently on her soft lips. Not wanting to be dry-humped anymore, Dora helped him get out of his clothes so she could really feel it.

Once all his clothes were off and he was back on top of her, he soothingly kissed and licked all over her neck and chest, making her nipples even harder. Zeek continued to kiss down her body, until he was face to face with her freshly waxed box. It was completely bald. He hadn't seen one that hairless since Chelsea's. Zeek was never big on giving oral sex and would only go down on Chelsea if he had to. The strange way he was feeling about Dora made it impossible for him not to please her.

He closed his eyes, and then stuck his tongue into her sticky sweet goodness. Zeek was amazed. He swallowed her juices and kept on going. Dora's tasted like Chelsea's did, but a little bit sweeter. He continued to lick away at her sugar spot, while moans of bliss escaped out of her. Suddenly, Dora's pelvis tightened as she started to release. Her walls collapsed and her body shook. This wasn't her biggest orgasm ever, but it was her first one that came by surprise.

"Put it in me, papi," Dora softly commanded, when Zeek lifted his head up and looked into her eyes.

This was the moment he was waiting for. *It's really about to happen*, he thought. He wiped off his mouth with the bed sheet, and then climbed on top of her. He slid his hard pole into her tight pond and began to move rapidly.

"No, Zeek. I want it slow. You can take your time with me," Dora said with passion, as she held his face with both of her hands.

Dora was different from all the other girls Zeek knew. She wasn't a hit-and-run or a girl who needed to rush the moment. Beyond that she was composed and traditional. He realized Dora was like him. She didn't enjoy rough sex or needed to have countless orgasms from every encounter. She wanted someone to make love to her, so that's what he did. Zeek softly kissed her lips as he slowly inched his way in and out of her narrow tunnel. He kissed around her neck as he rubbed his hand down to her waist until he reached her knee. He lifted up her leg and licked it all the way down to the top of her foot.

Zeek came back up and kissed her along her shoulder as he penetrated her deeply, sending shockwaves up her spine. Dora gasped as she wrapped her arms around him tight and drove her tongue into his ear. Zeek felt so at ease for the first time in his life. He didn't have to worry about being aggressive or proving how long he could last. Dora didn't demand that from him. Zeek's only assignment was to provide Dora with an assurance of affection. As Dora's body vibrated underneath his, Zeek was confident that he had done exactly that.

CHAPTER TWENTY-FIVE

Memorial Day Weekend was near, and everyone already had their plans made. Chelsea and Dya were going back to Cancun while Fawn was going to Miami with her cousin. But Qwanda was still waiting around to see if Zeek would take her away with him, while Shawnna did the same. Both girls thought they were going with Zeek to Aruba, but he had secretly decided to take Dora instead. Qwanda and Shawnna ended up becoming very bitter when they didn't go with him and thought each other was to blame. Qwanda ended up in Miami with Fawn, while Shawnna visited her family in St. Louis. Neither one of them really wanted to be where they were. They only wanted to be with Zeek.

Qwanda lay on the beach at the Sagamore Hotel with Fawn and her cousin, Tia, from New Orleans. The sun was out and the weather was just right, but even that wasn't enough for Qwanda to ease her mind. All she could think about was Zeek. Fawn and Tia were the only ones she felt she could talk to about her ongoing dilemma.

She took a sip from her Miami Vice daiquiri before she spoke.

"Y'all, this nigga's drivin' me crazy. I really love the shit out of 'em. Y'all might think I'm lunchin' on this, but I think I want to marry 'em. I'm tryna start a family 'n' shit. What y'all think?"

"Marry 'em? You haven't even told Chelsea that you even fuckin' wit'em yet. You got to think if this nigga's even worth losing your girl over," Fawn responded.

"I know Chelsea's ya dog. But do he feel the same way about you?" Tia asked.

"I honestly don't know, but I know he don't give a fuck about Chelsea. That's for sure. And I think he's messin' wit' this other broad, too. He only do that since nobody is supposed to know about us."

That's when Tia gave her a serious look. "Is you cool wit' that? Only being that nigga's creep? Girl, if you tryna be wifey, then you got to let that nigga know that shit. She gotta know it, too."

Qwanda knew Tia was right. If she wanted to be with Zeek, she had to let him know what she wanted, and also tell Chelsea what she'd been hiding from her. Qwanda had no problem telling Zeek. It was confessing to Chelsea that was the hard part. Chelsea was one of her best friends and she never wanted a man to ever come between them. But to Qwanda, Zeek was no ordinary man. He was the love of her life and she couldn't help whom she had fallen in love with. She had to let her know.

Chelsea and Dya were living it up in Cancun looking sexier than ever. The girls had wanted to get away by themselves for so long, and now had to capitalize on their fun in the sun adventure. They were going to parties every night, staying out until the sun came up, and slept until noon. This was their second time there, so they pretty much knew where everything was. They even kicked it with people they'd met from their first visit. Fake ballers kept trying to holler at them, but they weren't with it. They were only interested in those with major chips.

"No, we a'ight," Chelsea said as they passed a group of men trying to talk to them. "Girl, I'm so tired of these fakin'-ass niggas down here. If I wanted a broke nigga, I could get one back home."

"I know that's right. D.C. is full of 'em," Dya replied. "But I know one nigga from around the way that's ballin' fo' real," Dya boasted.

"Who?" Chelsea was curious to know.

"Ya boy, Zeek. I heard that nigga's sittin' on millions. I don't know if that's true, but that's what I heard."

"Yeah, I heard somethin' like that as well. Damn…I had that nigga, too."

"Don't think you can't get him back," Dya suggested.

Chelsea poked her lip out. "I can't. That nigga hates me."

"He don't hate you. That shit you did was almost a year ago. He probably over that by now."

Chelsea twisted her lips. "I doubt that."

"Why? That nigga loved you. Don't you still love him?"

Chelsea thought for a second. "Yeah. I do."

Dya gave her a big wink. "See. Love don't go away like that."

Chelsea was taken by the message that Dya had given her. She didn't know if Zeek would take her back or not. She never even tried. She was too embarrassed to even approach him on it, so she avoided him altogether. *If Zeek still loves me, he'll forgive me for my mistake,* she thought. It wasn't all about Zeek having money now that sparked her interest in him. Chelsea still loved him. She needed to get her man back, and that's exactly what she was going to do.

❖ ❖ ❖

Zeek had finally returned from his vacation with Dora. The time Zeek spent with Dora was the most exhilarating experience he'd ever had. He connected with Dora on a level that was unachievable with any other girl, especially Chelsea. They had shared endless nights on a private beach talking and being extremely intimate with each other. Zeek caressed her body gently while expanding her insides with his manhood, as the warm Caribbean water rolled up around them. He was feeling Dora so much. His relationship with Chelsea was like puppy love compared to what he now felt for Dora. Zeek had fallen for her hard and it was only a matter of time before no one else in his life mattered.

Zeek wanted to catch up on some well-deserved rest, so he decided to take a nap before he got back to business. Zeek was asleep for about two hours before his mother called. It didn't matter what he was doing, if his mom wanted to talk to him, he had to answer. His mom called to make sure he had gotten home from his trip safely and wanted him to come over for dinner. Zeek advised her he would be on his way in a few and ended the call. She also said for him to come by himself because she only had made enough for him.

Zeek kept thinking about his mother's cooking all the way to her house. He was tired of tourist food from Aruba and wanted some good soul food from his mother's kitchen. She was his favorite chef and his mouth watered as he looked forward to indulge in her cooking. He hoped she'd made baby back ribs, mac and cheese, and collard greens. That was his favorite meal.

Zeek finally arrived at his mother's house and couldn't wait to get out the car. He was so hungry he thought he could smell what his mother had prepared all the way from the street. He visualized a hot plate with steam rising from it already waiting for him on the table. When Zeek opened the front door, his body froze from who he saw, as his mother walked over to greet him.

"Hey, Zeeky, baby. We've been waiting on you," his mother said as she hugged him and held his hand. "Haven't we, Chelsea?" she happily asked.

Chelsea didn't respond and sat on the couch with an uncomfortable look on her face. Chelsea could see in Zeek's eyes that he wasn't happy she was there, and she was right.

I can't believe this bitch used my mom to get to me, he thought.

Zeek's mom always had a strong liking for Chelsea. She wasn't aware of Chelsea's foul ways, and Zeek wished he would've told her a long time ago. But Zeek was somewhat impressed by her tactic. Chelsea knew the best way to get to a man was to go through his momma. It worked every time.

"I know y'all hungry. Come on in here, so we can eat," his mother said, as she walked past Chelsea giving her a wink.

Chelsea took a quick glance at Zeek and followed his mother into the dining room. Zeek shook his head and proceeded to walk behind them.

Zeek dug into his favorite meal, not even stopping for conversation. Even if he wasn't hungry, he still wouldn't have had much to say at the table, especially while Chelsea was there.

"So, Chelsea. How's your mom doing?" his mother asked, to kill the silence at the table.

"She's fine. She got a new job."

"Oh, really? Doing what?"

"She's a paralegal."

His mother gave her a big smile. "Good for her. What about yourself? Are you working?"

"Yeah. My girlfriend opened up a hair salon out of her house. I braid hair there part-time," she said, lying with a straight face.

"Which friend is that?" Zeek asked, trying to call her out.

"Fawn."

"Fawn can do hair?" Zeek asked.

"Yeah. You didn't know that?"

"Nah."

Chelsea knew what Zeek was trying to do, so she did it to him right back. "So where are you working at these days, Zeek?" He looked at her and remained silent.

"He's a construction supervisor," his mother proudly answered for him.

"So that's what you do, Zeek? Construction?" she cunningly asked.

"Yeah," he said sarcastically.

Chelsea gave him a smile and Zeek couldn't help but to smile back. They realized they both had something to hide from his mother.

After dinner, Zeek found out that Chelsea didn't drive over to his mother's house, and had actually walked. She continued to surprise him with her cleverness. He felt obligated to take her home. In the car, Zeek and Chelsea talked about their trips during Memorial Day Weekend. They both made sure not to mention any juicy details to each other about the fun they really had.

"Could you come in for a minute?" Chelsea asked, as they pulled up to her house.

"That's okay. Tell ya mom I said hi."

"My mom's not here. She's out of town."

Zeek scratched his head. "I don't know about that, Chelsea."

"Please. I really need to talk to you. It's important to me."

Zeek looked at her sad face and gave in seeing how serious she was. He told himself he would hear what she had to say and get out of there.

Zeek sat on the couch waiting for Chelsea to speak her mind. She sat down right beside him and began to stare into his eyes. That's when she started crying. "Zeek, I'm so sorry. I know I hurt you. Even if you never forgive me, I want you to know how sorry I am. I miss you so much."

Chelsea's outburst took Zeek by total surprise. He had never seen her cry that much in his life and knew she meant every word that she said. He put his arm around her and kept letting her know that everything would be all right.

Chelsea had eventually stopped crying and they were now watching a movie together. This moment reminded Chelsea of some of the good times they used to share. She felt like they were a couple again, and she wasn't alone. Zeek had a similar feeling. Watching movies was their thing, and he missed going to the movies with her, too. Chelsea lay across his lap until the movie was over.

"I got somethin' for you," she said, as she sat up.

"What is it?"

"It's a surprise. Come on. It's upstairs." Chelsea got up off the couch, and Zeek followed her to her bedroom.

When Zeek walked into her room, he saw a fancy wrapped package sitting on her bed. When he opened it, he was happy to see she had gotten him the complete second season of *The Wire*.

"Oh shit! Where did you find this? I've been lookin' all over for this shit."

"I found it online. I knew you would like it."

Zeek gave her a hug to express how thankful he was.

"Yo. I'm tryna watch these now," he said, letting go of her and starting to remove the plastic wrapper.

"That's cool. I'm gonna take a shower."

Chelsea then left for the bathroom, while Zeek put disc one into the DVD player. Zeek became hesitant to sit on her bed as he remembered that she'd had sex with Rodney on it. He didn't want Chelsea to start crying again, so he didn't hold a grudge. Besides, he was doing it to one of her best friends anyway. He was already paying her back.

Halfway into the first episode, Zeek noticed a *XXL* magazine under Chelsea's pillow. He took his attention away from the television and started to flip through the pages. Zeek's eyes got big when he saw who the eye candy of the month was. *Oh shit. It's Makeffa*, he whispered to himself.

Zeek quickly went to the middle of the mag to find her centerfold. He found Monica's section and couldn't believe she was the same girl he'd met on the Greyhound bus.

Daammmnn. I ain't know she was doin' it like that. I wish I would've hit that. She's phat as shit. I hope she still got the same number, he thought.

Makeffa's pictures were so sexy to him that he wanted to jump through the pages. His favorite picture was of her lying naked on an ice-covered floor in a meat freezer. Her poses were so nasty, and he loved them.

Chelsea walked into her room wearing only a towel while Zeek was still looking through the magazine.

She sucked her teeth. "What you over there lookin' at?" she asked, as she walked over to her dresser.

"Your *XXL* mag. The eye candy girl in here is a friend of mine."

Chelsea became a little jealous, especially since she was naked herself, and he acted like he didn't notice.

"That skinny-ass, dark-skin girl? You know her?"

"Yeah, I know her, and she ain't nowhere near skinny."

"Yeah, whatever."

"You hatin'."

"Well, I guess I'm a hater then," she said, as she dropped her towel and slid her apricot-colored thong on, followed by a matching lace bra, that she took off of her dresser.

Zeek missed looking at her body. He got hard while staring at her completely round backside. He was falling into her trap, and he knew it.

Chelsea walked over to the bed and grabbed Zeek's hand. "Why look at pictures… When you could have the real thing," she said, moving his hand down her smooth, lotioned body. That was all Zeek needed to get himself going. He pulled her onto the bed and started kissing and rubbing on her.

Zeek missed smelling the sweet fragrances that she wore, which drove him crazy, and this time he could tell she had on Mambo. Zeek's arousal level went even higher. Zeek had all his clothes off and was about to put on a condom. Before he could do so, Chelsea stopped him and put his hard pipe in her mouth. Chelsea didn't like performing oral sex, but she had to prove she meant every word she said. After several minutes of licking and sucking on him, she let him put on the condom, so he could enter her.

The sex was hot and heavy. They had been doing it for almost ten minutes now, and Zeek still hadn't busted yet. This caught Chelsea off-guard. She was expecting him to be a minuteman as usual, not the aggressive lover he'd turned into. Chelsea was in the zone from all the deep penetrated strokes he was laying into her. He was twisting and turning her into positions she'd never been in before. She was biting down on her bottom lip, as Zeek pulled her hair, while giving it to her from the back.

Shawnna had taught Zeek everything he knew about sex. She showed him how to make a girl cum fast with his tongue and to produce multiple orgasms with his magic stick. Most importantly, she taught him how not to cum fast by strengthening his pelvic floor muscles. After the first time Zeek had made love to Dora, he went to Shawnna, so she could help him with his foreplay skills. Shawnna told him that good foreplay was the best way to get somebody turned out. Zeek took what he learned from Shawnna and tried it all out on Qwanda. After he went down on Qwanda for the first time, she was giving him head every chance she got. This time, Chelsea was the one Zeek was going all out for.

When it was all over, Chelsea lay there, captivated by Zeek's performance. She was tired, sweaty, and her kitten was throbbing after a long hour of getting pounded out by Zeek. Chelsea could only come to one conclusion. This was the best damn sex she'd ever had, period. Even better than Mister.

Qwanda had been tossing and turning all night long. For some reason, she was having a hard time sleeping. Maybe it was because she had to tell Chelsea about her and Zeek's relationship. If that wasn't it, she had no way of figuring it out. It was 8:22 a.m. when Qwanda finally decided to get out of bed. She needed to smoke a blunt before calling Chelsea, so she could calm her nerves. After she put the roach in the ashtray, she picked up her phone and made the call. She couldn't recall another time she had been more nervous.

Zeek shut Chelsea's front door at the same time her phone rang. Chelsea decided to only answer the phone because she was already up, and it was Qwanda calling her. *For her to be callin' this early, it must be important*, she thought. "Hello?"

"Hey. What's goin' on?" Qwanda asked nonchalantly.

"Girl, I'm walkin' on clouds right now! What's up wit' you?" Chelsea asked with a smile on her face.

"I gotta holla at you about somethin'." She paused. "Wait a minute. Why you walkin' on clouds?" Qwanda asked suspiciously.

"Girl, Zeek got done blowin' my back out."

Qwanda was shocked. "Zeek? He was there?"

"Yeah, he left right before you called. I gotta tell you, girl. Youngin's dick game came up! Everythang is so different about him now. It's crazy. I feel like I'm in love all over again."

Chelsea was laughing while Qwanda didn't find anything funny. She was heartbroken. It took everything she had in her to hold back her tears. That's when Chelsea remembered, "Oh yeah, girl. What did you wanna talk to me about?"

"Nothin'. It ain't that important," Qwanda said as tears rolled down her face.

"Are you sure, girl?"

"Yeah, it was about Cancun, but I'll talk to you about that later. I'm goin' back to sleep."

"Aight. Call me when you get up." *Click!*

Qwanda hurried to end the call. She couldn't believe this was happening. *How could Zeek do that to me*, she cried.

Qwanda tried to convince herself that Chelsea was lying. *But why would she lie about that? Especially somethin' about Zeek. Unless he told her about us, and that bitch was rubbin' it in my face.*

Qwanda then thought there could be some truth to what Chelsea was saying since she'd noticed herself that Zeek's sex game had vastly improved. Qwanda couldn't separate a lie from the truth right now. She had to call Zeek to get some answers.

Zeek was trying to keep himself awake while he was driving. He had the window down, so the cool air could hit his face. That's when Qwanda called.

"Hello?" he answered.

"Where you at?" she asked softly.

"I'm on my way to the crib."

"Which one?"

"Number two."

"I'll be right there." *Click!*

Qwanda knew right then where he had come from. The way Qwanda hung up the phone, Zeek thought that she couldn't wait to see him. He was right. She couldn't.

Zeek dropped his keys on the dining room table when he heard loud banging on his front door.

"What the hell," he said, as he hurried to the door.

Qwanda pushed him hard, as soon as he opened the door.

"You was over fuckin' Chelsea's!"

Zeek didn't know what was going on.

"You was fuckin' her?" she shouted as she pushed him again. Zeek was now aware of what she was getting at. Chelsea had told her everything. Qwanda waited for him to open his mouth, so he could tell her what she'd heard wasn't true. Zeek couldn't stand there. He had to say something.

"It's not what you think."

Qwanda snapped, "You gonna go fuck her again! And you tellin' me it's not what I think? Why would you do that shit to me?" she cried.

Zeek had never seen Qwanda this emotional. He'd never thought about what the consequences would be if she were to find out about him and Chelsea. Now, it was too late.

"I'm sorry," Zeek said with sadness.

"Yeah. You are a sorry mothafucka! And I'm a fool for thinkin' you loved me! And to think...I was about to fight Chelsea over your stupid ass."

Qwanda wiped the tears from her face, walked out and slammed the door behind her. Zeek stood by the door in a complete daze. He couldn't believe what had happened. His plan wasn't supposed to turn out this way, but somehow it had. Zeek realized how much he cared for Qwanda and didn't want to lose her. He wished he could convince Qwanda that his sexing Chelsea was only a one-time thing, and that it would never happen again. He wondered if she would ever want to see him again. *Damn. I really fucked up.*

CHAPTER TWENTY-SIX

Zeek's voicemail had come on once again and Chelsea couldn't believe it.

"Why the fuck isn't this nigga answerin' his phone?" *Beeeeeppp!* "Shit! Zeek, this is Chelsea. I'm tired of leavin' ya ass fuckin' messages. Call me back!" *Click!*

Chelsea was furious that Zeek hadn't called her ever since the night they were together. Every time she called him, he promised he would call her back, but never did. After a while, he stopped answering her calls altogether. Chelsea was left to assume that Zeek wanted to hit it and quit it, but she wasn't feeling that. She needed an answer to why he was avoiding her. She persisted to keep calling him.

Chelsea continued to make a fool out of herself, and Qwanda let her as they drove down the street.

"Girl, you better call him back. Don't let him do you like that," Qwanda said as she continued to instigate, so she could laugh every time Chelsea cussed him out on his voicemail. It was obvious that Zeek didn't care about Chelsea. Qwanda wanted her to feel some of the same frustration she felt. She also figured out that Chelsea didn't know anything about her and Zeek, either. Qwanda decided not to tell Chelsea the truth yet. She was going to get Zeek back first. He needed to get his.

Qwanda rushed back to her house so she could take a shower before she called Zeek. She wanted to make sure she would be ready for him when he came over. While she was straightening up her house, her doorbell rang. *Who could that be?* she thought.

Qwanda went to the door not sure of who would be visiting her. When she opened the door, she didn't understand what was going on. It was Shawnna.

"Is Zeek wit' you?" Qwanda asked sharply.

"No, I came alone."

"Then, how the fuck you know where I live?" she spat.

"I was with Zeek when he bought this house."

Qwanda became irritated. "You was wit' him? You stepped foot in this bitch before I did?"

"I know you're upset, but…"

"You damn right I'm upset!" Qwanda said, cutting her off.

"Look," Shawnna said peacefully. "I didn't come here to give you any problems. I came here to talk to you. There's somethin' I think you would want to see."

Qwanda put her hands on her hips. "What is it?"

"Can I come in?" Shawnna requested.

Qwanda was hesitant at first, but she moved to the side so Shawnna could walk through. They both took a seat on the couch.

"So what do you want me to see?" Qwanda hoped she would show her a positive pregnancy test, so she could beat her ass, and then kick her out of her house. But instead, Shawnna reached in her purse, and handed her something completely different.

"Who the fuck is Cadora Mendosa?" Qwanda asked, while looking at the boarding passes to Aruba.

Shawnna shrugged her shoulders. "I don't know."

"Where did you get these?"

"I found them when I was goin' through Zeek's pockets. I was washing his clothes and that's what I found."

Qwanda couldn't take her eyes off the boarding passes. This changed her whole perception about Zeek once again.

"I know how much Zeek cares about you," Shawnna admitted. Qwanda quickly took her eyes off the passes to listen to her. "And I understand if you think I'm a grimy bitch, but I love that nigga as much as you do. I can accept knowin' about you, and you knowin' about me. But I can't except him lovin' some other bitch more than both of us," Shawnna said as she wiped tears from her eyes.

Qwanda was in total astonishment. Not only did Shawnna admit she had been with Zeek physically, but she opened her eyes to a bigger threat to her heart. It wasn't Shawnna or Chelsea. It was Cadora Mendosa. Qwanda was furious. She realized something had to be done. She was going to inflict pain on Zeek or Cadora. She couldn't decide which one yet.

Shawnna and Qwanda were both tired of being hurt and emotionally drained by Zeek. For months, Shawnna was fed up with competing with Qwanda and wanted Zeek to leave her alone. She was deeply in love and wanted to have him all to herself. He had been singing the same song for months, and Shawnna was through with hearing his broken promises. She no longer wanted to play the mistress role. She wanted to be his one and only, but Zeek would never make that possible. That was clear to her now.

Shawnna figured that Qwanda and she should band together to get their revenge. If Qwanda was willing to listen, she had a plan.

"Now, what am I supposed to be lookin' for?" Qwanda asked.

"It's a safe he keeps in his bedroom closet. I need you to get it for me. There's somethin' special that he's keepin' in there. We need to find out what's in that shit."

"Why can't you do it?" Qwanda asked suspiciously.

That's when Shawnna grinned. "Because I ain't got the key to that house…you do."

Qwanda thought about the upper hand she had on Shawnna. *This bitch don't even got a key.* She smiled back at her and agreed to do it.

Qwanda quickly ran up the steps and into Zeek's bedroom. She had to move fast since she didn't know when he would return. She rummaged through piles of clothes in his closet looking for the safe. A certain bag caught her attention.

"What the hell. Pam. Sheka…Courtney. This nigga got all these bitches' drawers in here. Grimy mothafucka," Qwanda said angrily as she stumbled across his underwear collection. She walked a little further into the closet and found the safe. She grabbed a garbage bag out of her pocket and put the safe in it. She didn't even take a second to look at it. She ran out of the house as fast as she could, hoping not to leave a visible trace that she was there.

Putt! Putt! Putt! "What the fuck could be in here?" Qwanda shook the safe as they stood in the woods.

"I don't know, but we about to find out." She took the box from Qwanda, and placed it on a tree stump.

She pulled out a .38 Special that Zeek had given her and shot the safe open. She yanked the hot safe apart and pulled out its contents.

"What the hell is King Kong?" Qwanda asked as she held up the big, labeled Ziploc bag of powder.

"I think it's some type of heroin. All the stamp bags in this other Ziploc have King Kong on them, too."

"Why would he keep this locked up? Wouldn't you think he would be tryna sell this?" Qwanda questioned.

"Yeah, but this could be his personal stash," Shawnna implied.

Qwanda's eyes grew wide. "You think he's on that shit?"

Shawnna shrugged. "Possibly. This probably is what he uses to keep his dick hard so long. You know…like a lil' young man's Viagra."

"I hope not. If he is…I ain't never seen no track marks on him or noticed him sniffin' a lot, either. Have you?"

"Nah, but some people can hide their symptoms real good. I'll tell you this, doe, when he find out this shit is missin', he ain't gonna be able to hide shit." Shawnna smirked.

Even though it all sounded risky, Qwanda still went along with Shawnna's plan. She only hoped they were doing the right thing.

It was after midnight, and Bink and Riff continued to hold down their slow corner. Bink and Riff were average height and both were a dirty shade of paper bag brown. Their usual summer attire consisted of black tees, blue jean shorts, and Timberland boots. Bink kept his hair in little locks, while Riff always rocked a fresh baldy. Bink and Riff used to have a good part of the game on hold. Things changed when they got chased out of the Trinidad area and were forced to relocate. Following that, their crew leader, Durty, was killed by Cook because Durty had forced Zeek out of the alley where he had first set up to hustle.

Ever since, Bink and Riff both were lost in the game. They were tired of the struggle and wanted something different.

"This is real fucked up. Shit is slower than a mothafucka. I remember when we used to have all these streets," Bink complained.

"Yeah, thangs was good when Durt was around. Now, we got weak product and them U.B.N. niggas is runnin' every fuckin' thang."

"Man, fuck them niggas," Riff barked. "I'm tellin' you, young. We should build up our muscle and take our shit back."

"You ain't sayin' nothin'. I'm wit' that shit."

Bink was down for the comeback. Bink and Riff thought about who would be crazy enough to go against U.B.N. That's when they were approached by a young girl.

"What's up, pretty baby? You rollin'?" Bink asked.

The girl sucked her teeth. "Come on, Bink. Don't even come at me like that."

"How the fuck you know my name, young?"

"It's me. Shawnna."

Bink was impressed with her new look. "Damn, boo. I heard you got clean, but you lookin' good as hell."

Shawnna smiled.

"If you ain't rollin' or on that shit no more, why you out this time of night?" Bink asked. He was curious to know what was up with Shawnna.

"I got somethin' for y'all," she said as she handed him a shopping bag.

Bink and Riff quickly looked in the bag. They were both surprised by the contents.

"Damn. How much you want for all this?" Bink asked.

"Nothin'."

They were both confused. "You goin' to give us all this dope for free?" Riff questioned.

"Yeah. Just make sure you get rid of all of it."

"Who did you take this from?" Bink asked.

"That's not important. Make sure y'all come up off of it."

"Aight. And you positive you don't want nothin' from it?" Bink asked again to make sure.

"Just throw me a favor in the future," she said, giving him a wink.

Bink nodded his head as Shawnna walked away into the night.

Shawnna didn't mind giving Bink and Riff the hook-up. As many times as she'd stolen from their stash house, she felt she had to pay them back something. She also knew Bink and Riff hated Zeek for having Durty killed—at least that's what they thought. They also thought Shawnna had given them dope, too. But King Kong was its name.

CHAPTER TWENTY-SEVEN

On the other side of town, Joseph sat in the bathroom stall while at the Sala Thai restaurant. He planned to stay there and cry until he had no more tears left in him. He cried so hard that tears were even falling on his shattered cell phone, thrown on the floor in anger. His boyfriend had told him that he was done with him for good this time. His heart was broken once again.

Gavin was fed up with Joseph's jealous and insecure ways. He kept giving Joseph chance after chance to change, but he never did. Gavin needed someone in his life that could trust him. He wanted someone who wouldn't fight with him every time he was out of their sight. That's why he had told Joseph that he'd left him for Amir. Amir happened to be Joseph's best friend.

Joseph felt that he had done everything he could to be the best boyfriend to Gavin. He even checked himself into a ninety-day rehab so he could kick his drug addiction. Now with Gavin no longer wanting him, he had a strong desire to go back to the one thing that never let him down: heroin. Thinking about Gavin made Joseph's heart ache. He had bought him whatever he wanted and had remained faithful to him for two-and-a-half years, and yet, that wasn't enough.

Joseph finally pulled himself together and came out of the stall.

He stared at himself in the mirror and started to cry again. *Why am I not good enough for him?* Joseph had developed a complex about himself. Yet, he had no reason to. He was tall with chocolate smooth skin and had mild feminine features. He was a fly dresser and had everything going for himself. Looks definitely weren't his problem. It was Gavin.

Joseph later went back to the table where his brother and their associates were having dinner together. His brother was none other than Glimpse, the one and only Southeast drug boss. Glimpse took one look at his brother and knew something was wrong.

"Aye, lil' bro. You a'ight?"

"I'm feeling sick."

"That's all? Just sick?" Glimpse asked suspiciously.

"Yeah. Could one of y'all take me home?" Joseph asked as he looked around the table.

Glimpse then nodded at Trish. She nodded back and got up from the table. "Come on, yo," she said to Joseph. Joseph got up and said his goodbyes to everybody.

He was about to leave out when Glimpse stopped him. "Aye, Joe. I hope you feel betta."

"Thanks," Joseph said softly and then followed Trish out of the restaurant.

While Joseph rode along in the car with Trish, he stared out the window. Thinking about Gavin leaving him for his best friend made him feel so bad. He needed something to ease his pain, and he needed it now.

"Aye, Trish. Do me a favor. Drop me off out my friend's way."

"Where they stay at?"

"Northeast."

"A'ight," she said, while trying to call somebody she could go see herself.

Joseph sat and closed his eyes as his body trembled. He prayed he would find what he was looking for.

"Yo, Joe. Joe! Wake the fuck up so you can tell me what street to turn on," Trish said as she drove into unfamiliar territory.

Joseph was still halfway asleep, while trying to lead Trish to where he wanted to go. After a few turns, they found themselves on West Virginia Avenue.

"You can let me out here."

Trish stopped the car and let Joseph out.

"You sure you goin' to be a'ight here?"

"Yeah. My friend lives right there and I'm strapped so I'll be cool."

"You sure they there?"

"Yeah. I talked to 'em before we left the restaurant. You can go 'head and roll out. I'm goin' to smoke a jack before I go in."

"A'ight. Be easy, young."

Trish didn't want to keep pressing him so she gladly went on her way. She had a lady friend to go see anyway. Joseph continued to smoke his cigarette until Trish was out of sight. He threw down the cigarette and headed toward two men that were standing on the corner.

Joseph hoped that the men had what he wanted or at least knew where to get it from. When he got closer to them, he was glad he knew who they were.

"Bink. Riff. How y'all fellas been doin'?"

Bink was surprised to see him. "Look who it is, Riff. A blast from the mothafuckin' past. What's up, Joey?"

"Nothin', yo. Just chillin'. I'm glad to see y'all still out here."

"Yeah. We still doin' our thang."

Joseph cut to the chase. "Y'all still got that boy?"

"Yeah, we got this wild shit called King Kong. Mothafuckas is fallin' out off this shit, too."

Joseph nodded. "That's what I'm talkin' 'bout. Let me get a hundred of that shit." Joseph handed Bink two fifty-dollar bills and Riff handed Joseph fifteen stamp bags.

"You got ya own needle?" Bink asked.

"Nah. I ain't got shit."

"It ain't nothin'," Bink informed. "Go see my man. He's in front of a vacant around the corna. He got what you need to get ya blast on."

Joseph gave him dap. "Good lookin'. I'm out."

Joseph hurried around the corner to find who Bink was talking about. Just like Bink said, his boy was standing right there in front of him.

"Bink told me I could go up in there," Joseph said to the young boy.

"Yeah. Go 'head. Everythang you need is inside."

Joseph walked into the vacant house and right by the door was a bucket full of syringes, lighters, and spoons. He grabbed one of each item and walked upstairs to an empty room that didn't have anybody inside getting high. He picked a corner to sit in, and then began to prepare his dose.

He dumped out a baggie onto the spoon, and then spat in it. He wanted his saliva to help the dope cook up faster. Once it was ready, Joseph filled up the syringe and tied his belt around his arm. Once his vein shot up like an earthworm buried under his skin, he injected the dosage into his arm. It didn't take long for the dose to take effect. Joseph began to nod and drool as the powerful substance took over his body. In between nods, he started crying thinking about Gavin. He managed to pull out his wallet so he could retrieve a picture of him and Gavin together. One look at his face took his anger over the edge. "Fuck you, Gavin! Fuck you, fuck you, fuck you!" he cursed at the picture before ripping it up.

His depression heightened so he reached for another bag from the pile he had on the floor. When he leaned over, he found that it was hard for him to breathe. Joseph held his chest, gasping for air. The nausea and dizziness hit him at the same time. He kept trying to rise to his feet, only to fall down each time. He rolled over onto his back and began to lose consciousness. Soon after, his lungs collapsed, causing him to suffocate. Of all the times Joseph had shot dope, this was the first time he had ever overdosed. Joseph was only looking for a temporary escape from his estranged and bitter life. Instead, King Kong gave him a one-way ticket on a deadly voyage. A journey that no user had ever made it back from. Now Joseph didn't have to worry about being in pain any longer. King Kong had taken that all away.

Glimpse badly needed to use the bathroom before he left the restaurant after having too many drinks. When he walked over to the urinals, he noticed something in one of the stalls that caught his attention. He saw it was his brother's cell phone smashed, along with balled-up pieces of paper towel on the floor. That's when it hit him what was really wrong with his brother. Gavin had broken up with Joseph once again. Glimpse was heated. "I'm goin' to kill that faggot," he yelled as he rammed his fist so hard into the wall of the bathroom stall that he realigned its structure.

He hated when Gavin hurt his brother's feelings. He didn't like that his brother was gay, but he dealt with it. He at least wanted his brother to be with someone who would treat him right. He hoped for Gavin's sake, this would be the last time he would ever make his brother cry.

The very next day Glimpse couldn't find Joseph anywhere. Since he had broken his phone, Glimpse had no way of reaching him. He checked his house, but he wasn't there. His last resort was to ask Trish, since she was the last person seen with him. When he went over to Trish's spot, he hoped she would be able to help him.

"Aye, Trish. Did you drop my brotha off at his house last night?"

"Nah. He had me drop him off over a friend's spot. I took 'em out Northeast."

Glimpse was confused. "Northeast? He don't fuck wit' nobody out there. Did you see who it was?"

"Nah. He told me to go 'head. He wanted to hit a jack before he went in. Why? You think something's wrong?"

"I don't know, yet. I got a funny feelin' about this shit. Show me where you took him." Glimpse and Trish got in her car and rode over to Northeast.

"I let him out right around here," Trish said, as she pulled up along the curb.

Glimpse looked around. The rundown area didn't look like a place Joseph would go. Glimpse was more suspicious. "Drive down there. I want to see if them niggas seen 'em."

Trish pulled up right where the two men were standing. "Yo, I'm lookin' for my brotha. He came out here last night. Have y'all seen 'em?" Glimpse said as he showed the men a picture of his brother that he had in his cell phone.

Bink stepped forward to get a closer look. "Yeah, I know Joe. I did see 'em last night."

"How you know 'em?" Glimpse asked.

"He used to come out here all the time and niggas would serve 'em. Last night was the first time I'd seen him in a while."

Glimpse was afraid his brother had turned back to drugs. He

needed to find him. He hoped it wasn't too late. "Do you know where he went?"

"The last I know, he headed to a crackhouse around the corna."

Glimpse was desperate to find his brother. He held up a hundred-dollar bill. "Show me."

Bink took the money and got in the car with them. He thought he was making some easy money. *There was no way Joey would still be in that house*, he thought. He hoped he wasn't wrong.

Bink walked Glimpse and Trish into the vacant dwelling. Glimpse wanted to be sure his brother wasn't still there, so he wanted to check every room. When Glimpse stood in the doorway of one of the bedrooms upstairs, his lips tightened and his body started to shake. He was devastated at the sight of his brother Joseph, dead on the floor. Tears ran down Glimpse's face as he knelt down to cry over his brother's body. Bink and Trish were shocked by what had happened. Glimpse was so hurt. Words couldn't describe how he was feeling. He became so emotional while looking at the bags of heroin that had taken his brother's life. Not too far from the bags, he saw a torn-up picture of Gavin. *This mothafucka got you back on this shit!* He cried to himself.

Glimpse picked up all the bags of heroin and held them tight in his hand. His thoughts were to tie Gavin up and inject him with all the remaining bags. He wanted him to die the exact same way his brother had, only worse. Glimpse opened up his hand to take another look at the bags. *King Kong?* The name on the bags jogged his memory. King Kong was a name he was somewhat familiar with. His rage grew even greater.

"This ain't heroin," he said as he looked at Trish and Bink.

"It ain't? What is it?" Trish asked.

"It's fuckin' fentanyl."

Trish or Bink had never heard of it and didn't have a clue.

"How you know what it is?" Trish asked.

"My supplier asked me to get it about a year ago. I told 'em I didn't want to touch the shit."

Trish didn't understand. "What's wrong wit' it?"

"This shit's almost fifty times more potent than morphine. Anybody who takes this could die in minutes," Glimpse said, handing Trish one of the bags.

Trish looked at the bag closely herself. She remembered seeing it somewhere. "Yo, I remember this shit, young. The boy we was havin' a problem wit' 'round the way had this shit," she declared.

"Then that means this whole thing is bigger than my brotha dyin'. Whoever's at the top of this shit needs to come down." Glimpse paused and turned his eyes on Bink. "My man, you know who I can blame for all this?"

Bink froze. He knew by saying the wrong thing could cost him his life, so he played it safe and blurted out a name of one of his enemies. "It's Zeek. That's the nigga y'all need to be lookin' for."

"Who the fuck is Zeek?" Glimpse asked.

"He's the biggest nigga ova here, slim. He runs damn near everythang. I hear he be movin' some powerful shit. Some lethal-type shit, too."

Glimpse had heard all he needed to hear. He was going to find the one they called Zeek and kill him. Zeek became Glimpse's number one target. His brother's death had caused him too much pain and he needed someone to take it out on. Trish wanted to be the one to find Zeek for Glimpse. She felt responsible for letting Joseph go astray. This was her way of apologizing.

Bink was glad he left the vacant still breathing. If Glimpse or Trish had checked his pockets, they would have found his stash and killed him on the spot. Now, Zeek would have to be the one to watch his back. Bink hated Zeek and wanted him to die for killing Durty. Bink figured this was the best way to do it without it coming back on him. He also knew that in the hood, if someone said you did something, you might as well have. That's how it is in the streets. There ain't no time for talking. Only enough time for firing back. It was about to be on.

CHAPTER TWENTY-EIGHT

"Hold up. Come again, young. Who was lookin' for me?" Zeek asked Marcus while they stood out on the block.

Marcus shrugged. "I don't know. Some brown-skin broad wit' a fucked-up ponytail."

"Well, what did she want?"

"She was asking 'bout you and wanted to know if I knew you. She talkin' 'bout she was tryna get some weight of that King Kong shit you be havin'."

Zeek was caught off-guard. "King Kong? I wonder how she knows about that shit."

"Hold up, nigga. I know you ain't holdin' out on us. You got us movin' the regular, and you keepin' the Scarface shit for ya self." Marcus laughed, while Zeek didn't find anything funny. "I'm fuckin' wit' you, Zeek. I know we got the best shit," he said, still laughing. "But what is that King Kong shit anyway?"

Zeek thought about if he should tell Marcus what he had done to Rodney. If there was anybody Zeek could trust, it would be him. "Yo, you remember that nigga Rodney I had beef wit'?"

"Yeah, what about 'em?"

"About ten months ago, he came to me tryin' to get on wit' some dope, but dope wasn't what I gave 'em. He got straight fentanyl."

"Fentanyl? What's that shit?"

"Some shit that's way stronger than heroin. A small amount could kill a fuckin' elephant, and that nigga got murdered for sellin' that shit."

Marcus looked at Zeek and admired him for being so gangsta. "Damn, Zeek. You's a grimy-ass nigga. I didn't know you had it in you, slim."

Zeek looked at Marcus like he wasn't proud of what he'd done.

"I don't get it. If that shit happened last fall, why was youngin' comin' around askin' 'bout it now?" Marcus asked.

"I don't know," Zeek said, shrugging his shoulders.

Marcus tried to make sense out of it. "I think somebody else besides Rodney attached ya name to it. You still got some left?"

"Yeah, but don't nobody know I got it."

"You sure? 'Cause somethin' ain't right," Marcus suggested.

Zeek paused for a minute. *Somethin' wasn't right*, he thought. *Somethin''s not right at all.*

"Where the fuck is it?!" Zeek shouted as he tore up his closet. He looked desperately for his safe, but he couldn't find it anywhere. "Where the fuck did I put it?!" he wondered. He realized that he only kept it in his closet. It had to be there. *Somebody stole it*, he thought. *It could only be one of two people: Shawnna or Qwanda.*

There was no sign of a break-in, so Zeek didn't have a choice but to suspect one of them. *Why would they do that?* He had to find out what was up with them.

Zeek rushed over to Qwanda's house. She was the first one he would confront since she was the last one who was mad at him. Qwanda was on the couch watching TV when Zeek came banging on the door. By the knock, she quickly figured out who it was.

"Hey, boo," she said once she opened the door.

Zeek said nothing as he pushed her back and slammed the door behind him. Qwanda could see it in his eyes that he was pissed about something.

"Where is it?"

"Where is what?"

"You know what I'm talkin' 'bout."

"What?" Qwanda still decided to play dumb.

"The fuckin' safe! Where is it?"

Qwanda thought his actions were funny. She couldn't believe that Zeek was a dope head. She busted out laughing.

"What the fuck is so funny?"

"You, nigga. You really on that shit, huh?"

"What the fuck you talkin' 'bout?"

"That dope, nigga. Shawnna was right about you. She knew you'd come lookin' for it." Qwanda gave him a devilish grin. "I guess you need that King Kong so you can stay hard for that Dora bitch."

"How the fuck do you know what's in there?" Zeek asked, grabbing her arms and shaking her.

Qwanda was scared. She never had seen that type of aggression from him and didn't want to get beat up for playing with his dope. So she gave in.

"A'iight! Get off of me and I'll tell you."

Zeek released her and waited for her to start talking. "Shawnna shot ya safe open and found your dope in there, but I'm the one who took it."

Zeek's blood boiled. "What the fuck is wrong wit' you bitches! That wasn't dope!"

"Well, how the fuck was we supposed to know? You got the shit hidden."

"I hid it for a fuckin' reason, you nosey bitches! Now where the fuck is my shit?"

Qwanda didn't want to answer him, but she had to. "Shawnna gave it away."

"She did what? Who the fuck she give it to?"

"Some kid named Bink."

"She gave it to Bink? Why would she do that shit?"

"Because she was mad she found out about Cadora." Qwanda started to cry as she continued. "And I was, too. She gave it away to someone who hated you."

Zeek started to pace the room. "I can't believe you'd do this to me. You, of all people." He stared into her eyes. "If somethin' bad happens to me, it's all y'all fault."

Qwanda developed a guilty conscience. "I'm sorry. I shouldn't of gotten involved. The only reason I took it is because Shawnna ain't have no key to get in."

Zeek suddenly stopped pacing. "Shawnna has a key."

"She does?"

"Yeah. That girl used you," Zeek said, as Qwanda put her head down in shame.

"Just so you know: that shit you took was fentanyl, not heroin. It's way fuckin' stronger, and almost everyone who takes it dies. When word gets around that I'm passin' out death, you'll have yourself to thank for that shit." Zeek stared her down one last time and slammed the door behind him.

When Zeek left, Qwanda realized she didn't get the outcome she was looking for. She didn't find out anything about Cadora or Zeek's drug habit. She'd only found out that Shawnna had played the hell out of her. She had to call her right away.

Shawnna answered, "Hello."

"Shawnna! You fuckin' bitch! Zeek told me you had a key! Why the fuck you lie to me?"

"Who the fuck you callin' a bitch? Hoe, you better slow ya roll."

"I ain't gotta do a mothafuckin' thing. Zeek ain't fuckin' wit' me now because of you. And that shit wasn't dope, dumb ass."

"So what, he ain't fuckin' wit' you. Get over it, bitch." Shawnna sucked her teeth and continued. "Anyway, what did he say about that Cadora broad?"

Click! Qwanda hung up on her.

"Oolll! I'm goin' to kill that bitch!" Qwanda shouted. Qwanda realized that Shawnna didn't give a damn about her and only used her to get what she wanted. If Shawnna messed her up with Zeek for good, she was really going to kill her. Qwanda now hated her that much more.

Zeek ran to one of his spots and got his gun. He loaded up the .40 caliber and took an extra clip with him. He was going to find Bink and get his package back. He knew where Bink hustled, so it was going to be no problem finding him. Zeek hoped Bink would give up his stash without giving him any problems. He didn't want to have to kill him.

It was around 1:00 a.m. when Zeek spotted Bink and Riff out on West Virginia Avenue. They were unaware that Zeek had passed them right before he had parked his car around the corner on Central. Zeek didn't know if he was walking into a dangerous situation or not, but he really didn't care. He was only there for one thing. Riff was the first one to see Zeek walk up to them. Riff nudged Bink to show him who was coming toward them.

"Bink, I know this ain't how the game go, but that shit Shawnna gave you…I'ma need that back."

Bink might have figured someone would come looking for their package one day. He never imagined that it would be Zeek himself. Bink had him right where he wanted him.

"So you're the one that be havin' that shit? I guess I was tellin' 'em the truth after all. Huh, Riff?"

"What the fuck you talkin' 'bout, young?" Zeek asked, looking at both of them.

"This nigga and some broad came through here lookin' for whoeva had that Kong. I told 'em it was you."

Zeek got heated. "Look, mothafucka! Don't be tellin' nobody shit about me! That ain't none of yours or their fuckin' business what I got, bitch!"

Bink smiled. "I had to tell 'em. That shit killed his brotha, man. And now he wants to kill you."

Zeek couldn't take it anymore and put his gun to Bink's face. "I'm gonna kill ya bitch ass if you don't hand over my shit!"

"You ain't got the heart to kill me, nigga," Bink said as he stared into Zeek's eyes.

"Oh, I got the heart. I'm tryin' to give you a chance to live."

Blink saw the frustration in Zeek's face. He couldn't tell anymore if he really would pull the trigger or not so he decided to play it safe.

"Riff, give this mothafucka what's left of that package."

"Slim, is you crazy?" Riff protested.

"I said give it to him!"

Riff hesitated for a second, then went around the corner to get the package.

Bink looked back at Zeek and smiled again. "You know they still gonna kill you, right?"

Before he could answer, Riff was firing shots at him. Zeek quickly started firing shots back, trying to take Riff's head off. Bink tried to draw his gun, too, but Zeek fell back and shot at Bink, hitting him in the neck. The shot caused Bink to lose control of his movements and stumble in the way of Riff's fire. Bink's body dropped from a single shot to the back of the head.

Riff's rage was now on high because Zeek had made him shoot

his best friend by accident. He was really trying to kill Zeek now. Zeek continued to scramble from bullets and ducked down behind a parked car as broken glass fell all around him. Riff shot at Zeek so many times that he ran out of bullets. He quickly bent down and pulled Bink's gun from his hand. Before he could get a good grip on the gun, he caught a bullet in his knee and screamed in pain.

Zeek saw that Riff was wounded and decided to make a run for it. Zeek took off and Riff fired the whole clip at him, missing every time. After feeling like he had been running for miles, Zeek finally got to his car and sped away. Riff suddenly heard police sirens in the distance. He crawled over to Bink to see if he was still alive. When he saw that Bink was gone, he picked up both guns and hopped away leaving Bink's dead body on the sidewalk.

Zeek drove onto New York Avenue and felt he was out of danger. He didn't get to leave with his package, but he had left with his life. Everything happened so fast that he didn't have time to think. This was the first time he ever shot anybody and didn't know how to feel about it. He was a wanted man and had to protect himself at all times. Since Shawnna was the cause of all his problems, she was going to have to pay for her mistake. He mind raced as he was on his way to pay her a visit.

Gavin and Amir finished a romantic dinner together at an elegant French restaurant in Dupont Circle. They went back to Amir's place where they listened to some jazz music and enjoyed a twelve-year-old bottle of Chardonnay. The mood was right and the lights were dim. A few glasses later they found themselves in bed loving each other's bodies. Gavin and Amir had been having sex for months now, but this was the first time they could do it guilt free.

Gavin hadn't heard from Joseph in two days and thought he got the point. Amir was so glad that Joseph was finally out of the picture. Amir was tired of competing with him for Gavin's affection and wanted to be his only lover. Amir knew he could give Gavin the kind of relationship that Joseph couldn't.

They were in the middle of their lovemaking when a gunshot was heard over the loud music that blew the lock off the door. They both jumped up as Glimpse kicked in the bedroom door.

"My brotha wasn't good enough for you, mothafucka?" Glimpse shouted, waving his .357 magnum at both of them.

"I'm sorry. Please don't kill us!" Gavin cried.

"Y'all in here doin' my brotha wrong, and I shouldn't kill y'all two gay bitches?"

"No! Please don't kill us! Get Joseph over here, and we can straighten' this out!" Amir pleaded.

"I wish I could call Joe, so he could see what the fuck y'all doin', but I can't. 'Cause my lil' brotha's dead!"

Gavin and Amir couldn't believe what they'd heard. They started crying even harder thinking about their bad situation.

"I don't know what y'all did to him, but Joe overdosed off some bad shit," Glimpse continued. "Y'all two boney faggots owe me for his death, but I'm not the one that's goin' to kill you. Y'all gonna kill each other." Glimpse pulled out the bags of Kong and threw them on the bed. "Now feed each other," Glimpse commanded.

"Please! Don't make us do this," Gavin said, trembling with fear.

"It's either y'all take this shit or get a bullet in the fuckin' head. Now do it!"

Neither one of them budged. They didn't want to give each other what was in those bags and wished they didn't have to. Without either one of them taking the initiative to make a move, Glimpse lost his patience.

"Oh! So y'all ain't goin' to take it?" Glimpse said as he went over to Amir's side of the bed and put the gun to his head. "Pick it up," Glimpse commanded of Gavin.

Gavin sobbed as he stretched his naked body across the bed to grab one of the bags.

"Now, give it to 'em."

Gavin didn't want to hurt Amir. Even with a gun pressed against his temple, he still couldn't do it. Gavin looked at Glimpse and shook his head no. Glimpse frowned and pulled the trigger. Amir's body fell on Gavin, leaving blood all over him. Gavin began to panic. Amir's body lay across his lap, and he couldn't take looking into his dead eyes. He started crying uncontrollably.

Glimpse turned the gun on Gavin. "If you don't want to die like your boyfriend, you betta swallow that shit and make it quick."

Gavin quickly weighed out his options, and then realized he didn't have any. Now with Joseph and Amir dead, he thought he had nothing else to live for. Gavin quickly swallowed the bag that he held in his hand and then swallowed all the other bags that were on the bed. If Glimpse wanted him dead, he would rather do it himself. After all the bags were empty, Gavin looked up at Glimpse and screamed from the top of his lungs as tears poured out of his eyes. "Are you happy? I took 'em all! Are you fuckin' happy now?"

"No," Glimpse said as he pulled the trigger once more, shooting Gavin in his face. His lifeless body hung off the bed dripping blood all over the floor.

Glimpse held no regrets for killing them. It was something he had to do, at least for his brother's sake. His path for revenge was almost over. Two down, and one more to go. Zeek was next.

CHAPTER TWENTY-NINE

Shawnna sat on her couch all night taking out her micros. She skipped going to the club so she could finish removing her extensions and get her hair redone for the weekend. In between braids, she would try to call Zeek to find out what was going on with him and Cadora. She placed another call, but Zeek still didn't answer. Instead of leaving a voice message, she kept calling back until he answered the phone. *This nigga's probably wit' that bitch right now*, she thought. As she attempted to make another call, he stormed right through her front door.

"Yeah, nigga. Just the person I wanted to see," she said as she got off the couch and walked toward him.

Shawnna was full of jealousy and rage. She was tired of not knowing what was going on and needed some answers from him right away.

"Who the fuck is this Cadora bitch?!" she shouted.

Zeek grabbed her hair, and smacked her across her face. Shawnna was in total shock from getting hit. Zeek ultimately disrespected her. She vowed that if any man ever put his hands on her, she would fight them back and that's what she did.

Shawnna swung wildly, trying to hit Zeek anywhere she could. While Zeek still had a hold of her, he smacked her again, causing her lip to bleed.

"You fuckin' bitch! I almost got killed tonight 'cause you want to be a stupid jealous bitch!"

"Get off of me!" Shawnna was kicking and clawing his fingers, hoping he would let go of the tight hold he had on her hair. He smacked her once more, throwing her down on the floor and kicking her in the stomach.

"You goin' to give my shit to some bitch-ass niggas! You had Qwanda steal from me 'cause you a jealous bitch! That's what I get for gettin' a crackheaded-ass, dope junkie bitch clean! Huh?" Zeek shouted as he kicked her repeatedly. "You're cut off, bitch. I'm done witchu."

Shawnna cried in pain after Zeek delivered another kick.

"I'm gonna kill you, mothafucka...and Cadora!" She cried as Zeek stood over top of her.

Zeek got even madder and pushed her head into the floor. "Keep fuckin' wit' me, bitch. You betta hope I don't get no one to kill ya ass."

Zeek's rage had taken him to a place he had never been. He realized that things had gone way too far. After he'd done physical harm to a woman he cared about, there was no turning back. He would never be the same. He suddenly lifted his weight off of her head and walked out of the door. Shawnna stayed on the floor and cried while rubbing her rug-burned face. Her mind had drifted further than it ever had.

"Fuck Qwanda and fuck Cadora! Let's see what those bitches do when Zeek's ass is dead. He's gonna die! That's my word!" She really wanted to get Zeek killed now for hurting her. She had the perfect person in mind to do it, too.

❖ ❖ ❖

Trish was on her way to the D.C. Jail to visit Glimpse. Glimpse was charged with the murders of Gavin Smith and Amir Johnson. He became the prime suspect after a week-long investigation gave authorities enough reasoning and evidence to arrest him. Patrick "Glimpse" Shaw was being held with no bond. Trish couldn't believe what was happening. Since she'd found out about Glimpse's arrest in the middle of the week, she had to wait until the following Monday to go see him.

Glimpse was only allowed visits on Mondays. This was a rule for all inmates with last names starting with the letters Q-Z. They were only allowed two half-hour visits that same day. Trish couldn't wait to talk to him so she could hear his side of the story.

Trish stood in the long visiting line that went out the door and around the corner. She didn't know so many criminals' last names began with Q-Z. The hour-long wait in line bugged her out. Once she got to the counter to sign up for her first visit, she found out that she still had to wait for her name to be called. Trish realized that she was probably going to be there all day. This made her hate jails even more.

"Patrisha Barnes!" the male officer at the front counter called out.

"It's about fuckin' time." She sighed as she got up.

A guard walked her into the room where Glimpse was already seated. They waited until the guard walked away before they started talking.

"Damn, young. How you doin' in here?" She still asked, even though she saw he was fucked up.

"I'm a'ight. It don't look like I'm gettin' out, doe," he said, assuming the worst.

"How they get chu?"

"They got recorded phone messages that Joe told Gavin that his brother was gonna kill 'em. They found out Joe was in a drug program and the same drug they found in Joe's system was the same one in Gavin's, but five times more. Then the slugs they found in both bodies. They're tying all that shit together as my motive for revenge. I'm done, Trish," Glimpse said, sadly.

Glimpse knew he probably wouldn't see daylight for a long time and Trish knew it, too.

"So what chu need me to do? You want me to fall back on ol' boy?" she asked.

"Yeah, put our protégé on 'em. If they can't get it done, then you do it."

"A'ight. Bet on that."

Trish was going to have to hold everything down whether Glimpse was released or not. She didn't have to try hard to fill the position. She was already built for it.

Glimpse and Trish continued to talk about business until the guard came back around.

"A'ight. Time's up," the guard said.

Trish looked up at him with attitude. "What chu mean? I still got the other half of my visit left."

"You can't combine your visits, ma'am. If you want your other visit, you'll have to get back in the visiting line and wait to be called again."

Trish looked at Glimpse, then back at the guard. "Man, fuck that. I ain't goin' through that shit again. Not today. I'll holla at you later, G."

Trish got up and walked out. Glimpse hoped she would have some good news for him the next time they spoke. He hoped she would tell him that Zeek was dead.

CHAPTER THIRTY

Shawnna had been looking for Bink and Riff for a few days now. When she finally found Riff, she noticed that he had a cast on his leg. She wondered what had happened to him.

"Damn, nigga. What happened to you? I've been lookin' for you niggas everywhere."

"Yo, you ain't hear? Bink's dead. Zeek killed 'em and shot me, too," Riff explained to Shawnna, not telling her the whole truth.

Shawnna was shocked. She thought Zeek was crazy for hitting her, but didn't know he was crazy enough to kill somebody. Now, she was even more eager to get him gone.

"Riff, I need this nigga dead. I'll give you ten stacks if you do it."

Riff gave her a serious look. "To kill Zeek? I'd do that shit for free."

"For real?"

"Yeah, but I'll still take the money."

"That's cool. I'll give you half now, and the other half when you kill 'em. You cool wit' that?"

Riff took the bag of money confirming his answer. Even though he was getting paid, he had questions of his own. "Damn, girl. First, you steal his shit, and now you want 'em dead. What he do to you?"

"He's been cheatin' on me wit' this bitch named Cadora. Then when I asked him about her, he starts beatin' on me n'shit. The nigga's crazy. I want him gone."

"A'ight, mami. Don't worry. Some other people want to kill 'em, too. We gonna take care of 'em. Believe that."

Shawnna was thankful, but still had another request. "And if you could…kill that Cadora bitch, too. I'll give you another twenty."

Riff nodded. "Yeah. We'll take care of her, too. That's if we see her."

Shawnna wanted Cadora to feel some pain for interfering with her life. She had threatened her well-being and needed to be punished. Shawnna felt Cadora owed her life to her, and Shawnna was going to take it.

"This is the D.C. Jail with a collect call from…"

"Patrick Shaw."

"Would you accept the charges?" the voice prompter asked.

"Yeah," Trish answered.

"Yo. What up, G?"

"What up. I'm checkin' on that problem I got out there."

"Everythang cool, young. Our protégé is already on his ass. I'ma give 'em a few days to make a move."

"A'ight. But remember. If they start fakin' on it, then you take care of it."

"I gotchu," Trish continued. "Oh yeah. There's a chick named Cadora that's connected to ya problem. I get extra paper if she fall, too."

"Cadora? Shit. She'll be easy to find," Glimpse said sarcastically about the odd name.

"I know, right?"

"A'ight. I'll hit you back."

"A'ight. Stay up, G." *Click.*

Trish hung up the phone with a smile on her face. The trap was set, and all she had to do now was catch the mouse, or the "mice," that is.

Zeek had fallen madly in love with Dora; so much so, that he took her to finally meet his mother. Zeek knew if his mother approved of her, then she would definitely be perfect for him. He hoped she would like her more than she did Chelsea. He actually wished his mother would like anybody more than Chelsea, yet it never happened. Zeek was real nervous when his mother opened the door and set her eyes on Dora for the first time.

"Hey, Zeeky baby. Come on in." Zeek walked in with Dora behind him.

"Hello, Ms. Harris," Dora kindly said.

Ms. Harris took a second to examine Dora and liked what she saw.

"Zeek, who is this pretty young lady that stands before me?" she asked with a big smile.

"This is Dora, Mom. She's the girl I've been goin' out wit'," Zeek said proudly.

"Well, how long have y'all been dating?"

"Three months," he said.

"You mean to tell me you've been with this girl for three months, and I didn't know?"

"Sorry, Mom. I was waitin' for the right time."

"Boy, please. Come on in here, Dora. I'm going to make you all some dinner," his mother said, walking Dora over to the couch by the hand. "Dora, baby, is there anything that you don't eat?"

Dora thought for a second. "No, I pretty much eat anything."

"That's my girl right there," his mother said to him, as she walked in the kitchen.

Ms. Harris prepared curry chicken and rice with cherry pie for dessert. Dora was so impressed with his mom's cooking that she wanted to take some home with her. Ms. Harris was more than willing to make her a take-home plate. She loved it when people complimented her cooking.

After dinner, Ms. Harris embraced Dora like she had known her for years. They sat and talked for a while, as Zeek listened and observed. His mother was taking on to Dora like he had never seen her with anyone. Zeek smiled knowing that Dora had taken the spot in his mother's heart that Chelsea once had.

"Okay, Ms. Harris. I'll see you later," Dora said, giving her a hug.

"All right, girl. Don't be a stranger like this boy over here."

"I won't. I'll make sure I'll call and come over."

"Okay, baby."

Zeek gave his mother a hug and kiss on her cheek. He wished he would've introduced Dora to her sooner. He would have had her blessings a long time ago.

Dora rode in the car thinking of how nice Zeek's mother was. Then she looked at Zeek. "Your mother's really a sweet lady. She reminds me of my mom."

"Oh yeah?"

"Yeah. She's really nice."

"So…when can I meet your mom?"

Dora looked oddly surprised. "You really want to meet her?"

"Of course. Why wouldn't I?"

"Okay. We have to go to the hospital, though. That's where she's at."

Zeek wasn't sure if her mother worked at the hospital or had been a long-term patient there. It didn't matter to him. He really wanted to know who had birthed such a beautiful child.

Rebecca Mendosa was at the District Hospital Center, awaiting a heart transplant. Dora's mother was a retired Spanish teacher who had spent her whole life caring for others. The woman, who Dora thought had the biggest heart in the world, was now in dire need for a new one. If Dora's heart was a perfect match, she would've risked her own life to give it to her. Even after three months without a possible match, her mother still continued to wait patiently for a donor. Dora's mother was eating Jell-O when Dora and Zeek had entered the room.

"Hey, Mama, how are you feeling?" Dora said, while reaching over the bed to give her a hug.

"I'm all right. It's good to see you. How's your sister doing?" she asked with a groggy voice.

"She's fine." Dora paused. "Mama, I want you to meet someone. This is Zeek."

"Hello," Zeek said, as her mother looked over at him and smiled.

Her mother said something to Dora in Spanish, and she responded back to her. Zeek wished he knew what they were saying. Whatever it was, they both thought it was funny.

Dora and Zeek talked to her mother for a few more minutes and then they left the hospital since visiting hours were over. She promised to return soon and bring Zeek back with her. Her mother wanted her sister to come along with them, too, but Dora didn't know if that would be possible. Her sister didn't like hospitals, nor did she enjoy watching her mother about to die. in her condition. She didn't believe her mother was going to make it, but Dora still had hope.

Zeek wanted to meet Dora's sister as soon as her mother mentioned her. He never heard much about her and was curious to know why Dora seemed to always talk about her mother, but not much about her sister. Every time Zeek would ask about her, Dora would change the subject or say she didn't want to talk. If there was something bad that had happened in Dora's past, her sister most likely had something to do with it.

But what could it be? Zeek wondered. *Was it a sibling rivalry? Or did her sister have a disability that Dora was ashamed of?* Yet, Zeek couldn't help but to assume that their fallout resulted over a man. What else would make a person stop talking to their own flesh and blood? A man.

CHAPTER THIRTY-ONE

"Stop callin' me!" *Click!* "That was them again," Dora cried to Zeek.

"Could you tell who it was this time?"

"No, this is so fuckin' crazy. I never had people say they wanted to kill me before."

Over the last two weeks, Dora had been receiving threatening phone calls and getting followed almost everywhere she went. For some odd reason, somebody wanted to kill her, but she didn't know who, or why. Every time Dora looked out her window, she swore they were outside waiting for her. She became so afraid that she didn't want to leave the house anymore. Anything she needed, she would send Zeek out to get for her. Dora was scared for her life.

"Calm down," Zeek said, while putting his arms around her.

"I can't do that shit!" Dora shouted after pushing away from him. "People want to kill me! I'm not ready to die yet," she said, trembling.

"You're not goin' to die."

"Can you guarantee that? Huh?" Zeek was silent. "I didn't think so."

"I can try," Zeek said sincerely.

That's when Dora began to cry. "This is my life we're talkin' about, Zeek! Tryin' ain't good enough! I need something better than that!"

She was right. Trying to survive wasn't good enough. He had to find a way to secure his life and hers. Zeek didn't know how, but Dora was aware what had to be done.

"I want you to take me away from this place."

Zeek was shocked. "You want to leave?"

"Yes. I don't want to be here anymore."

"Where would you want to go?"

"I don't care. Anywhere but here. I want to go. Can we go?"

Zeek knew Dora was serious and had to give her an answer. Leaving D.C. for good was never an option for him. Most of his family and friends were there, and it was the place he called home. Zeek never told her that her life was on the line because of him and he was getting death threat calls, too. The city wasn't safe for either one of them, and Zeek had to make a decision.

"A'ight. We'll leave tonight."

Dora was surprised. "Are you serious?"

"Yeah. If you want to leave, we can leave. I have to take care of a few things before we go."

Dora hugged Zeek as tears flowed out of her eyes. Zeek held her tight and felt her warm embrace. He tasted her salty tears in his mouth, as they started kissing passionately and were in immense need of each other's body. Zeek pulled Dora's T-shirt over her head and threw it on the floor, and then stepped out of his boxers, leaving both of them completely naked. They fell on the bed, as their kissing got even heavier. Dora's insides were instantly drenched and wanted to feel Zeek badly. Zeek felt her wetness and slid himself into her, causing her to moan and pant before she wrapped her legs around his waist.

Zeek pumped her hard and fast, which he knew she didn't like. This time, Dora invited him to punish her as she begged him to do it to her harder and harder. Dora wanted to unleash all the pain she harbored inside, and the more rapid and deeper he went in and out of her, the easier it was to let the pain slip away, producing the biggest and most fulfilling orgasm she'd ever had in her life. Zeek was indeed the perfect lover she'd been waiting for. He knew how to ease her, how to please her, and was soon going to find her a new place to start all over.

The first thing Zeek had to do was call Catch'em. He had to alert him he was getting out the game. Leaving the game wasn't an easy thing to do. Zeek hoped Catch'em would be okay with his decision.

"What up, Ike?" Catch'em spoke, realizing who it was.

"What up, cuz," Zeek said nervously.

"Is it that time already?" Catch'em wondered.

"Nah. I'm still straight on that."

"Good. So what's up?"

Zeek was going to have to tell him. "Remember when you told me that the day you throw in ya hand, nobody would be able to say you don't know how to play?"

"Yeah."

"Well. I'm throwin' mine in."

Catch'em was surprised. "Already? It's only been like a year."

"Yeah, but I know how to play. I got more than enough."

Catch'em couldn't disagree with that. Zeek had made millions in such a short period of time. There should be no reason why

Zeek didn't have enough money to live with for the rest of his life and Catch'em knew it, too.

"Yeah. You can certainly play like a mothafucka. When do you want me to stop sendin' you cards?"

"Nah. Keep sendin' 'em. I'm still playin' wit' a partner. He goin' to take over my hand."

"A'ight, bet. I'll keep it movin'. Just remember, Ike. If you ever want back in, holla."

"That's what's up. I'll keep that in mind. But good lookin' on everything you did for me, cuz. I love you for that shit."

"It ain't nothin', fam. Just keep in touch. I'll hit you up soon. Be safe."

"You too."

"A'ight, one."

Catch'em looked over at his mother when he got off the phone. He had to tell her the bad news. "Yo, Ma. Ya boy Zeek wanted out."

Maddy didn't understand. "Out? What the fuck you mean he wants out? He just got in this shit."

"I know, but he said he made enough money and didn't want to take no more chances."

Maddy was disappointed and shook her head. "My sista turned that boy into a pussy." She took a pull from her cigarette. "His ass will be back when he run outta money. They always come back. And I'll be sittin' here waitin' for 'em, too."

Maddy was sure of her prophecy, but Catch'em knew differently. He could tell by talking to Zeek that he was serious. He believed Zeek was out of the game for good. He hoped he was really doing it for the right reasons.

Now that Zeek was off of the phone with Catch'em, he left as he had to meet up with Marcus. He needed to tell him what his plans were, and what he wanted him to do. Zeek was going to leave Marcus in charge of everything. He was going to be the heir to the throne.

"What up, young?" Zeek said, as he got into Marcus's brand-new black Bentley coupe.

"What up," Marcus said while dapping him up.

"Yo. When did you get this?"

"This mornin'. Shit. I should've got one when you got yours. We could've got a betta deal on 'em."

"That's what I was tryin' to tell you."

"It's cool. I ain't ever worried. I'm still rich than a bitch." Marcus grinned.

"Well, you about to get a whole lot richer."

Marcus was confused. "We got extra birds comin'?"

"Nah. I'm getting out the game. It's gonna be all you now."

Marcus couldn't believe what he was hearing. "What? You gettin' out the game? Why the fuck would you wanna do that?"

"There's too much shit goin' on, and I'm tired of all the stress."

"Shit, nigga. Anything you do goin' to give you stress. It's all on how you handle it. You and me can handle anything. Don't let that stress shit fuck you up."

"I ain't, nigga. That's why I'ma take my money and chill the fuck out."

"Why chill when you could keep makin' money, nigga?"

"I got enough money."

"There ain't no such thing as havin' enough money. That's why we do what we do. We hustlas, man."

Zeek was frustrated that Marcus was giving him a hard time about leaving the game behind. It didn't matter, though. He was doing it anyway.

"That hustlin' shit is dead to me, young, but for you it ain't. I'm leavin' town tonight, yo. It's all on you now."

Marcus looked away as Zeek's words started to resonate. He took a deep breath and then looked at Zeek. "Aight, man, I know I can't change ya mind so I'm gonna stop tryin'. 'Cause you always been the type of nigga that said what they meant. But on some real shit, slim. I don't want you to stay in the game to make money. You's my mothafuckin' mentor, young. You was the only mothafucka in the game that looked out for me and my crew. You ain't never did no fakin' wit' me and for that shit I will always be loyal. I love you, my nigga," Marcus ended as his bottom lip quivered. His eyes glistened as his true emotions poured out of him.

"I love you, too, bro," Zeek said as he locked hands with his ace.

Zeek immediately felt the magnitude of what Marcus had confessed to him. Marcus respected his decision and also would never betray him no matter what.

Marcus helped Zeek get all the way to the top, and now he was going to be up there all by himself. Yet, he was ready for it. He had secretly groomed himself for the position by making U.B.N. one of the biggest drug organizations in D.C. history. Marcus was about to be a boss for real.

Later that night, Zeek went past his mother's house. This would be the last time he would see his mother before he left town. He told her he was relocating with his job for more money, and would send for her whenever he got settled. He hated having to keep telling her lies about what he did, but he had no other choice. She wouldn't be able to handle the truth anyway. Besides, how many mothers would be okay with their sons selling drugs?

CHAPTER THIRTY-TWO

Zeek printed out the MapQuest directions for Charlotte, North Carolina, and put them in his pocket. It was where Zeek and Dora decided they were going to relocate. Dora wanted to go to Charlotte, Los Angeles, or New York. She ended up deciding on Charlotte as she had heard it was slower and quieter than the other two cities. She really wanted to get away from the big city and be somewhere on the low. Charlotte was a good place where she could start a new life with Zeek and not be found.

Zeek was moving so fast that he forgot to think about what he was going to do with all his cars and houses. *Do I need to sell everything? What car should I take? Do I think I'm really not comin' back?* he thought. Zeek was so confused and felt he had very little time to figure it all out. The only thing he was sure of was that he had to get his money. Everything else he would figure out later.

Other than the stash houses, Zeek kept the bulk of his money at a storage building. E-Z Storage was where he kept his money and any other valuables. Storage space worked better for him instead of using a regular bank. Without a job, it was hard for him to deposit the large amount of money he had without being able to explain where he got it all from. Zeek preferred to protect his own assets in storage, so he'd always know their location. He looked in all directions to make sure he hadn't been followed.

Zeek opened up the storage room and went inside. Along the back wall were six light-green oversized duffel bags lined up next to each other. He didn't want to take all of them right away, so he only grabbed two. He looked over the bags and picked the ones that had a "1M" and "3M" written on them. The "M" on the bags meant million. He carried the heavy bags out of the building and put them in the trunk of his Cadillac Seville. He got in the car and started the engine, pulling away from the storage location. Zeek was about to drive away with $4 million. This was more than enough money to get him started with his new life with Dora.

It was now after 10 p.m. and Zeek had done almost everything he needed to do. The only thing that was left was to call Dora. He was now ready to pick her up so he could take her away. Zeek dialed her number and waited for her to answer. When he was sent to her voicemail, he didn't pay it much attention.

Maybe she's in the shower, he thought as he hung up. He waited ten minutes before calling back. Still there was no answer. Zeek still didn't think anything of it. To kill some time before calling back again, he would get some gas and something to drink. *Hopefully, by then, she should answer the phone,* he thought. When Dora failed to answer the phone for the third time, Zeek began to panic.

Zeek drove as fast as he could to her house, hoping not to get pulled over as he continued to think the worst. He prayed she hadn't been kidnapped, or worse, raped. He also had a visual of someone killing her and leaving her dead on the floor. Zeek's eyes began to water with the horrible thought. He loved her so much and didn't want anything to happen to her. It was hard for him to believe that she had finally decided to leave the house on her own. He prayed he would make it there in time to save her. Maybe Dora still had a chance to live.

❖ ❖ ❖

Meanwhile, Trish and her accomplice were parked on a street in a black Escalade. They'd been patiently waiting there for over an hour. Trish was getting tired of waiting. She perked up when she saw a blue Cadillac pull up across the street from them. This was one of the cars that Trish had been waiting to see. They then stared at a nearby building's entrance hoping to catch their target coming in or leaving.

Zeek looked at Dora's apartment building from out of his rearview mirror. Her building looked quiet and free from any disturbances. He saw that Dora's car was still there and if she wasn't home, she hadn't left on her own. Zeek had a strong feeling that Dora was still in her apartment. He thought it was a huge possibility that her attackers were still there if his assumption was right. He reached in the glove compartment to retrieve his chrome 9mm and tucked it in his waist. He then put two extra clips in his pocket before closing the compartment door. If it was going to go down, he wanted to make sure he had enough bullets to make it out of there alive. Zeek took a deep breath and got out of the car. He had never been this scared before in his entire life, but he was ready.

Zeek walked across the street and stood in front of the apartment building. He was about to walk through the door, when shots were fired at him. *Boom, boom, boom! Boom, boom, boom!* Bullets flew past him, hitting the building and shooting out the glass windows in the door. *Boom, boom, boom! Boom, boom, boom!* There was no car close enough for him to duck down behind, so he had no choice but to stand there and return fire. He pulled out his gun and pointed to where he thought the bullets were coming from. He got grazed on his thumb, causing his gun to fall to the ground.

Before he could reach down to pick it up, he felt his arm and chest area get extremely hot.

Several bullets hit Zeek, throwing his body to the ground. He lay there unable to move, paralyzed by the realization that he had been shot. He figured this would happen one day, but he didn't expect it to be so soon. His mind drifted as he took a few moments to reflect on his past.

He thought about the days when he didn't have a dime to his name and looking for a job was the biggest thing he had to worry about. Back then, Chelsea was his angel and could do no wrong, and he was her boyfriend and could do no right. After Chelsea got caught cheating on him, their relationship completely went sour. Zeek was desperate to change into the hustler Chelsea secretly desired. What started off with Zeek trying to show Chelsea he could be a hustler quickly turned into a drama-filled lifestyle.

Zeek's hunger for success grew along with his ability for deception. He not only messed around with one of Chelsea's best friends, Qwanda, but he was the reason Chelsea's ex-boyfriend, Rodney, was dead. His plot for revenge against Rodney backfired, causing a string of unexplained deaths and brutal murders. Zeek was blamed for it all and had to fight for his life. Lying face up on the stoop of his girlfriend's apartment building, he was left with the feeling that he had dug a hole for himself and was now about to get buried.

Why? He cried to himself, as blood flowed from his mouth. *How could I get so deep in this shit? Everything used to be so simple. This can't be the end for me,* he cried, continuing to cough up blood, trying to stay calm.

His vision blurred, but he could hear his shooter's footsteps getting closer to him. He lifted his head slightly to see who was trying to take him to the grave. Unfortunately, he was unable to make out the person, who was standing in the shadow of the night.

Zeek had a few enemies he knew of, and some he didn't. Anybody could have been out to kill him. *But who would set me up like this?* He thought.

As the footsteps grew louder, Zeek knew the gunman was getting near. When the gunman was only a few feet away from him, he was able to make out who it was. Zeek couldn't believe it. "What the fuck is goin' on?" Zeek muttered, spitting blood out of his mouth. His eyes widened as Dora appeared from the darkness.

"What the fuck are you doin'?" He tried to shout at her, spitting blood all over himself. "Answer me! I said answer me, bitch!" Zeek continued to yell at her, but Dora didn't respond.

She couldn't respond since she wasn't sure herself. All she knew was that letting Zeek live wasn't an option.

What Zeek didn't know was that Dora was part of the Eternal Blood street gang. She had been a member for less than a year. Dora had joined the gang because she badly needed money to pay for her mother's heart transplant. Instead of doing the right thing, Dora was under the bad influence of her adopted sister, Trish. Even though Dora and her sister had come from a good home, she still wanted to have the same respect her sister had out on the street.

Dora saw that Trish was tough and fearless and she wanted to have those same traits. She ended up joining her sister's gang out of complete desperation. She had been only a member of the Eternal Blood gang for two months before she'd met Zeek. If Zeek would've watched the news more often, he would have noticed there was a murder at the same corner store Dora was coming out of when he'd first met her. The storeowner was the fourth person she had killed. She never guessed that Zeek would be one of her victims.

Zeek stared into her eyes, trying to find the Dora he thought he knew so well. He hoped to find the Dora who would never bring him any harm or pain. Zeek felt guilty for all the hurt he had caused to those around him. He went from wanting to become a doctor that cared for the sick to a thoughtless drug dealer that sold poison to his people. He thought about all the girls he had treated wrong in the past. He would give anything to see Qwanda or Shawnna right now and do what he could to start all over with them. Most of all, he wanted to start over with Chelsea. She was the spark that ignited Zeek's entire transition. Zeek changed everything about himself to prove to her that he could. *Chelsea could have cheated on me a thousand times. I wouldn't care*, he thought. He felt that any wrong she could've done to him was way better than death. A tear fell from his eye mixing into the blood that was on his face.

Dora was oddly doing the same thing. She stared at Zeek, trying to erase the bad things he was capable of doing. He didn't look like a killer, but all the overdose deaths he was responsible for told her a different story. Dora truly loved him and wished he wasn't the one she was sent to kill. Doing this to Zeek wasn't easy. She tried her hardest to escape, but she couldn't. Dora was trapped. Dora flashed back to that dreadful day in her apartment with Trish.

"He wants me to do what?" Dora had asked, hoping her ears had deceived her.

"Glimpse wants your boyfriend dead," Trish had repeated slowly.

"No...no...there has to be a mistake. Zeek can't be the one," Dora had contested.

"Don't matter if it's a mistake or not, Dora. You already know. Once the money's put up, the price tag can't be removed."

Dora couldn't come to terms with what had to happen. Her

frustration grew as she searched heavily for a solution, one that would spare Zeek his life. "I'll cover it. Tell Glimpse whatever he's gonna pay me, tell him to keep it. And if that's not enough, tell him he ain't got to pay me for the next three hits…Zeek can't die."

"Sorry but ya money ain't no good on this one, big sis. That nigga killed Joseph…well at least the shit he was pushin' did. The same way it happened to a whole lot of other mothafuckas. It was one thing that Zeek was fuckin' wit' Glimpse's money, but his brother tho'…ain't no comin' back from that. He gotta fall."

Trish's stern words had hit Dora like a shotgun blast to her chest. Her heart had ached like her own life had been sold. Dora had turned and leaned against the kitchen counter so Trish couldn't see her tears forming.

"Sis, don't fold over no nigga. You ain't get into this shit for love. Keep ya mind focused on Mom who's layin' in a fuckin' hospital bed. That's the life you need to worry about savin'."

Dora had wiped her face with her forearm as she'd turned and watched Trish head for the door. Trish had reached in her pocket and tossed a stack of money on the couch as she looked back. "Glimpse wanted that shit done like yesterday so don't fuck around. You'll get the rest of ya paper after the hit. Don't let me down."

When Dora kept stalling, Trish had continued to call both of their phones. Trish had threatened Zeek while she had pressured Dora to get the job done. Dora had tried to run away with Zeek, but then realized she couldn't. Sooner or later, she would have to meet up with her sister. Dora didn't want to die over somebody's life that was already paid for. To Dora, Zeek's life was priceless, but Glimpse only gave her $20,000 for it. It wasn't a good deal, but she had to take it.

Dora could've easily asked Zeek to give her the money for her mother's heart transplant, but that still wouldn't get her out of the gang. The tattoo on the back of her neck would always remind her of that. She had to stay loyal to her family. Loyalty was more important than anything else. Without that, she had nothing. Dora broke her long stare and raised her gun at Zeek.

Zeek begged for his life, as tears ran down Dora's face. His pleading ended once she finally pulled the trigger. She shot him once more in the head to make sure he was finished.

"I'm sorry," she cried, as she watched blood pour from his head and onto the sidewalk. "I'm so sorry," she repeated, as she walked away from his body.

Dora's job was done, but there was something that she had to do for herself. She shot open Zeek's trunk and took out both duffel bags. Trish pulled up the truck, and got out to help Dora sling the enormous bags in the backseat. They both got in the truck and Trish sped off.

"Damn, big sis. You really took care of that nigga. You stretched that mothafucka out, and you got his money. You a bad bitch fo'real."

Dora didn't respond and put her head down. Any other day, Dora would have been proud to hear those words coming from her sister, but today they saddened her. The love of her life was gone and wasn't coming back. She started to cry again as they rode off into the darkness.

Zeek's bloody body lay on the warm pavement. If Zeek was still alive, he would have wondered what everyone would have done if they found out he was dead. His mother would have fallen apart, and Marcus wouldn't have gotten any rest until he found his killer. Catch'em would do the same. If he thought about everyone else's reaction, they would all be different. His own reaction surprised him the most when the white light started to appear. He wasn't afraid and looked forward to leaving the cruel world behind him forever.

The way Zeek was killed looked like he'd died from a long-standing street feud, but Zeek died trying to prove to Chelsea that he could be something that he wasn't. Unfortunately, his plan ultimately backfired. What Zeek didn't know was that Chelsea ended up loving him for who he was anyway. For Chelsea, Zeek realized that he didn't have to have all the riches or try and become a street king to win her heart. All he had to do was mature. Zeek's whole perception on what the meaning of life really meant had changed for the better, but unfortunately, his time had expired. Some might say Zeek died for all the wrong reasons. But, the only thing for sure was that Zeek died because he was wide open.

EPILOGUE

Back in Chicago, no one could figure out why two rival gang members were found dead together in such a heinous way. Some believed that crooked cops looking for drugs were behind the killings. Others thought that an ambush was set up by another gang to get two powerful drug dealers out of the way. It wasn't strange to many when Jaws was reported missing by his girlfriend a few days after Lunchmeat and Bumble were found dead. When Drake and Gripp found out that Bumble was killed along with Lunchmeat, they figured out exactly who to go after.

Drake and Gripp were tipped off that Jaws was hiding out in the Cabrini Green Projects on the Westside of Chicago. When Jaws got trapped between Drake and Gripp on a stairwell, he knew there was nothing he could do. Drake shot Jaws in the back of his head with a 44 magnum, sending his body over the banister and onto the lower landing. Once Drake and Gripp left the building, the hallway got crowded, and everybody looked at Jaws's dead body with his head halfway gone. Jaws had gotten exactly what he deserved.

"Hello, everyone. I'm Regina Post with a WMAQ Channel 5 news special report," the anchorwoman announced. "About an hour outside of Chicago in the town of Evanston, a junkyard owner sold all eighty acres of his land to a well-known Chicago development company. When a group of workers went out to the area to take some soil samples, they couldn't believe what they discovered. It was a body. When investigators finished scouring the property, forty-three corpses were found in all. The owner of the land couldn't believe that a cemetery had formed right in his own backyard. Most of the dead were of African-American and Latino descent, which led authorities to assume that the owner was not linked to any of the murders...so far, no suspects have yet to be charged in connection with any of the bodies found. We will continue to follow this story."

Poundcake never returned to Chicago. He didn't even come back for his cousin Pester's funeral, either. He had heard that some of Lunchmeat's people would be waiting for him outside of the service. He didn't want to risk putting any of his other family members in danger. A few days after the funeral, Poundcake was able to sell all his property and moved the rest of his family down to Texas. Poundcake and his family were now living in peace, while they owned and operated five apartment buildings in the Dallas-Fort Worth area.

Back in D.C., Alonzo signed his first cleaning contract with the Gallery District restaurant chain. "It's going to be great doing business with you," Lonzo said as he rose from the conference room table and shook his new employer's hand.

His company would start off making $30,000 a month and he could afford to hire ten workers to sign on with his company. Lonzo felt strong and confident as he strolled out of the office building in his inexpensive black Geoffrey Beene suit. He couldn't wait to celebrate with the people he loved.

"Now I can marry Jewel." He smiled as he danced along the sidewalk. He planned to propose to Jewel on her birthday in October, which was less than sixty days away. He also wanted to buy a house for his bride-to-be. Things were looking great for their future. "Thank you, Lord! Thank you, thank you, thank you! I can't believe this is happening to me! Wait 'til I tell Zeek! He's not going to believe this!"

No one had found out about Zeek getting killed yet, but when they did, someone was going to have a huge price to pay. A whole lot of blood would be spilled, and a new cycle of mayhem would ensue...

Unforgiven Love: Wide Open 2 coming soon...

ABOUT THE AUTHOR

S.K. Collins was born and raised in Pittsburgh, PA and is now living in Washington, D.C. This former aspiring rapper-turned-author brings out the heartfelt emotion in his writing from an edgy street life perspective that leaves the reader begging for more. S.K. describes himself as a fortunate new author to have received guidance, words of encouragement, and advice about the publishing industry from some of the veterans like Keith Lee Johnson, author of the series *Little Black Girl Lost;* and Teri Woods, author of the trilogies *True to the Game* and *Dutch.* S.K. already has numerous books in the works that he can't wait to feed the hungry audience looking for something new and fresh. Connect with the author on Facebook, Twitter and Instagram.

Tell S.K. what you thought about his book.

Contact Info
thewritersk@gmail.com
Facebook: SK Collins
Twitter & Instagram: @thewritersk

DISCUSSION QUESTIONS

1. Do you think Chelsea had a valid reason to dog Zeek the way she did?

2. Was Qwanda wrong for getting with Zeek even after Chelsea knew she wanted him first?

3. What was it about Qwanda and Shawnna that made Zeek unable to love them like he loved Dora?

4. Why didn't Dora ask Zeek for the money to pay for her mother's operation, when she ended up stealing it from him in the end?

5. Where do you think Drake and Gripp will bury their dead now that they can no longer bury them at the junkyard?

6. Should Zeek have gone about getting his revenge against Rodney in a different way?

7. Who was your favorite character(s) and why?

8. What character(s) did you dislike the most and why?

9. What was your favorite part in the story?

10. Out of all the women, who appeared to love Zeek the most?

11. Instead of bringing Chelsea to Chicago, could Lunchmeat have chosen another way for Chelsea to prove her loyalty to him?

12. Even though Poundcake was a certified gangster, did he make the right decision by bailing out of a war he started, knowing he couldn't win? Do you think he should have died instead of Lunchmeat?

13. What portrait did Lonzo's character paint of a positive image?

14. Why do you think Zeek kept the fentanyl in his safe after he gave it to Rodney? Do you think he was planning to give it to someone else?

15. If there is a sequel, who do you think will avenge Zeek's death? And who do you think will be blamed for it?

If you enjoyed "Wide Open," be sure to check out

CROOKED G's

by S.K. Collins
Coming Soon from Strebor Books

INTRO

"This is it," Shakita whispered softly to herself. "This is my last fucking chance." She nervously exhaled as her sweaty palm gripped the last five-dollar bill that was once part of a thick bankroll. Shakita had been sitting at the same slot machine in Hollywood Casino for over three hours trying to get it to crack. The alluring sound of big payouts and jackpots being won all around her on the casino floor, kept her optimistic that she would soon be a part of that elite winning circle. She deliberated about all the thousands of dollars that she had dumped into the slot machine she sat in front of, and had a good feeling it would give it all back to her, and then some. Her last pull on the lever may be the one that would bring her riches beyond belief. For her sake, it had to be. If it wasn't, Shakita would be penniless. Shakita wished she could increase her odds of winning, but with no more money to spare, all she could do was pray for a fucking miracle.

She slid the crinkled bill into the machine and waited for it to register. She placed her trembling palm on the lever. Her heart began to pound at an enormous pace. She closed her eyes, not wanting to perceive what would ultimately happen next. Shakita pulled the lever down hard and intensely waited for the dramatic outcome.

She heard the reels spin in rapid succession until each one came to its own abrupt halt. Then there was complete silence, which scared the hell out of her. She slowly opened her eyes, hesitant to face the harsh reality of what she had already known. Shakita looked frightfully at the number sevens on the reels that failed to accurately line up. At that moment she wanted to die. It was now lucid in her mind that she had completely lost everything. She was now in a world of shit. Shakita's life literally flashed before her eyes knowing that all the money she lost never belonged to her in the first place. The money had been property of the notorious Bay Jackson, all $250,000 of it.

Bay Jackson was a ruthless hustler from the Northeast side of D.C. He'd grinded his way to the top all by himself to achieve the status he obtained before going to jail. He left his immense stash with his ex-girlfriend, Latrice. Bay didn't trust anyone but her and knew she would hold his money until he was finally freed. Bay planned on starting a rap label when he was released, and Latrice was on board to be his trusted talent scout. Latrice was the only person Bay had in his corner, and she was also Shakita's best friend. Shakita didn't know how she would tell Latrice that she had blown all of his money, which Latrice never knew she had.

Shakita lit up a cigarette as tears rolled from her eyes. She smoked nervously as she reflected on how fucked up her situation had become. In two months she had gone through $250,000 and didn't have shit to show for it. She knew Bay was a no-nonsense killer and would flip on anyone who played with his money; Latrice would be no exception. He would kill her, too, if it came down to his paper, and Shakita would be all to blame. Shakita knew that Bay was getting out of jail in less than four weeks. She had to find a way to get all his money back, and she had to find a way to tell Latrice how badly she had betrayed her. Shakita smashed out her cigarette, grabbed her purse, and hurried out of the casino. She had no time to waste, because her and Latrice's lives were now on the line.

CHAPTER ONE

Two Months Earlier

"Just sit tight, lil' mama. I swear we're going to be in and out of this joint. All we need is five minutes," Kam assured Shakita. "Are you going to be cool?"

"Yeah, I'm fine," she said meekly as tension spread across her face.

Kam saw the strained look in her eyes and he had to console her.

"I know you're nervous as shit, but we going to be straight. I promise. All right?"

Shakita quickly nodded her head as she fought to hide her anxiety. Kam touched her cheek and smiled before he exited the car. Shakita watched as Kam and three members of his crew casually walked into Montgomery Mall. To the average eye Kam and his crew looked as if they were a group of regular browsers. They strolled across the mall floor not giving away any sign they were actually jewelry thieves. Montgomery Mall was set to be their fourth heist in the past eighty days. The only part Shakita had to play in the scheme was to get them out of the area before the police showed up.

Shakita pulled on her cigarette as she tapped her foot on the gas pedal. *Just chill, girl*, she said to herself, as she struggled to disband her paranoia of them getting caught. She suddenly got a bad feeling in the pit of her stomach that told her to get out of there. As much as she wanted to listen to her gut, she quickly shook the feeling off, and studied the exit doors, praying Kam would appear at any moment. She had to abandon her fear and remind herself the reason she was there. She needed money for gambling, and selling stolen expensive jewelry was her way of making it happen. Shakita had promised herself that this would be her first and last time taking part in a jewelry heist. She would be one and done, never again allowing herself to descend so low out of monetary desperation. All she had to do was sell the jewelry and she would have enough money to get back to what she did best: gamble to win it big.

"Where the hell are they?" she wondered as she lit up another cigarette. Too much time had elapsed and Shakita was falling apart. Her protruding eyes fixated on the exit doors hoping Kam would emerge, yet her racing heart told her that he wouldn't.

Kam and his crew walked casually through the crowded mall and headed straight toward Bertzman Jewelers. Kam checked his watch and smiled knowing their timing was perfect for the security shift change. Now all they had to do was get in and get out. They stepped into the jewelry store and one of the sales associate's eyes beamed. He thought about the huge commission he would make from whom he ignorantly assumed were rappers. He quickly dashed toward them eager to assist.

"Hello, gentlemen. Are any of you looking for something particular?" the sales associate asked as he displayed his preeminent charm.

"Yeah, I'm looking for a tennis bracelet or a pendant for my daughter. She just turned sixteen," one of Kam's crew members said. "I need something really special for my baby girl."

"I can certainly help you over here, sir," the sales associate said as he walked them to the other side of the store.

Kam walked over to a display case full of Cartier and Hublot watches. His eyes lit up green as he quickly added up the value of the watches in his head. He glanced up and saw that the other sales associates were assisting other customers. He knew his time was now and without warning, he pulled his mini sledgehammer from his pocket and then swung it heavily at the vulnerable glass. *Crack! Crack! Smash! Crack! Crack! Smash!*

Glass flew in all directions as Kam reached in the smashed case and pulled out all the display trays full of watches. The rest of his crew followed suit and almost simultaneously smashed out three other cases full of diamond rings and bracelets. They quickly packed as much jewelry as they could fit in their bags and headed for the exit. The once helpful sales associate tried to intervene as he grabbed at Kam's arm. Kam cracked the sales associate in the head with the steel hammer leaving him bloody and disoriented. Kam then pushed him to the floor as they rushed out of the store.

"Security! We need security! We've just been robbed! Somebody stop them!" the sales associate yelled as he wiped blood out of his eyes while trying to catch his balance.

A security guard finally heard the sales associate call for help, but by the time he was ready to react, it was too late. They were gone.

Shakita's heart fluttered when Kam finally busted from out of the doors.

"Let's go!" he shouted as they quickly piled into the car.

Shakita took off so fast that she almost ran over someone in the parking lot.

"What the hell took y'all so long? Y'all were in there for like twenty minutes. I was out here losing my fucking mind," Shakita emphasized as she put more distance between them and the mall.

"Girl, you tripping," Kam said as he shook his head. "We were only in there for four minutes... Five minutes tops. I told you we were going to be in and out."

"I swear this is some crazy-ass shit," Shakita said as her arms shook from the sudden rush of adrenaline. They were almost on the Beltway when Shakita realized that no one was coming after them; they had made it. She fell back into the headrest and exhaled deeply. They had just gotten away with grand theft and she felt like a true bad ass. The robbery put some hair on her chest as she felt bolder to take on the next challenge in her life.

"The spot's right there. Pull up in front of that Accord," Kam instructed as they made it to their destination. Shakita maneuvered the car into the tight space. She then smiled, happy that her required driving was finally over. Kam's men got out the car and then quickly entered into a small building while Kam waited behind. He opened up his bag giving Shakita a peek of what he had obtained.

"Damn," she said as her eyes marveled at all the diamond-encrusted watches. She pulled one of them out of the bag and held it up to the light. The diamonds glistened so much that they looked wet.

"I see you got eyes for that one." Kam smiled. "It's perfect for a girl like you."

"The diamonds on this thing are crazy. This is like a twenty thousand-dollar watch."

"Try more like forty. That's a big face Rolex. The diamonds alone are like ten stacks."

Shakita slipped the loose-fitting watch on her wrist and stared at it in admiration. The cold eighteen-karat gold band against her skin gave her the chills.

"This is so beautiful. I don't even want to take it off."

"You don't have to. Keep it," Kam replied.

"But don't you want to cash it in with the rest of them?"

"Don't even worry about it. Believe me, we have more than enough. We really made out on this heist. You'll still get your cut, too. Thank you for doing this for me. I really appreciate it."

"No problem." She smiled.

Kam returned her smile, then he opened the door. "I'll see you in a few minutes," he said as he placed his lips gently against hers. She tensed up from the sudden intimate gesture, but then pulled him in closer to her as her lips received his. The silent built-up tension between them had finally boiled over. The kiss had been long overdue, giving them clear indication that something was missing from their kinetic bond. The thought of them being together had often crossed her mind. They were both cut from the same cloth, they were reckless. They were outlaws in their own right, who made their own rules as they went along. They were supposed to happen and now that they did, together they would be even more dangerous.

"Can we celebrate tonight?" he asked as they clasped hands.

"Of course we can." She smiled.

"Okay cool. I'll be back in a few. I got to get this money." He gave her a wink and got out the car.

Shakita blushed as she watched him walk into the building. A feeling of joy touched her heart. It had been awhile since someone had shown her that they really cared about her. It was easy for her to get affection from men, but for them to actually care about her well-being was something totally different. When it came to Kam, there was no denying that she held a special place in his heart.

Shakita eagerly eyed the small store across the street and stepped out of the car. She was out of cigarettes and needed a fresh pack. She figured by the time she got back from the store, the exchange would probably be done.

"Thank you," Shakita said to the clerk as she took her change. She placed the coins in her pocket and then retrieved her lighter. She stepped out the store and immediately lit her cigarette. She then headed back to the car but suddenly stopped in her tracks. The cigarette fell from her lips as she frantically watched the dramatic scene that emerged across the street. Police cars had completely surrounded the building. All three of Kam's crew members were being detained as they were being led out of the building. Shakita couldn't believe what was happening. She was confused as to how they were found so quickly, or even at all. She had been convinced that they weren't tailed after leaving the mall. She drove around in circles making sure that no one was behind them.

"Something isn't right," she whispered.

Police officers cleared onlookers from the street as a tactical team van pulled up to the scene. Shakita's heart started to pound as she thought about Kam still being in the building. She knew he wouldn't come out willingly and would fight to his last breath. Tears escaped her eyes as the tactical team entered the building with their guns drawn. She prayed that Kam could somehow find a way to escape the surefire ending. She wanted to help him any way possible. It was almost too late for him to surrender, and she was the only one he would listen to. Kam trusted her over anyone in the world. She was putting herself at risk of being caught, but she didn't care. She had to get to him.

She started to run toward the crowd of officers hoping she could stop them. Before she could even take a step, her ears informed her that she was too late. *Bang! Bang! Bang! Bang!* The erupting sound of guns being fired caused her heart to drop to her stomach. Gun blast after gun blast continued to echo from the building until they suddenly ceased.

"It's over. We got 'em," one of the officers said to his team after he received confirmation over his walkie-talkie. Shakita fell to her knees as pain flooded her heart.

Everything had happened too fast for Shakita to fully accept that it was real. Then the sight of a morgue van that pulled onto the scene undoubtedly let her know that Kam's existence had been lost forever. Shakita cried uncontrollably knowing that Kam had died for nothing. The heist had produced no winners, and Kam's tragic death made it completely evident. She then remembered the watch that was stuffed in her pocket. Shakita knew she had the only unaccountable piece of jewelry left from the heist, and had no choice but to get rid of it. She wiped her face and quickly got off the ground. She walked to her truck that was parked a few blocks away and never looked back.

The next morning, Shakita pulled up to Pawnbrokers Unlimited. She placed her sunglasses over her eyes, then stepped out of her truck. The metal newspaper holder grabbed her attention before she entered the pawn shop. She kneeled down and read the top story on the *Washington Post*. "It was a setup," Shakita whispered in awe. The headlining article caused tears to stream down her cheeks.

"We were never supposed to make it," she cried.

Shakita continued to read the story. She was astonished to discover that the people Kam were supposed to make the exchange with were undercover cops. She finished reading the story and was assured that no other collaborators were being sought. She didn't understand how she had avoided being caught, but she was extremely thankful.

"Can I help you?" the chubby, light-skinned owner of the shop asked as Shakita approached the counter.

"Yes you can. I want to get cash for a piece of jewelry I no longer have a need for."

"Sure thing, baby girl. What you got?"

Shakita pulled the watch out of her purse and placed it on the glass counter. The man curiously looked at the watch and then back at Shakita.

"This wouldn't happen to be stolen from anywhere, would it?" the man suspiciously asked. "If it is, I don't want any part of it."

"No it's not stolen. It was a gift from my cheating ex-boyfriend. I don't want anything to do with him or this watch."

The man looked at Shakita with doubtful eyes. He knew about all the jewelry store robberies over the past few weeks and didn't want any unnecessary attention drawn to his business. He quickly glanced at Shakita's overall appearance. He knew without a doubt her raw beauty had gotten her a lot of costly things. It was way too often that scorned women came into his shop to sell their once-precious items. He saw that Shakita was another hurt soul trying to seek vengeance for her broken heart. He decided to help her. "I'll give you five thousand for it."

"You can't be serious. Five thousand dollars? Do you know how much this watch is worth?" she asked, feeling insulted by his offer.

"Yeah, I know how much it's worth. To me it's worth five thousand. To you it should be worth less than that. I think the cheaper you sell it, the more you'd piss your ex-boyfriend off. That is your purpose, right?"

"I know what you're trying to do and I won't let you take advantage of me. You can easily get twenty-five for this watch. I want ten or I'll just go somewhere else," Shakita threatened. She reached down to pick up the watch, but the owner quickly gave her a counter-offer.

"I'll give you eighty-five hundred. I respect your hustle, but that's the highest I can go. I guarantee you no one around will give anywhere near that much. Go 'head and shop it around, but if you come back here, my offer will go down to three thousand. The choice is yours."

Shakita didn't have time to hit every pawn shop in town hoping to get a better offer. She needed money fast and had to make a decision. The watch was the only thing that would forever connect her to Kam. If she parted ways with the watch, she would be left with nothing to symbolize their bond. All she would have left to remember him by were her cherished memories. She sighed deeply coming to terms with the choice she would have to make. If her conditions didn't progress, it would be inevitable for her to keep the watch regardless. If that happened, she'd be forced to sell it for an even lower amount.

She pushed the watch closer to him confirming her decision. He quickly picked up the watch and gave her a nod that she was doing the right thing.

"I'll be back with your cash and receipt," he said as he walked to the back of the shop.

Shakita rested her elbows on the glass counter and placed her hands under her chin. She felt stupid for what she'd just done but knew it was the only logical solution to fix her problem. The owner came back with her money along with the receipt. He counted every bill out loud to show her she wasn't getting cheated. "Thanks," she said placidly.

She hurried out of the shop not wanting to tear up in front of the store owner. She wiped her swollen eyes all the way until she got into her truck. She stared miserably at the shop as she thought of Kam. The keepsake that they briefly shared, which signified their irrefutable connection, would soon be sold to someone else. She assured herself that once she won a jackpot, she would return to reclaim the watch. Time was her only ally and she prayed she had enough of it to make all her efforts count. With a fresh stack of money in her possession, she felt the tide would surely turn in her glorious favor. She cracked a weak smile as she headed to Hollywood Casino.

Shakita pushed herself away from the crap table and rushed into one of the casino bathrooms. She screamed and pounded her fist against the wall, outraged and disillusioned about what had just taken place. Two Caucasian women quickly exited the bathroom as Shakita continued her emotional rant. She was sickened to her stomach and heartbroken that she had failed to win once again. Not only had she sold the watch that Kam had given her, but the amount she received for it had been completely diminished. She was back to being broke and felt like the most ill-fated person in the world.

"If I would have just kept my stupid ass at the slot machines instead of fucking around with that damn crap table bullshit, I would still be out there fucking playing. I could be up right fucking now." She screamed in her head. Her chest heaved up and down as she paced the bathroom floor.

She then dug into her purse and pulled out a cigarette. Her back slid down the cold wall as the nerve relaxant started to take effect.

She flicked her ashes onto the floor as she dwelled heavily on what she was going to do next. She needed money badly, and her avenues of opportunity were drying up fast. Now that she was without Kam, there were only two other people she could rely on. She would first go to her best friend, Latrice, for support. If and only if it really got chaotic for her, she would be forced to ask that certain individual for assistance. They would remain her ace-in-the-hole unless she was out of options. She swallowed hard, hoping that her predicament would never get to that drastic level.

"All I got to do is ask her to let me hold a few dollars until I get back up," Shakita said softly as she lifted herself off the floor.

She quickly headed to Latrice's house hoping her friend would be able to lend a helping hand. Her electricity had been disconnected in her apartment, and she had already been served an eviction notice on top of her other bills. Gambling had truly put everything she had in jeopardy, but once she won it all back, the risk would be worth it.